"That was quite the kiss, my lord."

Satisfaction sprawled within King Arthur. "There is no need for it to end."

Guinevere's posture shifted. It was a slight thing, but it seemed to put her worlds away. "I think there is."

He blinked. His need for her was like a runaway stallion. Hauling it back took effort. "There is?"

"One kiss does not heal everything." Guinevere took a step back from him, straightening the bodice of her dress. "You left me in the past to come here."

He frowned, confused. "I explained that already, but perhaps I should apologize instead."

Guinevere shut her eyes a moment, then met his gaze without retreat. "Nothing, not even an apology, makes up for being considered invisible for so long. The only times you noticed me was when I made you unhappy. I don't want to be that woman anymore."

"But you kissed me!" he protested, realizing how lame it sounded the moment he spoke.

"I did, and it was wonderful. It wasn't enough."

Sharon Ashwood is a novelist, desk jockey and enthusiast for the weird and spooky. She has an English literature degree but works as a finance geek. Interests include growing her to-be-read pile and playing with the toy graveyard on her desk. Sharon is the winner of the 2011 RITA® Award for Best Paranormal Romance. She lives in the Pacific Northwest and is owned by the Demon Lord of Kitty Badness.

Books by Sharon Ashwood

Harlequin Nocturne

ROYAL
ENCHANTMENT

———

SHARON ASHWOOD

Recycling programs
for this product may
not exist in your area.

ISBN-13: 978-0-373-13991-0

Royal Enchantment

Printed in U.S.A.

Dear Reader,

The Camelot Reborn series tells the tale of how King Arthur and his knights come to our time to save humanity from a deadly enemy. There is plenty of magic and adventure to be had—and also a generous helping of romance. One can't talk about the Round Table without including Queen Guinevere. It takes a strong woman to keep up with the king of Camelot, and an even braver one to take a second chance at love.

They've had a stormy marriage. As a princess, Gwen was married to Arthur in an alliance between kingdoms, not as the result of a love match. He's a mighty warrior, with a destiny and constant danger at his heels. Finding a place in his life was difficult for a young wife—even one with plenty of spirit.

Now Gwen is in the modern era, with a modern woman's choices. Suddenly Arthur has to woo his woman if he wants to keep her at his side. But he's not the only one making sacrifices. A happy-ever-after demands courage from both of them, and a devotion that transcends time and worlds...

Happy reading,

Sharon Ashwood

For all the princesses who wanted the sword *and* the frilly dress—and maybe the horse and the dragon, too. Why not?

Prologue

Once upon a time, King Arthur of Camelot made an alliance with the fae and the witches to keep the mortal realms safe for all the free peoples. The world back then was filled with peril, with dragons and ogres and much, much worse lurking in the dark places. The greatest danger came from the demons who roamed the earth, causing suffering wherever they went. With the help of the enchanter, Merlin the Wise, the allies waged war upon the demons and succeeded in casting them back into the abyss.

At least, that's what Queen Guinevere was told. Stuck in the castle with her ladies-in-waiting, all she heard was gossip and rumors and thirdhand accounts of how mighty Sir So-and-So had been that day. As a royal princess, her value was measured by the children she'd bear, not the strength of her sword arm—and certainly not by anything she had to say.

So she missed how Merlin's final battle spells had stripped the fae of their souls—and how the Faery people blamed Camelot for the disaster—until an enraged party of wounded fae burst into the castle threatening to crush humanity to dust. That's when fear rose from the soles of Guinevere's slippers, creeping up her body in chill waves of foreboding. Something had gone horribly wrong for her husband and his friends—but, as usual, Arthur had failed to send her word, and so there was nothing Guinevere could do.

In the end, it was Merlin who gave her a full account of the disaster. He came to her sitting room, dusty and disheveled from the road and with his dark face tight with worry. She set down her embroidery and stood, feeling as if she needed to be on her feet for whatever he had to say.

And then he told her. The fae would indeed carry out their threat against the mortal realms, but no one knew which day, year or even century their attack would come. So Merlin had put the king and his knights into an enchanted sleep and, when the fae returned, the heroes of Camelot would arise once more. As Merlin spoke, the mighty warriors of the Round Table were already stretched out upon empty tombs, trapped as effigies made of stone. In that form they would wait out the ages. They had sacrificed everything—fame, wealth and their very futures to stand guard over humankind.

But Guinevere had been left behind. Again.

Chapter 1

"Is this where you saw the beast?" asked Arthur Pendragon, High King of the Britons, as he slowed the Chevy SUV into the gravel beside a remote highway.

"Yes, about a half hour's walk off the road." His passenger was the dark-haired Scottish knight, Sir Gawain. "That's a wee bit close for comfort."

They were miles from civilization, but both men knew that meant nothing. A determined monster could find a town and crush it in the matter of an afternoon. Arthur parked and got out, a cold drop of rain making him look up. The October sky was baggy with clouds, promising a downpour.

Sir Gawain slammed the passenger door and walked around the front of the vehicle to stand beside him. The two men gazed toward the wild landscape of the inlet, a forest of cedars to their backs. Arthur glimpsed a distant sliver of water crowned with the ghostly outline of hills. The raw beauty of the place only darkened his mood. "Let's gear up."

They pulled weapons from the back of the SUV—swords, guns and knives—and buckled them on. Once armed, Gawain loped toward the forest at a speed that said much about the urgency of their hunt. He'd shrugged a leather jacket over a fleece hoodie and looked more like a local than a knight of Camelot. On the whole, he'd adapted to the twenty-first century with enviable ease.

Arthur followed, his heavy-soled boots sinking into the soft loam. Unlike Gawain, he'd spent his entire life as a king or preparing to be one, and blending in hadn't been a necessary skill. Until now, anyway. Waking up in the modern world had changed more things than he could count—but not his duty to guard the mortal realms.

As they crossed the swath of scruffy grass between the road and the trees, Arthur saw the tracks. He immediately dropped to one knee. "Blood and thunder," he cursed softly. The print was enormous, as big as a platter with three clawed toes pointed forward and a fourth behind. "Not to ask the obvious question, but what is a dragon doing in Washington State?"

"What's Camelot doing here?" Gawain countered with a shrug.

"Are you saying there's a connection?"

Gawain didn't answer, and Arthur didn't blame him. Sometimes there was no easy way to tell enchantment from sheer bad luck. As a case in point, after Merlin had sent the Knights of the Round Table into an enchanted sleep, an entrepreneur had moved the church and its contents—knights included—to the small town of Carlyle, Washington, to form the central feature of the Medievaland Theme Park. Arthur had gone to sleep in the south of England and awakened nearly a thousand years later as part of a tourist attraction in the US of A. After that, a fire-breathing monster hardly surprised him.

Arthur rose, dusting grit and pine needles from his hands. "A dragon can't cross into the mortal realms on its own. It doesn't have that kind of magic."

"Then it had help," Gawain muttered. "I suspect that's your connection."

Arthur shifted uneasily, the wind catching at the long skirts of his heavy leather coat. "So do we have a new enemy or an old one we've overlooked?" There were too many choices.

Gawain grabbed his arm in a bruising grip. "There!" He pointed, his hand steady but his face losing color.

Arthur sucked in his breath as a ripple of movement stirred the undergrowth. He reached for the hilt of his sword, Excalibur, but his fingers froze as the beast reared from the shaggy treetops. He was forced to tip his head back, and then tip it more as he looked up into a nightmare. "Bloody hell."

The dragon's green head was long and narrow with extravagant whiskers. Huge topaz eyes flared with menace, the slitted pupils widened as the beast caught sight of the two men. The eager expression in that gaze reminded Arthur of a cat spotting a wounded bird.

"I told you it was big," said Gawain helpfully.

Arthur's thoughts jammed like a rusted crossbow. The dragon was close enough that he could make out its scent—an odd mix of musk and cinders. Through the screen of trees, he could see a bony ridge of spikes descending from its humped back onto a long muscular tail that twitched with impatience. Or hunger.

"Ideas?" Gawain asked under his breath.

Arthur repressed a desperate urge to run. "Be charming. Maybe it will listen to reason."

Gawain gave a strangled curse.

"Hello, mortal fleas," the dragon boomed, its deep voice resonant with unpleasant amusement.

Arthur grasped Excalibur's hilt and drew the long sword with a hiss. It should have made him feel better, but fewer knights than dragons walked away from a fight. He adopted his most courteous tone. "Sir Dragon, pray tell us what brings you to this realm?"

"Are there only two of you?" The dragon's tufted ears cupped forward with curiosity as he pointedly ignored Arthur's question. "What happened to your armies, little king?"

Arthur flinched with annoyance. After transporting Camelot's resting place to Washington State, Medievaland's founder had sold off most of the stone knights as a fund-raising effort. As a result, Camelot's warriors now resided in museums and private collections, and there they would stay until awakened with magic. Counting Arthur, Camelot had exactly eight knights awake out of the one hundred and fifty that had gone into the stone sleep and no one knew where the rest of them were. Arthur was hunting his missing men one by one, but it was slow going.

There was no way he was sharing those details. "I don't need an army to say that this place offers you no welcome. The mortal realms have forgotten the old ways, and dragons are no more than myths. Not even the fae reveal themselves to the humans here."

The dragon snorted, twin puffs of smoke curling up from its cavernous nostrils. "And what does this world make of you, High King of the Britons?"

Arthur held Excalibur loosely in one hand, the tip resting between his feet. It was a posture meant to look relaxed, but he was balanced and ready to strike. "To my great sorrow, Camelot is forgotten. I keep my true name to myself."

Amused, the dragon rumbled with a sound like crashing boulders. "But you still tell me to go? You would risk a thankless death for the ignorant rabble who live here?"

"Yes," Arthur replied with outward calm.

Like a preening cat, the dragon stroked a huge, taloned forepaw over its whiskers. It looked casual, but Arthur detected something else in the dragon's manner. Anger or sorrow or even disappointment.

"You amaze me, little king," said the creature. "Once, your Pendragon forefathers held the deep respect of my kind. Now you can do no more than shoo me away as if I were a stray cat."

"This time is different."

"Is that why you left the mistress of your forgotten realm a widow?"

Arthur clenched his jaw. *Guinevere.* The memory of her made him ache with a mix of fury and regret. "That is not your affair."

"A shame." There was a dragonish, smoky sigh. "The minstrels of my world still sing of the Queen of Camelot's beauty. A dragon would have kept his mate close."

Arthur ground his teeth. Leaving his queen was the only thing he'd done right in their marriage. Back then, even the image of her delicate face and graceful hands had burned like acid crumbling his bones. He'd desired her so much, and yet they'd been so utterly mismatched. His crown and sword, his title and lands—none of it had meant a thing to her. All she'd wanted was—he wasn't even certain what she'd wanted. He prayed she'd found happiness in the end.

"Don't speak of my queen," Arthur growled, all pretense of civility gone. "I ask you again, dragon, why are you here?"

"Ask me rather what I want." The dragon arched its neck to angle one huge yellow eye at Arthur.

His words echoed Arthur's thoughts with almost-sinister precision. "Fine. What do you want?"

"It has been long years since I made humans tremble behind their flimsy doors. I was once a destroyer of cities, a fiery death that rained from the skies. The name of Rukon Shadow Wing was the refrain of minstrels' songs."

None that Arthur had heard, but he kept that to himself. "Our cities are not your playthings."

"They are if I make them so, and this mortal realm is ripe for plucking. My name shall be whispered in terror once again."

"Humans have weapons far greater than my sword," Arthur said, his voice hard. "You won't survive."

"But there your logic breaks down, little king. You don't have an army, and by your own admission, modern mortals think me a myth." The dragon gave a sly smile that was horribly full of teeth. "It will be too late by the time the modern generals gather their wits for an attack."

"I will stop you."

"Assuming you could find the men to do so, every accord with the hidden world, including the witches and even the fae, decrees that the magical realm must stay hidden. Breaking that trust means war with the few allies you have left, and you can't afford that."

Arthur said nothing. Unfortunately, the creature was right.

The dragon chuckled, smoke rolling from its muzzle. "Poor king. Even if you could convince the human world that I am real, the rules won't let you say a word. What will you do, I wonder? Stand aside and watch me rampage through the countryside, or try to stop me all by yourself?"

Arthur finally lost his temper, gripping Excalibur's hilt, but the dragon still wasn't done.

"That would be the finest song of all," the beast said with a growling purr. "Rukon Shadow Wing defeating the mighty King of Camelot. You see, at the end of it all, that is what I want the most. The trophy of your head in my lair."

"I will not play the games of a delusional lizard!" Arthur roared, his gut burning. "I will see you dead first."

The creature's gaze flashed. "Foolish and rude. An unfortunate move, little king." And it bared its scythe-like fangs, saliva dripping from their points.

Arthur heard Gawain's breath hiss with alarm. His friend had been so still, Arthur had all but forgotten his presence. Now, with quicksilver speed, Gawain drew his gun and fired, grazing the long, weaving neck.

The dragon stretched its head high and snarled.

White flame shot toward the sky, the heart of it a blue as pale and clear as gemstones. Terror shot down Arthur's spine, making his heart pound so hard he barely heard the branches shatter as the dragon crashed through the trees. It was coming toward them at a deliberate jog, tail lashing in its wake.

Gawain and Arthur fell back step by step, keeping just enough distance to avoid the wicked jaws. The creature was perhaps eight feet high at the shoulder, but three times that from nose to tail. The huge head bobbed on the snakelike neck, jaws gaping to show its flickering tongue. But despite the danger, Arthur's thoughts turned to crystalline calm as he tracked its every motion. This kind of impossible fight was what Arthur of Camelot had trained for.

They reached the grassy ground beyond the trees and used the room to run, drawing the monster into the open. Gawain fired again just as the dragon's shoulders pushed out of the forest. The weak sunlight shimmered along its scales as it twisted away from the shot, but this time the beast wasn't so lucky. Chips of scale flew as the bullet hit its side. It was no more than a flesh wound, but the dragon bellowed with fury, the sound so loud it was a physical blow.

The beast bounded forward and snatched up Gawain, quick as a heron plucking fish from the water. The knight's howl of surprise shut off as the dragon's jaws clamped around his chest. The gun flew from Gawain's hand as the long neck reeled him skyward. One burst of flame, and he would be cooked.

Arthur swung Excalibur, his only thought to save his friend. Rukon reared up as Arthur attacked, the long belly flashing creamy white. Arthur lunged for one of the pale gaps between scales. It was a suicidal move, but a man defended his brothers, and a king spilled his blood for them. Arthur felt his blade connect, the shock of the blow jolting his shoulder before he spun away. Blood spilled but Excalibur's edge did not slide far into the flesh. The beast seemed to be made of iron. Still, Arthur bolted in again, refusing to give up.

The next second Rukon's whiplike tail whirled through the air, hammering Arthur so hard he flew back into the forest. Branches crackled and clawed at his face, turning the world into a mosaic of green and golden leaves—but not before he saw the dragon toss Gawain into the air with a disgusted flick. Gawain spun, arms outstretched, and dropped into the bushes with a mighty crash.

Arthur scrambled to Gawain's side, dreading what he would find. Just as Arthur reached him, the dragon roared again, then thrust its head through the trees toward Arthur. He scrabbled for Excalibur, but it wasn't needed. The dragon simply wanted to mock them now.

"This match goes to me. Have a worthy army waiting for my return, and bring reporters so that they can sing the song of my victory."

"Reporters?" Arthur repeated the word with confusion. What did a dragon know about the human press?

He didn't get a reply. With a huff of smoke, the dragon drew its head out of the trees and turned its back to the forest. Then it broke into a thundering run across the grass and unfurled huge leathery wings, each spine tipped with a glittering claw. The wingspan was enormous, blotting out the light. With a thunderous flap, Rukon Shadow Wing sprang into the sky, beating hard until the long, twisting form soared above the wild landscape.

As it rose higher and higher, a bright spiral of light appeared in the clouds. It was no bigger than a coin to Arthur's sight, but he knew it was a rift into another realm—a doorway no dragon should have been able to create. Rukon dived through it, and the light winked out. The sky was suddenly empty of anything but the coming rain.

Gawain moaned and rolled onto his back. "Did I ever mention dragon breath smells like old barbecue?"

"How badly are you hurt?" Arthur asked, helping Gawain as he struggled to sit up.

The knight paused before answering, as if doing a mental check of his bruises. "Hitting the bushes hurt the worst." He peered at the sleeve of his leather jacket. The fabric was scarred by the dragon's fangs, but not torn. For some reason, Rukon had spared him.

Arthur clapped his friend on the shoulder, unable to speak. Relief had closed his throat with a burning ache. They had survived, but he had a feeling their good luck had just run out. Too much didn't make sense. How was the dragon traveling between realms? Was Rukon really so hungry for glory—for the chance to kill Arthur before the cameras of the human media—that it was willing to risk starting a war with every magical creature that preferred to hide from human eyes? And why hadn't it butchered Gawain?

"Have you ever heard of Rukon Shadow Wing?" Gawain asked.

"No," Arthur replied, getting to his feet. "And I'd remember if we'd met."

Arthur picked up Excalibur and scowled at the blade.

The strike against the dragon's scales had dulled the edge. He slammed the sword back into its scabbard and paced the loamy ground, anger and confusion prickling along his nerves. What was going on and, more to the point, how could he stop it?

Both men jumped when Gawain's phone rang with the sound of a tiny fanfare. The knight was still sitting on the ground, but he unzipped his pocket and extracted the smartphone in its shockproof case. "Hello?"

Arthur watched his friend's face pucker in confusion. He knew most of Gawain's trademark scowls, but this was different. The knight held out the phone with a faintly dazed expression. "It's your wife."

The clouds picked that moment to unlock their downpour.

Chapter 2

Minutes later, Guinevere handed the phone back to Merlin the Wise. They sat in his workshop, the light dim and the details of the room lost in shadow. It didn't bother her that she couldn't see much. Her mind was already far too crowded.

"That voice," she said, the words faint. "That was his voice."

She'd heard her husband speak through a tiny square of a slippery, unfamiliar material called plastic. Impossible. Disorienting. A bone-deep queasiness made her clutch the edge of her chair.

"What about Arthur's voice?" Merlin asked gently.

She wasn't sure what to say. That hearing Arthur speak had made the blood rush to her cheeks? That she'd thought him lost to her forever? That hearing his words—she could barely recall what those were, she'd been so flustered—brought back bitter disappointment that Arthur had left her behind?

No, she'd never reveal that much vulnerability to Merlin. He was too arrogant and too manipulative for trust. She had no wish to be a pawn on his chessboard.

"Has Arthur changed?" she asked instead. Despite the unfamiliar form of communication, she'd recognized the force of Arthur's personality through his shock. There had been something different, more grim.

"Yes, he's had to change. This is a new world," Merlin said, offering no details as he pocketed the phone. "And, no, he's the same as he always was. That's the strength and the curse of Arthur."

"He left you behind, as well," she said, suddenly putting things together. "That must have been a blow."

"There is no need to concern yourself with that. I am here with Arthur now, and so are you." The enchanter's eyes were an odd amber color that reminded her of a hawk. She had no idea how old he was, but he appeared to be a man in his thirties, lean and dark and with the air of someone too smart for his own good. He watched her now as if afraid she'd turn hysterical. Maybe she would.

Her eyes strayed to the tomb at the center of the gloomy workshop. On top of it was an elegant effigy made of white marble, every fold of cloth expertly carved. She would have admired its beauty, except the face on that statue was hers. *She* was that stone woman with the budding rose in her folded hands—and that Gwen was dead. It was a tomb for her, and it was very old. So why was she alive?

She tried to swallow, but her mouth was as dry as the grave. "Tell me again how I woke up inside that statue?"

"Magic," he said with an airy wave. "I cast the same spell on you as I did on the knights of Camelot. While you were part of the stone, you slept. No age or disease touched you. But now you are awake and fully mortal again. Your life picks up exactly where you left off."

"Oh." She didn't sound enthusiastic even to herself.

Had she asked for this? She couldn't remember Merlin's spell, much less discussing it beforehand—and yet somehow that seemed the least of her problems. "Does this mean I shall continue as Arthur's wife and the Queen of Camelot?"

Merlin gave an affirmative nod.

"Why?" The word came out before she could stop it.

"Why?" He tilted his head. "I brought you here because Camelot requires a queen." He said it casually, the way someone might say Camelot required a gate or a carpet or new furniture in the reception hall. She was an object taken out of storage.

Gwen had always done what was required of her, but a hot nugget of anger was coming to life, as if emerging from its own block of stone. She hadn't asked to be abandoned, but she hadn't asked to be turned into a gigantic paperweight, either. Of course, there was only one man who was ultimately responsible for anything that happened in Camelot. "I want to speak to Arthur. Take me to him."

Merlin gave a sly smile and bowed low. "At once, my queen."

Merlin's obedience was about as reliable as a cat's but, for the moment, she was at his mercy. She watched with unease while he sketched an arc in the air with his hand. Where his fingertips passed, a bright, tremulous light followed, as if he'd opened a seam in reality.

Gwen blinked and stepped back in alarm as the golden luminescence dripped across the air like honey from a spoon. She'd seen many of Merlin's tricks, but this was new. She swallowed hard, trying to look as if this sort of thing happened every day.

When the light had filled in the impromptu doorway, he bowed again and reached for her hand. Stiffly, she allowed him to take it, and they stepped through the brilliance. A buzzing sensation rippled across her skin and, in the time it took Gwen to gasp, they emerged into a long hallway punctuated with closed doors. Merlin began walking, Gwen trailing after him. When she twisted her head to look behind her, the arc of golden light had vanished.

"Where is this place?" Gwen asked.

Merlin stopped before a plain and very unmagical-looking door at the end of the hallway. "The king's dwelling, as you desired."

The enchanter put one long-fingered hand around the doorknob and spoke a word. Pale light flared around the brass knob, and a series of clicks followed. Gwen guessed that was the sound of the locks surrendering.

"Why not simply knock?" Gwen asked, suspecting Merlin was just showing off now.

"Arthur's not home, so we'll let ourselves in."

"I may have hurtled through centuries," Gwen said under her breath, "but I can't imagine any reality in which my royal husband welcomes uninvited guests."

"We're not guests," Merlin said smoothly. "This is your home as much as his."

He pushed the door open with a flourish. Gwen stood on the threshold, suddenly uncertain if she wanted to step inside. "This is Arthur's home? Where is his castle?"

The enchanter gave a nervous cough. "Things work slightly differently in this day and age. This is my lord's apartment, which he rents. These rooms are his, but not the entire building."

On one level, Gwen understood the concept. Merlin's enchantment had given her information about the modern world, but the tumult of facts had come too fast for her to grasp them all. Not yet, and what she had absorbed seemed random. Modern clothes were a blank, but she was certain the standard measurements for an entry door like this were thirty-six by eighty inches.

Merlin was waiting for her to react, a concerned frown creeping onto his face. She stepped inside, reminding herself she was queen of this domain. Ahead was a large room with a balcony beyond tall glass doors. There were dark leather couches suitable for sprawling males. There was a bowl of something on a low table she assumed was food, although it was nothing that she recognized.

She continued her inspection, keeping emotion from her face. She didn't need Merlin to see her mounting distress. The function of the other rooms—a kitchen, bathroom and bedroom—were clear, although they lacked warmth or interest or personality or the slightest hint of being a home. Even the grand castle at Camelot, with hundreds of inhabitants, said more about its king than this sad place. Arthur was utterly absent. Gwen bit her lip. Come to think of it, absent was rather his style.

She turned back to Merlin. "Is this everything? Where do the servants sleep?"

"There's an office." He pointed to the one door she hadn't opened yet. "No servants."

"No servants?" That explained the dirty dishes in the kitchen sink and the crumbs around the bowl of whatever it was on the table. Words formed on the tip of her tongue, hot and burning. This was an insult. Royalty had men and maids to do their bidding. Gwen curled her fingers, indignation sharp in her chest. Then she swallowed it down. Arthur, for all his flaws, did everything for a reason. There had to be an explanation.

"Will I have my own chambers?" she asked, quieting her voice. "Will there be ladies to tend me?"

Merlin actually shuffled his feet like an embarrassed squire. "That's a conversation you should have with Arthur."

Which meant she wouldn't like the answer.

"Very well." She walked to the nearest couch and sat down, folding her hands in her lap. "When will the king arrive?"

Merlin gave a slight shrug. "Not long. He's meeting with his men."

"I understand," she said with a touch of acid. "His wife returning from the grave is a small matter compared to his knights."

The enchanter winced. "There was a dragon."

"Oh?" She raised a brow. "This is not the Forest Sauvage. How did a dragon get here?"

"We don't know. That's half the problem."

"And the other half?"

Merlin opened his mouth, and then closed it. "Arthur will tell you."

Which meant Arthur had asked Merlin not to say more. This, at least, was familiar territory. Battling monsters was a man's business. Never mind that it was the women, left at home, who had the most face time with whatever horror was tearing the village apart. They typically had the beastie on the run by the time Sir Whatever showed up to poke it with a sword.

Gwen paused, wondering at her thoughts. Merlin's spell had introduced a lot of unfamiliar—and usefully sarcastic—words and phrases. She rather liked that.

"I can wait. There's always a dragon. Or a troll. Or a quest." Closing her eyes, Gwen leaned back against the squishy cushions, discovering the ugly piece of furniture was actually comfortable. "While we wait, you can tell me why Camelot needs a queen."

Merlin's voice was soft. "That's also something Arthur needs to say."

Gwen sighed. She considered trying out one of the useful modern phrases, but when she looked up again, Merlin had disappeared. The only thing left was a faint curl of smoke drifting toward the spackled ceiling.

Gwen huffed. *Coward.* It was Merlin's fault she was here. She hadn't asked to be dragged forward in time.

She rose, too nervous to stay still. The prospect of seeing Arthur turned her insides cold. She was angry with him, of course, but there were other emotions, too—ones that she really didn't want to examine. Fear, maybe? Shame? Anytime she'd tried to fix things between them, it had all gone wrong. They were just too different. And then there was the fact she'd never done the one thing required of a queen—she'd failed to give him an heir.

She drifted around the space, picking things up and putting them down again. The circuit didn't take long. To the left was an alcove with table and chairs, but she couldn't imagine it had ever seen a dinner party. The kitchen was filled with marvelous devices, but little food. She avoided the bedroom.

The office door beckoned. Why was it closed when

every other room was open for inspection? There was no lock, however, and in a moment she was inside. She froze before she'd taken two steps.

Now she understood the closed door. This was the room where Arthur lived. It was not large, but there was a substantial desk in the corner covered with papers. The clutter had the feel of determination and excitement, of boundless enthusiasm colliding with rigorous organization. She approached it, her hands at her sides, touching nothing.

A map hung on the wall, poked full of colored pins. Gwen studied it, not sure what it signified but recognizing the hand of the high king who had made a conquest of Britain. He'd been barely more than a child when the lesser rulers had bowed to his sword. Give Arthur something to conquer, and he was in his element.

Once upon a time, that confidence, that strength of purpose had stopped her heart. Who wouldn't revere a man who could pluck kingdoms like ripe fruit and make them his own? But she might as well have loved the sea or a range of mountains. Great works of nature had no time for mortal women. She had been a clause in a treaty between Arthur and her father, King Leodegranz. Marriage had been the price of peace, and her dowry had been the famous Round Table.

The table had got more of Arthur's attention. Gwen frowned and turned away from the map.

There was a computer on the desk, and she experimentally touched a key. The black screen jumped to life, displaying words and pictures. She bent closer to look, her brain catching up to the spell that made it possible for her to read the modern text. Once she began, Gwen lost all awareness of the room around her. She pushed the arrow buttons, making the lines of type move. The novelty of it intrigued her.

So did the words themselves. It was a report of mysterious destruction outside the town. Was this the dragon Merlin had mentioned? Her pulse quickened.

A thickly muscled arm caught her around the waist. Deep in thought, Gwen jerked away from the desk, surprise quickly turning to alarm. The grip tightened, pulling her back against a wall of chest. And then she knew him. She knew the scent, the feel of his body.

"Arthur." She put both hands on his confining arm, but he didn't release her.

"What are you doing in here?"

He'd spoken to her on the phone, but the device had done his voice an injustice. Up close, the deep, rich sound was something touchable, like warm fur. Gwen closed her eyes, wishing it didn't enchant her quite so thoroughly. He'd left her behind. That said enough about his true feelings.

"Shouldn't you be asking why I'm here at all?" She put an edge in her voice out of reflex, as if that would hold his magnetic effect at bay.

"You forget I spoke to Merlin. I know how you arrived." His tone was carefully neutral.

His coolness burned her. "And no more needs to be said?"

"What would you have me say?"

"You could begin with hello. I am your wife."

He relaxed his grip enough that she could turn and pull away. She took a step back, looking up into his face. Her breath hitched then. The encounter with the dragon hadn't been gentle. His left cheekbone was purpling over raw scrapes that said he'd skidded on hard ground. Without thinking, she reached up and cupped his wounded face. "How badly are you hurt?"

"Gawain got the worst of it, but he walked away."

Arthur's clear blue eyes finally met hers. Their expression made it plain that he was unsettled to see her. That made everything worse. His anger was easier to fight.

Gwen dropped her hand, her mouth gone dry. The bruises did nothing to hide the clean, strong symmetry of his face. He was eight years older than she was, but that only put him in his early thirties. His neatly trimmed beard had not changed, but his hair was longer. There was something lionlike about the shaggy mass—it was no one color, but a wealth of autumn shades from gold to dark auburn. She yearned to touch it.

He was dressed strangely in what she assumed was the modern style. Her hands fisted in her skirts—the same ones she'd slept in for centuries. The clothes made the gulf between them seem even wider.

They stared at each other for a long moment, teetering at the edge of…something. Could it be he was glad to see her? There was so much unsaid, so many hurts and so many things she didn't understand.

In all their years together, she'd never come to grips with what drove him. Most of all, she'd never known what drove him away, exactly, beyond the fact that she wouldn't sit still and say nothing for years on end.

All Gwen's unspoken questions rose up, almost a physical pressure under her ribs. At times—though not often enough—she would have swallowed her questions back, bowed her head and retreated. But she'd been ripped from her century and dumped here without permission, and she was done with silent obedience.

"Why am I here?" she demanded.

Chapter 3

Once, Guinevere hadn't been bold enough to hold Arthur's gaze, but she did so now. He could see her irises were not the perfect blue that minstrels described. Rays of green and gold gave them an iridescent depth. In a similar way, Guinevere was never just one thing. Arthur's life would have been so much more predictable if she were.

He took a step back, taking in her tall, slim form. By all the saints, she was lovely. Her golden beauty cut him to the quick, reminding him why he had tried so hard to wipe it from his thoughts.

"Why, Arthur? Why bring me here?" Guinevere asked again, her voice shaking.

Why had he brought her here? He'd done no such thing, but he wasn't ready to admit that. Not until he knew more. "Why are you rifling through my private space?" he countered.

"Your private space? Is there something here the Queen of Camelot cannot see?" Her color was rising to an angry pink.

"There are confidential matters that I would keep to myself." Such as the many places he believed stone knights might be languishing. If his research fell into enemy hands, their lives might not be safe.

Gwen clenched her fists. "You're not content unless I'm locked in a tower, deaf and blind to the dangers at our door!"

"You meddle," he growled. "You have from the first day you set foot in my realm."

That wasn't exactly true. Their disagreements had grown with time. At first, he'd been conquering a realm and far too busy for his young wife. After the first few years, they'd begun to get along. But then she'd been ill, and then trouble had started: the scandal with Lancelot. She'd always claimed he was just a friend, and Arthur believed her now. But that hadn't always been the case, especially after the incident with the Mercian prince. Then there had been their endless fights. In the end, he'd ridden off to war as often as he could. They couldn't make each other unhappy if they were miles apart.

Her eyes flashed. "The realm is not just your business, husband. I am the queen. These are my people, as well."

The air between them sang with frustration. Within seconds, they'd picked up the threads of their old argument. Arthur cleared his throat, cursing his anger. Her stubborn will ignited his temper at every turn.

"It's dangerous in this time," he said softly. "Even worse than before. This world is deceptive in its illusion of order and safety."

"And you would protect me through ignorance? I'm not a child."

His chest burned. "Remember the prince of Mercia."

The man had been rotten through and through—young, handsome, a good dancer and witty conversationalist. He'd flattered Gwen when she'd first come to court, and later that flirtation had grown more serious. In the end he'd coaxed information out of her that broke a treaty and all but started a war. Gwen hadn't even suspected trickery until it was too late. By then, both Gwen and Arthur looked like fools. It was plain he had no control over his wife—and any weakness in a king made their enemies bold.

"I know better now," she said through clenched teeth. "I've said a thousand times how I learned my lesson."

Anger made his voice cold. "Self-knowledge is good. Trusting you to stay out of the kingdom's affairs is another matter."

"When will you trust me?"

"I would take that chance if I was an ordinary husband with an ordinary life. I'm not that man."

She visibly flinched. "And what would you have me do?"

"I would have you at my side." He reached out, cupping her cheek and hoping to take some of the sting from his words. "As you say, you are the queen. A queen has a household to run and official duties to discharge. You make guests welcome, smile at our subjects and grace my arm at official functions."

She lifted her chin, the movement breaking contact with his hand. "In other words, you want me to sit quietly like a good little mouse."

It was a harsh statement but true. He didn't want

her involved in matters of state. Guinevere's intentions were good, but she had always underestimated schemers. And now? Nothing had changed. Enemy fae were skulking around every corner. Many foes would try to attack him through his curious, trusting wife, and that meant neither of them were safe with her here. But here she was, his greatest vulnerability wrapped in an exquisite female form.

Arthur released the breath he'd been holding. She hadn't moved—her arms still folded as if to protect her vital organs. Sadness took him then, an ache for the gulf that forever yawned between them. He reached out, taking one of her hands and unwinding that closed posture.

"Come sit down," he said, with all the gentleness he could muster. "We need to talk."

She frowned. "Why does no one say that for a happy reason?"

Despite himself, Arthur gave a rueful chuckle. "I don't know, but you're right." He led her from the office and closed the door firmly behind them. He hadn't been in the apartment long enough to invest in a lock for his office, but clearly it was time.

Arthur led Guinevere to the black leather couch and guided her to a seat beside him. The familiar swish of her long skirts stirred memories. At every step, a fresh storm of emotion ran through him—regret, desire and a strong conviction that she would bring nothing but trouble.

And yet…

This was Guinevere, the queen who made hardened warriors stand gaping like witless boys. Her beauty wasn't just flesh and features, but a lively kindness that burned like a lantern through a winter night. It was her forthright ease with strangers, her wit in conversation and the charm that had turned his warrior's castle into a shining court. In a small, secret corner of his heart, he was in awe of her. She made people love her with a smile. He'd needed an army before anyone would spare him a glance.

They sat and regarded each other for a long moment, as if neither knew how to begin. What was there to say? They'd faced the same problems so many times before: her independence and his need to rule, her curiosity and his protectiveness. There would be a fight, and usually he'd end it by leaving.

But what about reconciliation after the storm? That was the one consolation of their relationship, and he would rather begin again with sweetness than fury. Perhaps if he tried harder this time, maybe, just maybe he could make her accept his rule.

Arthur picked up her hand from where it lay on the black leather and kissed it. He lingered over the act, feeling her soft warmth. Her fingers were long and delicate, the palms slender and graceful. They smelled of scented oils and, beneath that, the richness of her skin.

When Arthur finally looked up, there was a flush high on her cheekbones. He felt a surge of pride that he had the power to stir her blood. But instead of smiling, the corners of her lush mouth turned down. "It has been a long while since you did that, my lord."

"Too long." He tasted her warmth on his lips, and it awakened old hungers. "An unforgivable oversight."

"You left for battle and never came home again."

He looked away, back into a battlefield strewn with carnage. "The fae swore to destroy Camelot, and then all the mortal realms. We just never knew when or how. We had to come up with a plan."

"Merlin told me," she replied. "You went into the stone sleep and woke up here. The fae have returned to carry out their threat."

He nodded. "Morgan LaFaye is their queen now, but she is in a magical prison. It should hold her long enough for Camelot to strengthen its forces."

Guinevere's eyes were intent. "How will you accomplish that?"

This was information she'd find out anyhow. There was no harm in answering. "The knights were scattered during the stone sleep, and I've had to locate them one by one. I've only found a handful of my warriors so far, but I will keep searching."

"Where did they go?" Guinevere's brows furrowed.

"The tombs have turned up in museums and private collections." Arthur was still holding her hand, but his grip had tightened. He released Guinevere, afraid of crushing her bones. Suddenly weary, he released a sigh. "I had to buy Percival at auction."

A smile twitched the corners of her mouth. "I hope you didn't overpay. That would surely go to his head."

For the first time since she'd arrived, they laughed together. Merriment was scant in his life. Female company was even rarer. For all their difficulties, he'd been faithful to his wife, and having her near stirred heated memories. Arthur's heart gave an odd skip at the thought of Guinevere's sleepy face in the pale light of early morning. They'd had their moments.

He snapped himself back to the present. "I shouldn't be troubling you with unpleasant tidings."

"Trouble me," she said. "How did you come out of the stone sleep?"

"Not easily. Gawain found my tomb in the Forest Sauvage."

"And then?"

"There was a battle. It's a long story."

"I want to hear it."

"Why?"

"First, you are my husband." She said it with a bittersweet smile that speared his heart. "And I'm part of Camelot, too."

She was more than that. Guinevere was royalty, but noble birth meant little in these modern times. A difficult truth struck him. With no skills, no occupation, how would she survive? Whatever he'd done in the past to protect her—and he would lay down his life in an instant—he had to keep her close now. Without him, Guinevere was alone. The thought filled him with an odd mix of dread and desire.

Her expression was expectant, waiting for him to say more. He smiled, feeling the bruises on his cheek and jaw. "I promise I'll regale you with the entire story, every last dull detail of it. But right now I'd rather tell you what this modern age has to offer."

Her eyes widened with interest. "All right. Please do."

"This is a strange world, filled with extremes. Most obvious is the wealth of information and experience. Books are readily available, and travel is breathtakingly fast."

"Really? And who are the books for?"

It was a reasonable question. They'd been born in a

time when relatively few learned to read. "Schools are available to everyone, rich or poor."

"Do women go to school, as well?"

"Yes, they are regarded as equals here."

Guinevere said nothing, but her breath had quickened, a sure sign of emotion. An uneasy feeling crept down Arthur's spine—had he just opened Pandora's box?—but then she put a gentle hand on his knee. The unexpected touch sent a flood of heat up his thigh. Without quite knowing what he did, he leaned forward, needing to be closer.

"Then perhaps things can be different," she said. "We can live as the modern people do."

Her words did not quite sink in—other sensations were elbowing their way to the fore. Enchanted, he reached over, touching the slight cleft of her chin. The skin there was like satin, beckoning him to explore further. She stilled, growing watchful again. Only the muscles of her long, graceful throat moved as she swallowed.

Arthur was mesmerized. Her scent enveloped him, the space between them growing warm. All his earlier reservations melted, and he didn't care that he was dropping his guard. Right then all that mattered was Guinevere. His Gwen. She should be at his side, where he could touch her silken skin whenever he liked.

"Things will be different," he said, believing it for a heady moment. "Things will finally be right." He would rule Camelot, and she would be at his side, bonded together in this strange new time. The challenge of finding their way in the modern world would give them the common ground they'd always lacked. An image formed in his mind's eye of them seated before the assembled knights, hand in hand and finally united. They looked deliriously happy.

"Right?" she asked softly.

"As they always should have been. As I always meant them to be."

His daydream faded when she rose with a sigh, crossing to the balcony door to look outside. Rain splattered the glass, blurring the lights outside. At some point, dusk had fallen.

"How do I know we want the same thing?" The question was hesitant.

A familiar knot of confusion made Arthur frown. He never understood exactly how her mind worked. It was as if tiny demons lived inside her skull, coming up with ways to torment him. "How could it be otherwise? You're my queen."

She turned from the window, her expression defiant. "You didn't ask me to follow you into the future."

Arthur got to his feet, wary of her mood now. "The fae had sworn vengeance on me. I was the one they wanted, so it was safer for you to remain in Camelot. With danger gone, I believed you'd find happiness."

"Happiness?" She gave a mirthless laugh that fired his skin with shame. "You left me alone."

His anger rose in self-defense, but he held it in check as she lifted her hands in a helpless gesture. "Never mind the past," she said. "What am I supposed to do now?"

Arthur took a deep breath, then let it out slowly. A moment ago, he'd been certain everything would be fine. He wanted to recapture that mood. "You're wondering if there's a role for you here, in this world?"

"Precisely." She looked ghostly in the soft light, twilight deepening behind her silhouette.

He covered the distance between them in a single stride. The energy of their argument prickled beneath his skin, and it made his hands rough as he grasped her slender waist. She went rigid at his touch, resisting until he ran a hand down her spine. Yes, she needed comfort. Another long stroke and she arched into him, her body remembering his. The skirts of her dress floated around her as he pulled her close.

Relief made him ache as he realized there was still a welcome for him in her arms. Arthur bent his head, murmuring into her ear. "Let me reassure you that there is no one else I would consider as my queen."

Lashes veiled her eyes, with a hint of mischief lurking beneath her sadness. "And why is that?"

"I wanted you the moment I saw you dancing in your father's garden. You were everything I was not."

Her lips quirked. "A girl, you mean?"

He buried his nose in the cloud of her hair, her scent filling his soul. "You knew nothing of the ills of the world. You were innocent."

She pulled back to search his face. "No one stays that pure. That ignorant."

"Not when you become a wife," he said, letting desire sharpen his smile. Then he kissed her.

He was forced to bend while she rose on tiptoe. They flowed into the embrace naturally, her arms winding around his neck. His hands inched down her ribs and over her hips, reclaiming her curves. Desire, already invading his thoughts, pushed its way to the fore.

He kissed her hard, reminding her that he was the master, and yet leaving coaxing nips behind. When they were together like this, there had never been a question about the spark between them. Her mouth opened, welcoming his exploration, letting their tongues twist and mingle. The gentle swell of her breasts pressed into his chest, demanding to be stroked and when he obeyed—even a sovereign sometimes obeyed—a sound of pleasure escaped her throat. Heat tore through his body, making him drive her back against the cool glass door. He held her head, gentle and yet not, as he plundered her mouth. Her fingers twined with his, her body arching up, straining to meet him.

How long the kiss lasted was impossible to know, but the sky was fully dark when they were done. The lights of the city shone behind his Gwen as if this new age had fashioned a celestial crown for his queen. Arthur ached with desire, eager to put his seal on this conquest. It was a healing, yes, and a reunion, but he also wanted her to know beyond doubt that she was his.

He took her hand, pulling her with him until he paused at the door of his bedroom. He touched a switch and a soft light bloomed from the bedside lamp. Praise all the saints that the room was acceptably tidy. He placed his hands on her shoulders, turning her to face him.

Guinevere's eyes were soft and dazed. "That was quite the kiss, my lord."

Satisfaction sprawled within him. "There is no need for it to end."

Her posture shifted. It was a slight thing, but it seemed to put her worlds away. "I think there is."

Arthur blinked. His need for her was a runaway stallion. Hauling it back took effort. "There is?"

"You want me as your queen. I understand that."

"And?" Arthur was confused. What more was there to add?

"Is that what I want now, in this new world? Did you ever think to ask?"

She waited, but he had no answer to give. That said enough, and they both knew it. He felt his temper begin to fray beneath the sting of awkwardness. Why should he ask? He was king and she had made her vows when she was little more than a girl.

Then again, was it fair to ask her to keep them when so much had changed?

"You left me behind—not just once, but over and over again." Guinevere shut her eyes a moment, then met his gaze without retreat. "I know you believed you were doing the right thing. You saw my desire to participate fully in your reign as naive and dangerous because of the fae and magic and the kings who hated the fact you'd conquered them."

She was completely right. "And?" he asked.

"And nothing, not even an apology, makes up for being considered invisible—dispensable—for so long. I don't want to be that woman anymore."

None of what she'd just said made sense to him. He'd never thought of her that way—not in the fashion she meant. "So what is it that you *do* want?"

"I've been in this world for only hours, but what you've said intrigues me. You say women have access to education? That they have equality? I'd like to find out what that means."

"How does that matter? You're the Queen of Camelot. What more could you desire?"

Gwen caught her breath, as if he'd slapped her. "There is a whole new world in which to answer that question."

She stepped into the bedroom and closed the door. "Good night." The words were muffled and very final.

"Gwen!" Chagrined, he pressed his palm against the hard barrier. He'd said the wrong thing. He'd known it the moment the words left his lips. *Stupid.*

And now the door was firmly closed. Arthur could easily break it down, but that was no answer. Reason demanded that they both cool off before the argument escalated to a fight, but his temper didn't want to listen. Self-discipline alone made him back away from the blank, infuriating blockade.

Right then, the dragon problem looked simple.

Chapter 4

Gwen's eyes snapped open. Bright sun streamed in the window, pooling on the carpet. Her eyes, sore and sandy from crying herself to sleep, protested against the glare. Squinting, she sat up, mind scrambling to reassemble yesterday's events. Statue. Merlin. Arthur. Gwen pressed a hand to her head, as if the memories might shatter her skull.

She'd shut Arthur out of his own bedroom. He was her husband. He was the *king*. What had she been thinking?

Gwen sagged back to the pillows. That was the whole point—she'd been *trying* to think, and with Arthur charming her, that was hard. He'd kissed her, and the heat of it still simmered under her skin. But bed sport, however delicious, wasn't the only thing she desired from her husband. She'd pushed him away, but she'd done it in hopes he would consider everything she'd said. If their marriage was to get better, someone had to make the first move.

She wanted Arthur's conversation, his confidence and his trust. She needed the same respect he gave to his knights. No, she demanded more. He should love her, Guinevere, and not just the idea of a wife or queen.

Gwen clawed her way out from under the covers. It was a large, soft bed, and it took her a moment to put her feet on the floor. When she finally stood, shivering slightly in her thin chemise, she could see the streets beyond the apartment window. She was high up, higher than the tallest towers of Camelot, and the men and women below seemed tiny. How on earth had these people built so many enormously tall buildings, with so much glass and so little stone?

She took a step closer, momentarily hypnotized. Merlin had said the name of this city was Carlyle, Washington. The streets ran in perfect lines, brightly colored vehicles speeding along them like ambitious beetles. Merlin's spell provided the proper words for what she saw— trucks, cars, buses and stoplights. But the knowledge had little meaning. She had no experience of any of it.

A sudden need to sit down put her back on the bed. Gwen pressed her face into her palms, willing her thudding heart to slow down. All the bizarre things that had happened yesterday were still true. She'd half expected to wake up in her own chambers far, far in the past.

She dropped her hands to her lap. She had to find courage. After all, this wasn't the first time her life had changed utterly from one sunrise to the next. One day, her mother had died. One day, she'd been betrothed. One day, she'd left the only home she'd known for Camelot. She would face this trouble like every other, even if she'd been catapulted centuries into the future. What other choice was there?

As she sat, she slowly became aware of the world around her. There were deep, rumbling voices sounding through the walls—Arthur's definitely, and perhaps Gawain's brogue, and then others she couldn't name. The last thing she wanted to do was to face the knights on her first day here, when everything was unfamiliar and awkward. But again, what choice did she have?

She padded into the tiny bathroom that adjoined the chamber. Merlin's spell had been helpful here, but the sight of water appearing without pumps or buckets— hot water, no less—was still fascinating. And oddly overwhelming. Taking a breath, she turned a tap over the sink. She must have turned too hard, because the water hit the porcelain with so much force that it bounced back, blinding her with the spray. She jerked it off again, panting with the surprise. An impulse to cry rolled over her—to cry and be comforted and told everything would be fine. But that was a weakness she couldn't afford if she was ever to earn respect.

Grimly, she washed and pulled on her gown, wishing for her ladies-in-waiting. They would have made sure her hair was perfect and her dress free of dust or wrinkles. Most of all, they would have distracted her with gossip and silly jokes. They had been her friends, and now she had none. She was alone.

Once Gwen had tidied herself, she stepped into the rest of the bland, spare apartment. The living room was crowded with big men draped over the black leather furniture. Arthur saw her first and looked up. As if that were a signal, everyone fell silent and rose to their feet, then, as one, they bowed.

"Be at your ease," she said, the words made automatic from long habit.

There was a rustle as they straightened, every face turned her way. She paused, frozen by the weight of their stares. She recognized the knights: Gawain, Beaumains, Percival and Palomedes. There was also a young woman she did not know, with short fair hair and a smartphone in her hand. Gwen scanned the young woman's clothes and the confident way she carried herself. There was no question she was from the modern age.

Gwen forced herself to take another step into the room until she faced Arthur, and then sank into a deep curtsy. "My lord."

"We're not so formal here," he said. "Please rise."

She did, feeling an unaccustomed shyness. She'd at least been able to count on her manners, but even that was different here.

"I'm glad to see you awake," said Arthur. "I trust you slept well." He, on the other hand, had dark circles under his eyes. Gwen wondered if he'd slept at all.

"Well enough." She barely noticed what she said, for she was studying her husband with care. The warmth of the night before had been replaced by a more impersonal friendliness. She knew it of old—the mask of Arthur the King, friendly, jovial and utterly impenetrable. It was as if they hadn't kissed or touched or had a real conversation. Disappointment throbbed like something wedged under her breastbone.

Gwen swallowed hard. Had she destroyed everything by pushing him? For asking for a voice in their marriage? She wanted to talk everything through, but now was not the time. As always, the business of court pushed her needs aside. She was aware of the others, staring as if she were an exotic beast. Her breath hitched, but she found her voice.

"How long did I sleep?" she asked with complete casualness. "It must have been some time, judging by the light."

"My lady," said Beaumains, who was Gawain's younger brother and her favorite among the courtiers. "We all crash when we first come out of the stone sleep."

"Crash?" The word confused her.

"Sleep for a long time," explained the woman, who was standing beside Gawain. "Don't be surprised if you feel disoriented at first. Everyone's reaction on waking is different. Arthur held my sister at sword point for the first few minutes after he regained consciousness."

The king gave the young woman a pained look. "I'm not a morning person."

"You were in a paranoid delirium."

"That's something like your resting state, isn't it?" Gawain quipped, giving Arthur a sidelong glance.

The banter didn't hide the tension in the room. Gwen looked quickly from face to face. The young knights—the ones she considered friends—were subdued. Gawain, on the other hand, scowled at Gwen. She groaned inwardly. He had always blamed her for making Arthur unhappy, and clearly that hadn't changed.

Well, she would just have to work around him. She gave a confident nod to the room. "I did not mean to disturb your conversation, but here I am." She approached an empty chair next to Arthur. "What were you discussing?"

"Nothing of importance." Arthur waved a dismissive hand. "By your leave, my lady, I have summoned a friend to take you into town. You need clothes."

Gwen stopped in her tracks. Arthur was close enough to touch, but she kept her hands by her sides. "My lord," she began quietly, "by your own account there is a dragon marauding through the countryside, and fae armies threaten Camelot's welfare. Surely my wardrobe can wait?"

Arthur met her gaze and held it with his own. Despite his smile, the warning in his eyes was clear—he would not tolerate defiance in front of his men. "You need appropriate dress," he replied, his voice reasonable. "You don't need to remain here. There is nothing you can do."

The urge to protest rose up, but something made her look at the others in the room. Their expressions were carefully blank, but she could read the discomfort in their eyes. That made her back down. They didn't need to witness a fight.

"I'm sorry," she said quickly, turning to the young blonde woman. "We have not been introduced."

"My name is Clary Greene," she said. She had a pretty, triangular face and bright green eyes. "I'm one of the new kids in Camelot."

Gwen marveled. Clary's manner was quick and assured, as if certain she was the equal of the knights. If this was what living in the modern age meant, Gwen craved it with her entire being.

She smiled at Clary, plans already forming in her thoughts. "I trust you will show me everything. There is a great deal I want to learn."

Shortly after, the two women left. The scene Gwen had viewed from the apartment window was twice as frantic once she stepped onto the streets. Perhaps she should have been frightened, but there was too much to know where to start. Cars—including the old Camry

Clary drove—intrigued her, but those tall buildings entranced. So did the more modest buildings, the houses and malls and gas stations. There was a dull sameness to many of the structures, but every one of them was airy and light compared to Gwen's old home. As they drove to Carlyle's downtown shopping district, Gwen tried to figure out how the seemingly flimsy walls held together.

"So what do you need to get?" Clary asked as she parked by the side of a teeming road.

"I don't know," Gwen confessed.

"What do you have?"

"What I'm wearing."

Clary grinned, green eyes filling with mischief. "We're going to have some fun, girlfriend."

Gwen narrowed her eyes. "Who are you?"

"My big sister, Tamsin, is Gawain's sweetheart." Clary made a gagging noise, which said everything about being a younger sibling. "She and Dad went back home to the East Coast to see the family, and I came out here to keep an eye on things."

"What for?"

Clary shrugged, gathering up the phone that seemed to be part of her hand. "Camelot needs a witch on hand to thaw out any stone knights they find. Merlin's not always around. Plus, a modern guide comes in handy when a medieval queen needs to go shopping." With that, she got out of the car and waited while Gwen figured out how to do the same.

Shopping in the modern era was a revelation. Gwen had always been required to select a fabric and design, and then wait for a seamstress—or herself—to make a new gown by hand. Now she could try on as many outfits as she liked, then walk out the door with her purchase in hand. And the choices!

"I want some trews like you're wearing." Gwen had worn boy's clothes when running about the farms as a child. As much as she loved miles of swishing skirts, the option to choose something else once in a while was attractive.

"We call them pants," Clary corrected her. "Or slacks. They're on the list. So is lingerie."

The lingerie was intriguing, the pants marvelous and the three-way mirrors hateful. She dressed and undressed more times in a single afternoon than she had during her entire life. And there were so many colors and shapes of footwear! Every shoe had a personality, and Gwen saw a slice of herself in each—feminine, adventurous, bold or hardworking. Picking a pair—or several—was almost impossible.

Nowhere, not even in Camelot's greatest markets, had she seen so many goods for sale. The abundance was dazzling at first, but after a few hours of rambling from store to store, it became overwhelming.

"I need to stop," Gwen finally admitted. "Surely I have enough shoes."

She was wearing her latest purchase, low ankle boots of maroon leather. According to Clary, they paired perfectly with Gwen's new black skinny jeans and turquoise silk sweater. Compared to the gown that was now packed away in the trunk of the car, the clothes felt tight but almost weightless.

"It's not possible to possess enough shoes," Clary said, threading her arm around Gwen's. "Trust me on this. I'm an expert, and you have the king's credit card. I won't be happy until it melts."

"I need to sit down," Gwen moaned. "My new boots are pinching my feet."

The restaurant Clary chose was cheerful, with large windows overlooking the street. They crammed a mountain of shopping bags in beside them as they squeezed into a booth. A moment later, menus sat open before them, promising an abundance of treats. It was sunny, and the golden light felt good on Gwen's skin. She turned her face toward it for a moment, soaking in the warmth.

Her companion typed on her phone, engaged in a world as ephemeral to Gwen as the Faery kingdom. Over the course of the day, Gwen had learned Clary and Tamsin were Sir Hector's daughters, though they had been born in modern times. The circumstances of it all formed a convoluted tale she'd have to hear again before she understood it. It was enough to know the young woman was part of Camelot's extended family. Finally, Clary closed the case of her device.

"We've been talking nonstop all afternoon, but it's mostly been about clothes. I'm sure you have more questions about this time," Clary said. "Feel free to ask whatever you like."

Gwen didn't hesitate. "What is a woman's life in this time like? Surely you don't go shopping like this often?"

"Not often," Clary said. "Arthur doesn't usually loan out his charge card."

He probably never would again, judging by the number of shopping bags they'd accumulated. They gave their order to the waitress as Gwen smothered her guilt about everything she'd bought that day. She liked nice things, but had no desire to empty the treasury. "But what else makes up your daily routine?"

Clary played with her napkin. "I'm not sure a witch is the best person to ask about the average experience."

"Because you used your power three times this afternoon to summon clerks to help us?"

Clary shrugged. "In some department stores, it's the only way to get service. It helps with finding parking spaces, too."

Coffee and blackberry pie arrived, the sturdy dishes filling up the table of the booth. Gwen was hungry, and the pie wasn't that different from what she was used to, so she ate it with relish. The coffee was hot, but bitter and she spooned a lot of sugar into it before she could get it down.

"Then again, maybe I'm wrong. I don't think magic makes us all that different from other women," Clary said once the first few bites were savored. "We go to work and pay our bills just like everyone else."

"What do you work at?" Gwen asked.

"Computers." Clary shrugged. "I'm bored with the job I'm in and looking around for something else. While I've been visiting in Carlyle, I went for a few interviews. I'd like to get into social media marketing."

"And you can find employment wherever you wish?"

"Pretty much. I have good skills."

Gwen pondered that. Such independence! She'd never earned money herself.

No wonder she felt invisible. How was she supposed to be equal to someone who paid for everything she ate or wore? "How did you learn your skills?" Gwen asked, suddenly aware this was important.

"I went to school," said Clary. "That's normally how people learn their trade."

That fit with what Arthur had said.

Gwen chewed her lip. *Could I study at a school?*

Maybe she could learn how the great, towering buildings of this time were made. "I've always had a knack for constructing things—fences and sheds and even my father's war machines. I understand siege towers and catapults better than most soldiers."

Clary looked impressed. "You're an engineer at heart?"

"I don't know," Gwen said. "Some people carry a tune or bake perfect bread. I know what makes things stand up or fall down. Is there a school for that?"

"Yes." Clary nodded. "People pay well for that expertise. It's a long course of study, though."

Gwen didn't say more. This was a ridiculous conversation. She hadn't been in this world for a day, so any plans she made were castles in the air, without foundation or substance. And yet, the idea intrigued her. She'd always envied the monks their great libraries. Here, she could read her fill and become whatever she liked.

Or could she? What would Arthur do if she spent her days with her nose in a book, too busy to meddle with Camelot's affairs? Would he be grateful to be rid of her, or would he consider it disloyalty?

Sudden doubt seized her, and she stared down into her coffee cup. The drink was half-gone, for all she disliked it. Sugar only masked some of the taste, but the bitterness lingered. She'd swallowed it because it was expected of her, just like she did most things.

"Is there something wrong?" Clary asked.

"I'm sorry," Gwen said. "I don't think I like coffee."

"Then try something else," Clary said with a laugh. "There's lots to choose from on the menu."

Would it be that easy, Gwen wondered, *to place an order for a completely different life?*

Chapter 5

Swords rang and whistled in an elaborate dance, splashing shards of light on the walls. Tall windows opened onto a vista of wind-tossed trees, but inside the long fencing gallery, all was pristine order. Except, of course, for the deadly dance of the fae.

Talvaric executed an expert feint, swinging in a circle to cut high. His step was light, barely making any sound—though the force of his blow sang against his opponent's saber. Barto, Lord of Fareen, was almost his equal, which was saying something. Though of insignificant lineage, Talvaric had made his fortune as a professional.

Barto doubled his attack, striking over and over in a pattern that should have brought Talvaric to his knees. For an uneasy moment, Talvaric retreated. Fear needled through him, exhilarating and rich. It was said the fae had no souls—not since Merlin's spells had stripped them away at the end of the demon wars. It was also common knowledge that the lack of a soul meant a lack of feelings. That was and was not true. Fae were immortal, but they could be killed. The desire to survive and the fear of defeat remained. That was why Talvaric had taken up the sword as his life. It was a splash of red against an otherwise-eternal gray.

With a pounding heart, he let Barto drive him back another step, then twisted away. He went low this time, aiming for his opponent's legs. It was a move of cool precision, but Barto escaped with a backward leap. It didn't matter. With a turn of the wrist, Talvaric changed direction, sweeping the blade upward until it pricked Barto's chin.

There he stopped, his control of the weapon absolute. Talvaric held Barto's gaze, waiting for acknowledgment. Talvaric could have taken his head with ease. Slowly, Barto nodded, the gesture releasing a drop of scarlet blood where the sword tip pierced his skin. Talvaric waited until the trickle reached Barto's collar before he withdrew. They were both panting hard.

"A good match," Barto conceded. He wiped his neck and looked at his blood-streaked hand with clinical interest.

Waiting servants—two of the many dryads Talvaric kept as slaves—hurried to attend the two males, taking their weapons and handing them soft white towels. Barto wiped his face. Like all the fae, like Talvaric himself, Barto was tall and slender, with dark olive skin and hair so pale it was almost white. The coloring made a startling contrast to the brilliant green of fae eyes.

"You are a worthy opponent," Talvaric returned,

compliment for compliment. "I fought for many years at the pleasure of the queen and rarely saw the like."

Barto bowed and finished mopping his face. When he dropped his towel to the floor, a servant dashed forward and gathered it up.

"I appreciate the compliment," Barto said. "I would like to fight in the palace games this winter. There is no better preparation than practicing against our foremost swordsman. Will you compete?"

"Perhaps."

Barto shrugged. "You have won several times. I suppose the honor of victory begins to pale."

"Not really. But I wonder if the games will go forward in the queen's absence."

"Good point," Barto sighed. "This business with LaFaye is tiresome."

Queen Morgan LaFaye was under lock and key, captured by the allies of King Arthur of Camelot. That left an interesting vacancy on the throne, but none had immediately jumped to fill it. If the queen ever got free, she would not welcome a usurper.

"It's a pity I could not cross swords with Arthur," Barto said lightly. "He is said to be almost your equal."

Talvaric narrowed his eyes. "I doubt it's a fair comparison. His blade is enchanted by the Lady of the Lake. Excalibur has magic enough to cut through even Morgan's spells."

Which was why the queen feared it. Excalibur was the only real weapon the mortals had against a fae invasion. Morgan had been on the cusp of attacking the mortal realms when she'd been captured. Now hostilities were suspended while the leaderless fae milled about like sheep.

"I suppose you're right." Barto wandered over to the rack of swords suspended on the wall. He fingered one hilt, then another. "Is this the weapon you used in the last contest?"

"The same."

"And this?"

"I used that one in the match against the Giant of Trevayne."

"That was quite the contest. I wagered on you and won."

Contests? Talvaric felt a twinge of impatience. Who cared about sports when the whole of the mortal realms were ripe for plucking? But Talvaric knew better than to blurt that out. Barto was Lord of Fareen, and Talvaric was a commoner with no right to an opinion. Yet.

"Would you care to see my other collection?" he asked.

Barto looked up, curious. "Your beasts? Yes, I would."

Talvaric led the way through his manor. It wasn't a palace or a castle, but it sprawled through an endless maze of corridors and wings. Although his property sat far from the fashionable cities, the inconvenience was made up for by privacy. Soon they were traversing a long passageway lined with cages on either side.

The rooms were bright, with plenty of windows, and clean. The steel of the bars was polished, the floors of the cages always strewn with fresh straw. The pristine conditions weren't due to Talvaric's love for animals; it was simply that his collection was expensive and hard to replace.

Each cage held something unusual. Barto's gaze whipped from side to side, his eyes wide with wonder. "Wyvern. Manticore. Pixie. I'm not even certain what that is. How do you control them?"

"A variety of methods. The dragons are hardest to manage, but I've found a way."

"Dragons?"

Talvaric gave a careless wave. "It's always easy to impress your friends when you have dragons."

Barto's expression hardened, but he said nothing.

"There is a great deal of power here." Talvaric tapped on the bars of a particularly large cage. "Any magical beast can be a weapon if you know how to control it. And the study and acquisition of such creatures is never dull."

Barto said more nothing, but peered into the cage. It contained a large black dog with red eyes and shaggy dark fur. It smelled like something dead. "A barguest?" The question was sharp—not quite fear, but recognition of something dangerous. Barguests were best known for devouring lone travelers, especially after dark.

"Yes."

"How long have you been building this collection?"

"Hundreds of years." About the same amount of time as his ambition had been growing. The two were closely intertwined.

Barto straightened, his eyes cautious now. "You call these creatures weapons. That makes this manor a vast armory. Why have you gathered all this?"

Talvaric was forced to concede Barto was smarter than expected. Talvaric could all but taste the tang of his anxiety, and liked it. "I occasionally send my beasts abroad to deal with annoyances."

"Annoyances?" Barto really was starting to sound like a parrot.

"The goblins of the Crystal Mountains developed an irritating attitude. I sent them a gift. A troll."

Barto blinked in surprise. "On whose authority? The fae trade with King Zorath's people! This could start a war we don't need."

Talvaric almost wanted to laugh. "Trust me, the goblins are too busy for that at the moment."

Barto's mouth dropped open a moment before he snapped it shut. "That's unbelievably irresponsible."

Talvaric lifted a brow. "Are you actually angry?"

After Morgan's capture, some fae seemed to be regaining scraps of their souls. That raised some interesting questions, especially since many fae, including Talvaric, now regarded emotion as a weakness.

"No." Barto flushed, proving his denial a lie. "But I think it's time for me to leave."

"Come now, won't you stay and drink wine with me? I never like to see a guest depart without showing him the best hospitality I can offer."

"I—no." Barto had gone stiff, his shoulders rigid. "I have other commitments to attend to."

Talvaric didn't argue. If he'd had the capacity, he would have been amused. The servants showed Barto the door, because no one ever found the door in Talvaric's manor unless he wanted them to.

Talvaric poured himself a glass of ruby wine, made from the wild snowberries that grew high on the Crystal Mountains' peaks. That's where he'd found his dragons and formulated his plans. Rukon had performed his first task well and Arthur had received the message. Talvaric hadn't been sure the dragon would cooperate, but his added controls had worked. Of course, the message had only been the first step in a long progression of calculated mayhem, but one thing at a time.

Talvaric watched from an upstairs window as his

erstwhile guest mounted a fine gray stallion and galloped off across the manor's rolling lawns. A minute later, he returned to his collection and unlocked the barguest's cage. The huge, black nightmare backed to the far corner of its cage, cowering like a terrified puppy. Talvaric felt a knot of something warm and tingling in his gut. This display of subservience was the best part of mastering his beasts.

"That male I was with has annoyed me, and I believe he might just squeal to the council about the troll. I trust you have his scent?"

With a nod of its huge head, the creature crouched still more, its nose almost resting on its paws.

"Dispose of him, but bring the horse back unharmed. It looked valuable."

In a rush of fetid air, the barguest vanished to do his bidding. Talvaric finished his wine and dreamed of what he would do next.

Morgan's throne was vacant, and someone had to fill it—someone with courage enough to seize the opportunity and brave the consequences. Why not Talvaric? The titled fae might look down their noses at an upstart commoner—but not if he could prove, very publicly, that he was the most powerful of their number.

Talvaric would succeed where Morgan had failed, and destroy the fae's greatest enemy, Arthur of Camelot. And, he would do it in a way no one could ignore.

"See?" Clary turned her cell phone toward Gwen. "Wedding dresses look like cakes. Wedding cakes look like dresses. There's a kind of weird symmetry involving layers and fluff."

They'd been talking forever, still sitting in the coffee

shop. They were becoming fast friends in a matter of hours, and Gwen was thoroughly enjoying the process. "So when will Sir Gawain and your sister wed?"

"When she's done planning, which could be never." Clary shrugged. "Tamsin wants what she wants, and Gawain lets her have her way."

"That hardly sounds like the same man," Gwen said, shaking her head. "The knight I knew was gruff, to say the least."

"That hasn't changed. If he was a dog, they'd say he was unsuitable for adoption."

"Except for Tamsin?"

"Yeah." Clary sounded unimpressed. "Meanwhile, it's all wedding, all the time. Plus, she's a historian, which means a medieval wedding has to be accurate to the period."

"Why?" Gwen wondered. "What's the point of that?"

"It's a thing historians do. So what was a real medieval wedding like, anyway?"

"Mine was—it was not at all what I had expected for myself." Gwen had switched to tea and held the cup in her hands, warming her fingers. She hadn't been cold until a moment ago, but memory changed everything.

Gwen recalled standing at the window with her nurse, looking out on the summer-green hills. Below, the sound of saws and hammers broke the morning peace. Growing bored, she leaned on the wide stone sill, her chin in her hands. "What are they making?" she asked.

"A great wooden table, I'm told." Nurse smoothed Gwen's hair. She was a plump, homely woman who had been with Gwen since infancy. She'd fed and bathed her as a baby and been a mother when the lady of the castle died and Gwen had just turned eight. "The table will be your dowry."

"A table?" Gwen said with disgust. "That's a silly thing for a dowry."

"A special round table," Nurse said, "so all the knights who sit there will be equals. It will be grand, large enough to seat all of your Arthur's mightiest warriors, and he has many and more champions, let me tell you. It will fill the whole of his feast hall."

"That's a stupid idea," said Gwen with all the certainty of her sixteen years. "I'll go down in history as the queen with the silly table."

"You mustn't call your father's gift stupid, chickling. Men don't like that."

"It's my dowry, and it's a poor design if it's going to fill up a whole banquet hall. They should build the table like a ring. If they did it in sections, the servants could serve the food from inside the circle. It will take less wood that way."

"What a clever girl you are," Nurse said, but she sounded sad. "Don't tell your father."

Gwen didn't understand why, but the wisdom of her nurse's advice became clear once she went ahead and shared her idea with King Leodegranz. Her father saw the advantages of her design at once, and the round table was built her way. Gwen was delighted until he told everyone the innovation was his own. The world of men had no place for young girls with ideas.

By the time she married Arthur, the table had been finished and delivered to Camelot and Guinevere had turned seventeen. The wedding itself was a dream—or a nightmare. Camelot was far larger than her father's lands, the castle grander and filled with strangers. Gwen was expected to be a fine lady, fit to rule at her new husband's side. She felt like an utter fraud.

It was easy to stand tall and proud during the wedding and the feast afterward. Her gown was so stiff with gold embroidery it might have stood on its own. Her handsome new husband was all merriment, drinking and dancing with everyone. He danced with her of course, but only a few times. Gwen knew that was proper, that the host had to make sure everyone had a little bit of his attention, but she selfishly wanted more. She hardly knew anyone there, after all.

That was when she first met the Mercian prince, who told her she was a beautiful bride and saw to it that her wine cup was filled and filled again. For a lonely young country girl, that kind of attention was balm to her nerves. She hadn't yet learned to smell betrayal.

If only Arthur had known how naive she was—but he'd been a king since he'd pulled that sword from a stone as a child. He'd won wars, conquered tyrants and had an enchanter at his beck and call. She was good with chickens.

At the end of the long feast, he'd taken her to his bed. Nurse had told her—or tried to tell her—what would happen. Gwen had all but died of embarrassment and covered her ears. But in that moment, after her ladies had put her in her nightgown and brushed out her hair so that it lay like a shining cape almost to her knees, she wished she'd let Nurse speak. Gwen shook like an aspen leaf.

When he came to the queen's bedchamber, Arthur wore only his shirt. One would have thought removing his fine clothes and crown would have made him seem smaller, but the opposite was true. She could see the deep chest and the hard muscles of a swordsman's arms.

"Don't be frightened," he said, leading her to sit on the edge of the bed. "I'll make this as pleasant as I can."

Gwen bit her lips, stifling a nervous giggle.

"What?" he asked with a frown.

"Nurse says that before giving me medicine. She at least gives me a spoonful of honey to wash it down."

Arthur's expression went strangely blank. "You don't believe in sparing a man's pride, do you?"

"I'm sure you have enough to spare." She regretted her tartness almost at once, but she couldn't help herself. Her claws came out when she was afraid.

Arthur paced a few steps to the door and back again. Was he nervous? That was utterly impossible, of course, because he was the mighty King Arthur. He finally came and knelt before her. "I will give you sweetness," he said.

She had a good idea of what he meant. Despite her father's watchful eye, she'd kissed one or two of the younger knights at the last Yuletide feast, and at least one squire had sworn undying love. But the look in her husband's eyes had nothing to do with a youngster's flirtations. He was a man of five and twenty.

I will give you sweetness. With effort, she marshaled her thoughts and formed a word. "How?"

He held her hands, just that, and leaned forward, brushing her lips with his. "A little at a time," he said, and then did it again.

Gwen raised her eyes from her cup, meeting Clary's. "My wedding didn't start well, but in the end it was a very fine event."

Chapter 6

As the last knight left Camelot's council about the dragon—Sir Gawain with the last slice of pizza in one hand—Arthur stifled a jaw-cracking yawn. They'd been talking since the morning, examining every theory about where Rukon had come from and why. Now it was nearly four o'clock and they'd talked the matter of the dragon to death. Merlin had been invited, but, as usual, was never there when he could actually be useful.

After Gawain's footsteps retreated toward the elevator, Arthur shut the door and turned the dead bolt, relieved to be alone with his exhaustion. Sleep had been impossible last night, with Guinevere in his bedroom and him not.

Anger had slowly spiraled around and around his gut as the clock had ticked toward dawn. A lesser man might have raged and demanded, but Arthur had his pride. He'd reacted the only way he knew how—by being the king. And so he had summoned a council to deal with Camelot's problems and pushed his own away.

Not that he'd accomplished much. There wasn't enough information to track the creature to its lair. They were at a dead end until it appeared again. With a frustrated grunt, Arthur returned to the living room, stacked the empty pizza boxes and carried them to the recycling bin.

Basic cleanup complete, he poured himself a mug of coffee and went to his office. Immediately, a feminine scent distracted him. There was no mistaking the light floral musk of Guinevere's perfume, left over from her invasion of his space. It was faint, but his senses were attuned to its sweetness. Arthur set down his mug and scanned the papers on the desk, seeking any evidence that she'd disturbed his methodical chaos. Finding no signs of meddling, he woke his computer and saw the screen was just as he'd left it. Clearly, she hadn't had time to wreak her usual havoc.

Not like the time she tried to play peacemaker between the dwarves and goblins and nearly started a war, or the time she amended the peace treaty with Cumbria by giving away a forest or two because it seemed fairer that way. She'd been utterly sincere when she'd tried to make a match between a fae noble and the elven Queen of the Isles. Arthur closed his eyes, almost smiling despite the memory of drawn swords and angry oaths. No, as a newly minted queen, Guinevere had never stood aside when she thought she could make things better. Disaster after disaster had kept things…interesting. It would have been amusing if the kingdom hadn't been on the constant brink of war.

To be fair, she had learned her lesson after the prince of Mercia had played her for a fool. Arthur had been relieved but strangely sad, and a voice had nagged at him to say none of it would have happened if he'd been a mentor instead of consigning her to a life of embroidery and love poems. But politics was a bloody game, and he'd wanted her to be safe. Somehow, that never worked with Gwen.

Stifling another yawn, he sat down at the desk, determined to put in another few hours of work despite the need for sleep. There was no time for rest. The knights supported themselves by staging tournaments and feasts at Medievaland, Carlyle's medieval theme park, and there were schedules to make up and special events to plan. And then there were missing knights to find and fae to battle and... Arthur rubbed his eyes and willed himself to focus. Kings didn't get to take naps.

He opened his email program, his sword-calloused hands feeling clumsy on the tiny keys. He used the computer because that's what the modern world required, but he didn't relish the confined world of screen and desk and keyboard. This would be Guinevere's domain, once she discovered it—a place with more information than even her boundless curiosity could devour.

There was the usual slew of unread emails waiting, most of them routine items related to business at Medievaland. He scanned for something from Merlin, but there was nothing. However, one unfamiliar sender caught his eye: BeastMaster13@spellbound.com. A fan? Someone selling sword polish? Or another fellow with a make-believe quest? Medievaland attracted some very odd people, even by the standards of a time traveler with a magic sword.

With mild trepidation, King Arthur opened the message. It had only a single line, written in capital letters.

YOUR QUEEN IS BEAUTIFUL.

Arthur stared at the words, cold spreading from his core as if melting ice were trickling into his veins. Who knew his Gwen was here? Although the words were nothing, Arthur could read the threat beneath. Gwen had caught BeastMaster13's notice.

He jumped up from his chair and paced the tiny room. His logical side—the one that had been trained from boyhood to understand the ways of war—told him not to react. Threats were sent to goad. But his imagination conjured a thousand dangers—madmen, evil fae, sorcerers and demons. Logic didn't help when the enemy came this close to home. All he wanted was to find his queen and guard her with his own sword—and he wanted it with a fury that made him shudder.

Arthur took a deep breath. He knew better than to reply, but that was as far as his discipline went. Guinevere was out of his sight, wandering around the city without a care. She was his beautiful wife, and as the Queen of Camelot, she was also a symbol of his power. Harming her would hurt Arthur on several fronts—not just as a man, but as a king.

This was his fault. He had carelessly allowed Guinevere to run loose. That had to end at once.

Gwen noticed Clary looking toward the door and followed the woman's gaze. Arthur was striding toward them with a thunderous expression, and every thought about her future evaporated with an almost-audible pop.

His mood radiated outward, clearing a broad path on all sides. Although the people of Carlyle had no king, they recognized his absolute authority as if by instinct. Arthur wore a long coat that hid Excalibur, but he may as well have been holding it in one of his massive hands. Everything about the commanding giant said he was a warrior king on a mission.

From the force of long habit, Gwen rose as he entered and barely stopped herself from dropping into a low curtsy. The gesture had the unintended consequence of showing off her new clothes. Arthur stopped a few feet away, his gaze lingering on her soft sweater before sliding over the curves of her tight black jeans. Gwen knew she looked good, and his expression sparked a glow of satisfaction. Unfortunately, it wasn't destined to last.

"May I join you?" he said in a tone that wasn't really a question.

Gwen sat down again and he slid into the booth beside her, waving away the waitress before she could offer to take his order. "What brings you here?" Gwen asked.

"I came to ensure you were well," he said in a quiet voice that didn't carry beyond their table. "I am not positive, but I think the enemy may be aware that you are in Carlyle. I received an email that concerned me. I did not recognize the sender's name."

Gwen stared. Arthur rarely shared information in such a straightforward manner. The fact that he'd bothered to explain himself meant he wanted her to understand. She nodded slowly, feeling the weight of his clear blue gaze. It seemed to pierce through to her bones, as if gauging her response at the deepest level. "Thank you for the warning," she said.

Irritation flickered in his expression. He'd been expecting more. "It was a simple matter to find you. You're sitting in the window in full public view." He gave her another look up and down, as if he found her dress slightly indecent.

"Are you telling me to go back to your apartment now?" she asked, although she was sure that was exactly what he meant.

To Gwen's surprise, it was Clary who spoke up. "We're not without our defenses, my lord." Her look was polite but full of meaning. "I've spun a few battle spells."

His brows lowered. "I don't know who this enemy is or if he wields a gun or a pack of wolves. I would not be overconfident."

"Are you saying that there is danger here, in the full view of all these people?" Gwen aimed the question at both of them.

"Based on what's happened since yesterday," Arthur replied, "I'd assume nothing."

Clary toyed with her phone. "But as I said, my lord, you can trust me to get Gwen home safely."

Arthur's nod was stiff, as if he didn't want to agree but knew he was being unreasonable. He turned stormy eyes on Gwen, their expression possessive. "Very well, but I will assign guards to accompany you in the future. I will not have you walking the streets alone."

The words were roughly spoken, almost rasping. It was as close to emotion as Arthur would show in so public a place. Gwen stared, hating what she was hearing. Guards?

He rose with seeming reluctance. "When will you be home?"

Clary looked as if she was about to say something, but Gwen put a hand over hers. "Soon. We have one more stop to make." Gwen had no idea what that would be, but she was grateful for a moment to think.

Arthur hesitated a moment, but then bent and kissed Gwen's cheek. "Hurry home, wife."

"Of course," she said, suddenly awkward, but he was already halfway to the door. He never seemed to hurry, but his stride ate the distance at a pace few could match.

Silence fell over the two women, all their previous lightness gone. Gwen's thoughts of the future, of an expanding world unfolding before her shriveled to nothing. Cold nausea weighed in her stomach, but she sucked in a deep breath, doing her best to dispel it. "I don't want guards. I had them in Camelot, and I felt like a nuisance—or a prisoner—every time I wanted to go for a walk."

Clary stared at her, no doubt hearing the strain— and the uncertainty—in her voice. "Seriously? He's done this before?"

"He's worried," Gwen said, trying and failing to bury her bitterness. "I had a talent for trouble when I was younger. Years have gone by, but he's never forgotten." *And he's never trusted me.*

Gwen knew she'd said too much. She began gathering her parcels, the rattle of shopping bags hiding her confusion. Clary followed suit.

As they left, Gwen walked two paces behind Clary, her thoughts slowed to a dead crawl. She knew how to make drawbridges and catapults work, but not her marriage. An all-too-familiar confusion dragged at her like quicksand. A wife's first duty was to please her husband, a subject's first duty was to serve her king, and yet Arthur was a puzzle she'd never solved.

Once they reached the street, Gwen's fortitude ran out. She stopped walking, unable to push on. The cycle of unhappiness that was her marriage had started all over again. "I can't go home. I don't want to do what I'm told anymore. I can't be invisible, and I can't be a precious object always under guard. It's too much."

Clary turned and walked back to Gwen, coming to stand at her side. Clary's lips were thin with anger, but it clearly wasn't aimed at Gwen.

"What do you want to do?" Clary asked. "I won't take you anyplace you don't want to go."

The witch held Gwen's gaze with her own, her expression gentle. It was oddly unsettling, for Gwen had never had many female friends, especially after becoming queen. She wasn't sure how to respond. "Merlin has to send me back."

A car honked, and all at once Gwen was aware of the busy street around them. Vehicles swooshed past at unimaginable speeds. Pedestrians pushed by, arguing into their little squares of plastic. All around was color, sound, signs and a thundering bounty of objects and ideas. Gwen wanted it all with a sharpness that made her want to weep.

"I doubt Merlin has that power," Clary mused. "Even if he did, are you sure that's what you want?"

Gwen gripped the handles of her bags, feeling the weight of the pretty, bright clothes that should be part of a new freedom. She blinked hard, refusing the impulse to cry. "No, but where else would I go?"

"I don't understand," Clary said flatly.

Gwen sucked in her breath, letting it out in a heavy

sigh. She wasn't allowed in Arthur's office, but couldn't leave their rooms without a guard. Arthur didn't trust her to take part in Camelot's councils, and yet he wanted to keep her close. She was too naive and impulsive to let roam free, and yet he didn't want her in his private business. He judged everything she did, and he judged it harshly. "I was far less trouble as a piece of history."

Clary made a rude noise. "Sister, this world is full of opportunity. Forget Arthur and his chain mail boy band."

Clary slipped an arm around Gwen's shoulders, pulling her close. "You're in our time now. You get to decide what you want to do, and I think Arthur needs to know that."

Gwen's mind went blank, a hollow sensation stealing over her. It took her a moment to recognize it as a species of fear. "This is going to cause trouble."

They began walking again, drifting in the direction of Clary's car. "You don't need to decide everything at once," said Clary. "In fact, you shouldn't. You need time to breathe and clear your head, and so does he."

"But where?"

"You stay with me at my hotel," Clary suggested, warming to the plan. "I have a double room, and we've got all your clothes right here. It's as if this was meant to be."

It made sense. It made *perfect* sense, and Gwen's instincts grabbed at the offer. Yet, old habits died hard. "What do I tell Arthur?"

"That there is one more thing you need to buy," Clary replied. "Every independent woman needs a suitcase."

Chapter 7

The king pushed his way out of the café and strode down the street, his temper steaming. Other pedestrians cleared a path, pulling dogs and children to safety. He was aware of it all, but barely, as he stormed down the sidewalk with no sense of direction or purpose.

Arthur had reassured himself that Guinevere was safe, but he was far from satisfied. There had been a few moments when he'd seen her before she'd noticed him, and those moments had been a revelation. She'd glowed from within, as if a long-forgotten hope was awakening. It was a glimpse of the girl he'd first met, the one he'd wanted for himself before danger and politics and arguments had crushed that light out of her. And then, of course, there had been the modern clothes, with those tight black jeans caressing her thighs. He had witnessed many unanticipated marvels in his lifetime, but those legs had pride of place at the top of the list.

And then he'd seen the life die out of her the moment he'd opened his mouth. It was one thing to believe she was better off without him, and quite another to see the evidence with his own eyes.

Arthur crossed the street, dimly aware of the bustle around him as he grimly replayed the scene in the café. The image of Guinevere's soft curves, so evident in those modern clothes, tangled his thoughts badly enough that he almost didn't hear his phone ringing. He pulled it from his jacket pocket, finding a quiet doorway before he answered. "Yes?"

"Pendragon?"

"Who is this?" One more misgiving crowded into Arthur's mind. The male voice was unfamiliar, and no one addressed him by his surname. It was always "my lord" or "Your Majesty" or simply "Arthur."

"We haven't met, but you encountered my associate in the woods."

The statement cleared Arthur's head in an instant. This was about the dragon. "You mean your associate with the fiery temper?" Arthur asked drily.

"The same. I assume you got my email?"

Arthur cast a quick look around the street, just in case he spotted someone else talking into a phone. There was nothing but the usual busy street under a fitful sky. "What do you want?"

"I'm curious."

"About what?"

"I'm conducting an experiment."

The voice was rough, but the timbre and accent suggested it belonged to a fae. That was enough to make the skin at his nape prickle with foreboding. Still, Arthur let the moment stretch on. As a king, he'd learned the power of silence long ago.

Finally, with a quick sigh, the fae spoke again. "I'm standing at the gas station on the west side of town. Do you know it?"

"Yes." It was on a busy highway a few miles from the medieval theme park where the knights worked.

"If I tell you my dragon is about to burn it down, what will you do?"

"Find you and kill you like I do every other psychotic fae," Arthur replied without emotion. "That's why I took a long nap in a stone suit."

"You have a high opinion of yourself."

"The modern term is *badass*. I'm the one with the big, shiny sword not even your queen can survive."

"And I'm the one with the dragon. You don't have much time to get here before the show."

The line went dead.

Arthur swore as he put the phone away. A wave of unreality stole over him as the pedestrians swept by him, laughing or talking or hurrying with heads down in thought. They were ordinary humans with no idea what the enemy could do. He'd seen the soulless fae steal human lives for the sake of pleasure, drinking their life essence like a drug. It was Arthur's job to stop the fae from making these people their slaves.

If the dragon was in partnership with a fae, that changed everything. This wasn't just a large, scaly bully in need of a fire hose. With another oath, Arthur strode down the street, shouldering his way past a knot of idling boys. Was this threat a trap? Probably. But a warrior king took his share of risks to save the people in his charge. Anything less wasn't worthy of Camelot.

Pete's Pay and Go sat on the corner where a six-lane truck route crossed paths with the four-lane artery that ran into Carlyle. There was nothing remarkable or attractive about the place. It had gas, groceries and a fast-food drive-through that sold a chemical approximation of burgers and fries. As usual, there was road construction because the highways department never dug a hole unless they could tie up traffic for months at a time.

Arthur dodged the traffic cones and pulled into the last parking spot. When he got out, the first thing he saw was a van decorated with the call letters of the local news station and a cluster of equipment mounted on top. Whatever happened next would be beamed to every TV in town. Arthur's stomach went cold. Magic was a secret kept from ordinary mortals, but this fae ignored that rule.

Arthur wheeled, looking for explanations. Instead, he saw one of Camelot's knights getting out of a battered pickup. Sir Owen of the Beasts walked across the parking lot, pushing wavy brown hair out of his eyes and glowering at the highway traffic. Like the animals he befriended, the tall, young Welshman was happiest in the wilds. He hadn't been at their council earlier, but on his way back from a weekend in the woods.

"Sir Gawain texted me as I was driving back into town," Owen said in his soft, lilting voice. "He will be here presently but suffered an unforeseen delay."

Gawain hadn't mentioned anything when Arthur had phoned him en route, but Owen's careful courtesy discouraged questions. Arthur forged ahead. "You missed some excitement while you were gone. I'm expecting a dragon."

Owen's expression was eager. "Well, that will be

something. I've only ever seen a wyvern up close. It was quite fond of dried salmon."

"Rukon Shadow Wing isn't friendly."

"That isn't unusual," the Welsh knight replied, his enthusiasm firmly in place. "Dragons are touchy and intolerable braggarts to be sure."

Arthur nodded to the news van. "This one seems to want an interview. We should look around for any sign of his fae friend."

Owen fell into step beside him. "I don't understand why the dragon came here. They don't typically travel beyond their own domain."

Arthur grunted agreement. "If he's in league with a fae, no doubt the idea came from Queen Morgan's court."

"Of course, sire, that's quite possible, but I've heard of Rukon Shadow Wing. He lives in the Crystal Mountains."

Surprise made Arthur pause. Not that Owen had information on Rukon—if something had four legs, chances are Owen of the Beasts knew about it—but the mountains were deep in goblin country. Goblin and fae didn't mix. Ever. So how did Rukon cross paths with a fae? "That poses some interesting questions."

"Indeed, sire." Owen frowned in apology, as if he were somehow responsible.

Arthur didn't get a chance to reply. A young brunette with high heels and a microphone bore down on them with a predator's determination. "I'm Megan Dutton, Nighthawk News. I know you fine gentlemen are from the Medievaland jousting tournaments. Arthur Pendragon, isn't it? And you?"

She turned to Owen with a look Arthur recognized. The knight charmed more than just puppies and wounded fawns. "Owen Powys, mistress."

The reporter blinked rapidly, as if dazzled. "Yes, well, our newsroom received a tip regarding an imminent attack by fire-breathing dragons. Isn't that why you gentlemen are here? As part of a promotional event for Medievaland?"

She plowed on before Arthur could think of an answer. "And aren't you afraid that this kind of stunt might cause panic among the population? Care to comment on this irresponsible action by Medievaland's management?"

She thrust the mic toward him like a badly handled blade. Behind her, a minion with a camera edged closer. As one of the primary performers at the theme park, Arthur had some experience with press doing puff pieces for the tourist season, but Megan Dutton was after controversy.

He didn't have time for this. The longer she had him trapped, the less time he had to stop whatever was about to happen. "I'm sure I speak for the management of the Medievaland Theme Park when I assure you that there is no intention to panic the citizens of Carlyle."

"Then what are your intentions, Mr. Pendragon? What are we about to see?"

There was no opportunity to say anything more. Owen pointed to the sky, and then Arthur became a far less interesting part of the story. The camera swung away and Arthur followed the knight's pointing finger, squinting against the sun. Far, far up was a scrap of black with a long tail and it was spiraling downward in erratic loops. It was so distant one might have mistaken it for a child's kite if not for the long, sinuous neck.

Arthur watched, calculating where the beast was going to land. The wings were spread, but the creature was struggling to control its descent. Something was wrong.

"That's not Rukon—that's a female," said Owen softly. "Look at the slender shape of her head."

Arthur couldn't tell the difference. It was still the size of a truck and falling from the sky right over moving traffic. Whatever was beneath the dragon would be crushed. He spun to the reporter and her cameraman, putting the snap of authority into his voice. "Do something useful! Get everyone back."

He turned to Owen. "Help me clear the road."

With that, he bolted for the intersection, holding up a hand to stop the steady stream of cars. Owen was on his heels, intercepting the other lanes. It was foolhardy, but the dragon's shadow was steadily spreading as seconds ticked by. He looked up, estimating one more time where she'd land. She'd stopped trying to fly and was hurtling for the highway.

A truck started to turn and gave a furious honk as Arthur sprang in front of it, waving his arms. He danced back as a sudden wave of heat and fumes washed over him. His hands went out, slamming against the hot grille, but it stopped. He looked up expecting to see the driver's scowl, but the man gazed skyward, transfixed.

No one was moving now. Eerie silence muffled the scene. Arthur turned, putting his back to the vehicle, and felt his jaw go slack. The creature was still falling, close enough now to make out more detail. *Ten seconds until it hits the earth.* For an instant, he could see the dragon's iridescent blue hide and the slender taper of her wings. *Eight.* She seemed to shudder, as if heaving her last breath. It was then he saw the weave of golden magic tangling her wings, like a dog wound in its own leash. Whoever controlled her had bungled things, and now she couldn't fly. *Five.* Arthur watched, appalled as the dragon struggled, then loosed her fire. She blazed like a falling star, the thin membranes of her wings a corona of blinding white. She was trying to burn the chains of magic away. His gorge began to rise in pure, unadulterated horror as she roared in agony. *Zero.*

She vanished. Utter silence reigned.

Arthur's heart pounded. He'd expected a crash, a crumpled mass of bone and flesh, but there was nothing but the charcoal stink of dragon flame and spent magic. Arthur buried his nose in his sleeve as he backed away. He'd guessed the dragon's landing site correctly—if it had actually landed. A little bit more to the left, and the gas station would have been alight.

And yet none of that mattered now because the creature was gone, yanked back to her own world before her chains could break. Whatever the fae had wanted to do here, he'd failed.

Owen appeared at Arthur's elbow, his face white. "The dragon burned herself trying to get free."

The fae, whoever he was, was about to be dead meat. Arthur swore it in the depths of his heart.

The howl of sirens broke through his stunned dismay. Emergency lights flashed as a fire truck and ambulance pulled into the parking lot. A policeman was shooing the crowd back. Megan Dutton was still there, yelling into her mic about heroes and disaster and mysteries.

Arthur shot a glance at the reporter, and then at Owen. "Let's go before she starts asking us questions."

They slipped through the crowd to the parking lot.

There, they found Gawain waiting, worry creasing his face. "What happened?" he asked. "Someone said a flaming cow dropped out of an airplane. Is Merlin involved?"

Arthur heaved a sigh, half in relief and half in irritation. *Flaming cow?* People only saw what they expected to see. "A dragon was supposed to destroy the gas station, but something went wrong."

Gawain looked at the Pay and Go, which was clearly not burning. "Wrong in what way?"

"We don't know," Arthur said. "At least no one was hurt."

"Except the dragon," Owen put in. "How could she possibly have survived that fall, regardless of what world she was in?"

"Right." The beautiful, agonized dragon. Arthur closed his eyes, fighting back a rage so large he could barely breathe. They still didn't know anything, but Owen had a solid point. "Spread out and search this place. No doubt the fae is watching. He didn't orchestrate all this without a front-row seat."

Owen nodded and strode away, face thunderous. Arthur moved to follow, but Gawain caught his arm. "I'll take over here. You're needed at home—or rather, at Clary's hotel."

"Why?"

Gawain grimaced. "That's where Guinevere is sleeping tonight."

"What?" Blood rushed to Arthur's head. This wasn't the time for Gwen's antics, not with fae and burning dragons and reporters crawling all over Carlyle. And the Crystal Mountains—what was a fae doing crossing the goblins' lands? There were too many questions. He couldn't deal with another distraction. "There are no guards at the hotel. She's not protected."

"I think that might be the point." Gawain's face was carefully neutral.

"Doesn't she understand what's going on?" snapped Arthur.

Gawain raised his hands in a gesture of surrender. "Ask her, not me."

"After all the problems she's caused over the years, has she learned nothing?"

No sooner did Arthur say it than he snapped his jaw shut, remembering the light going out of Gwen's eyes when he'd approached her in the restaurant. She'd learned he was willing to walk away and leave her in the past for her own protection. Was that what he still wanted? Had he really just thought of her as a distraction?

Is it any wonder she wants her freedom?

So what was he going to do about it?

Chapter 8

Gwen had never dated and therefore needed advice.

Clary's first move had been to search the internet for tips on planning a romantic evening with an estranged spouse. This involved answering a number of quizzes and the application of Smoking Surrender Coral nail polish. Clary had then bullied Gwen into a dainty black dress and sent her to the hotel bar in time to meet Arthur for drinks. The two women had agreed a public place was a good choice, at least to begin the conversation. Finally, Clary had gone out, leaving the room unoccupied until at least midnight.

Gwen should have been pleased. For once, she was in control of the situation and Arthur was the one asking for attention. It took a lot for him to bend. Clary had attributed that to shutting the bedroom door last night, but Gwen wasn't sure his reasons were that straightforward. The King of Camelot was a complicated man.

She wondered if he'd ever loved her.

Guinevere took the elevator up to the cocktail lounge on the top floor. She'd been told the room rotated slowly, so that diners got a view of the entire city skyline by the time the night was done. To someone born in a stone castle that seemed both wondrous and enormously silly. What was the point when it took far less effort to simply walk around the room?

She pushed the thought out of her mind as soon as she entered the lounge. Arthur sat near the far wall, but he rose as she stepped into view. He'd been watching for her. He hadn't done that for a long time.

The space between them suddenly seemed enormous, as if she had to cross a vast plain in her high heels instead of a little bit of carpet. She wasn't used to the shoes, and her ankles wobbled slightly, but she kept her chin high and her bare arms relaxed at her sides. The only way to face Arthur, ever, was with courage.

The dress Clary had made her buy was a backless halter style with a tight waist and a skirt that flared just above the knee. The black satin whispered as she walked to Arthur's table by the tall glass window. He continued to stand, a frozen look on his face that she couldn't quite read. He'd dressed, too, in a well-cut suit and plain white shirt that showed off the taper from his broad shoulders to trim waist. He wore no tie, the casual touch somehow putting him above the formal crowd. Nothing marked him as a king, and yet the whole lounge seemed to acknowledge his status. Waitstaff hovered, and every other male had chosen a table far away.

Courage, she repeated to herself as she drew closer. She could see his eyes now, the heat in that bright blue like the fire of diamonds. The hunger in them was a physical touch, a hot lick from her ankles upward to the low plunge of her bodice. There was no pretense of manners in that look, just raw male appreciation. A sword-swinging warrior's appetite, despite what the costly suit implied. For that alone, she wanted to thank Clary for insisting on the dress. She needed confidence now.

He took a few steps, meeting her before she finally reached the table. He placed a hand at the small of her back, guiding her forward. "You look amazing," he said, bending to murmur in her ear.

That close, she could smell soap and skin. The scent and his nearness brought memories of lying beside him, exploring the landscape of his hard body. She snatched her mind back to the present, needing to keep her wits about her.

"Thank you," she said with a cool nod as he held the chair for her. She sat carefully, the short skirt making her feel exposed. She noticed a long black bag beneath the table and guessed Excalibur was inside. The sword never went far from Arthur's side.

A beat of silence followed, filled with questions and an undercurrent of hurt. It didn't show on their faces— they were both too skilled at court politics for that— but Gwen felt it like fingers along her skin. He was edgy, filled with nervous energy. Arthur took his seat and signaled a waiter with a flick of fingers. The man quickly returned with an ice bucket, champagne and delicate glasses.

If there had been any doubt before, Arthur was trying to impress her. By the rules they'd grown up with that meant showing his wealth and status. He might not have a castle here, but he wasn't a pauper. According to Clary, Medievaland was doing extremely well since the knights had arrived, and the management of the theme park had given them generous contracts. They were, in fact, becoming local celebrities with a dedicated fan base.

The waiter poured the champagne and retreated on silent feet. Arthur raised his glass. "We haven't had a chance to drink to your arrival. Be welcome, my lady."

Gwen tasted the bubbling liquid, decided she liked it and set it aside. Again, she wanted a clear head. It would be too easy to surrender to Arthur simply because he asked. She'd only imagined a path of her own choosing for a few hours, and she was unsure of herself.

"The lights are very beautiful," she said, looking out the window because it was easier than looking at him. "What is that ring in the sky?"

"A Ferris wheel," he said. "Those colored lights belong to Medievaland."

"Oh." She looked more closely, actually interested now.

"Did you find everything you required at the stores?" he asked, gaze intent on her.

"Everything to wear and to groom myself," she replied. "And a phone. Clary insisted I need one, although I'm not sure of all its uses yet."

"Give it to me," he said, holding out a hand.

She hesitated, fingers tightening on the black silk clutch purse she held in her lap. "Why?"

"I want your number."

She slowly handed it over. She'd chosen a green leather case painted with exotic birds, but he barely noticed it as he thumbed the screen to life and began tapping in numbers. Once, he said he'd been trained to ignore distraction on pain of a beating. She believed the story. It said as much about him as his great victories.

He handed her phone back. "I put my number in. Now you can phone me."

"Thank you." She closed the case and put it away in her purse.

"How did you spend the rest of the day?" he asked, his tone forced now.

She noticed the tight lines of his face, a sure sign of strain. She wondered what he'd been doing in the hours since she'd seen him last. "Reading. I borrowed Clary's laptop and just looked and looked. There's so much to know about this time. So many marvels." She'd searched for schools, too, falling in love with the idea of being a student. But that dream belonged to a new Guinevere that Arthur hadn't met yet. She wasn't ready to expose that vulnerable piece of herself to the man across from her. Not until she had a chance to find her feet.

Arthur looked down at his hands, clearly gathering his thoughts. The brief awkwardness of small talk was over. "Why are you staying here and not at home?"

"I—"

He fixed her with the piercing blue gaze that had made kings and sorcerers quail. "What do you want that you can't have beneath my roof?"

You, she thought, but knew he wouldn't understand. "Me," she replied instead. "I'm not there."

It was plain to see he didn't understand that, either. His brow furrowed in irritation. "Please explain."

Gwen cast a furtive look at her champagne glass, suddenly wishing she'd drunk more. Even liquor-induced courage was something, and he clearly thought her a spoiled child. "I don't know if I can."

"If you don't try, then we will achieve nothing."

As if this was just another project to be tackled and conquered. She felt the heat rise to her face and looked away, staring at the bubbles floating in her glass.

"Clary told me what has gone on here." Her body was rigid. "She said Gawain held her sister at knifepoint when they first met. The night Nimueh and Lancelot found each other again, they battled the Queen of Faery's assassin. That they both nearly died before all was over. And here we sit in a hotel lounge."

"Is that what you want? Knives and violence instead of this?" Arthur waved a hand at the half-darkened room. "I didn't take you for a warrior queen."

Gwen flinched. "You know I'm not." It would have been easier if she had been, but she preferred building things to killing.

"Then what is your point?" An edge of frustration crept into his voice. Not quite sarcasm, but its cousin.

She gave him a hard look. "Those men and women have passion between them."

"So do we."

She flushed. "There is a difference between passion and pleasure. Passion involves the heart and mind as well as the flesh."

The corners of Arthur's lips turned down. "You are frank, my lady."

"I am saving us pain. We had six years of doubt. Do we need a seventh? An eighth?"

The flush of temper crept up his neck. "Yes, I doubted you. After your illness, you kept company with Lancelot and Lionel and any of the other young knights who would sit at your feet and adore you. What was I to think?"

Agitated, she picked up the tiny paper napkin the waiter had placed under her drink and began tearing it to bits. After her illness, Arthur had kept her confined. She'd been depressed already and his overprotectiveness had made everything so much worse. "You left me alone, day after day. I was lonely and very young."

"And so you let them court you under my nose?"

"Yes, I did." She lifted her chin. "Did you ever stop to think why?"

"A girl's game." He said it with contempt, probably because her ploy had worked. She knew he'd been jealous and still felt guilty about it. And yet, what tools did a girl that age have?

Gwen met his eyes. "Perhaps I wanted you to fight for my affection. I was dazzled by you when we wed, and then you put me in your castle and rode away. I was no more to you than a chair or a tapestry. If I'd been a dog, at least you would have had a use for me."

They stared at each other, gazes hot with resentment. She'd never been so blunt before now. Arthur had to visibly unclench his teeth before he could speak. "Did those men ever touch you?"

She made a strangled noise, resentment bubbling up like a fresh wound. "No. They were my friends, not my lovers. And you've asked that a thousand times before."

He fell back in his chair with a hiss of breath. "I know. You have no idea how well that arrow flew."

"Then why did you never change?" It was a simple question, but she'd never dared to ask it. Now, though, there was no chance of retreat. She'd already shown too many cards.

Arthur glanced from side to side, fingers fidgeting on the tablecloth. Another couple was sitting down at a nearby table, close enough to overhear. "Is there another place we could go?"

"My room. Clary will be gone for hours."

He nodded, rising at once and ordering the champagne to be delivered. Arthur led the way to the elevator, not touching her and not offering a word. He held the bag with his sword instead, gripping the handle in a white-knuckled fist. Gwen didn't attempt to break the silence, but pushed the elevator button and waited stiffly. This standoff lasted until the hotel-room door clacked shut behind them.

The champagne arrived barely a minute after, and the fuss of delivery and tipping stalled the conversation further. Gwen kicked off her shoes, feeling more secure in the refuge Clary had offered her. The room was large, with a comfortable sitting area. Compared to Arthur's apartment, it was pretty, decorated in blue and yellow. Nevertheless, the place seemed smaller with Arthur in it. Gwen sat down in one of the overstuffed chairs, purposefully avoiding the intimacy of the couch.

He went to stand at the window, looking out with his hands clasped behind his back. "I knew you turned to others for friendship. I never understood why you didn't trust me. I did everything to protect you, whether or not you appreciated my methods. It was my duty and desire to keep you safe."

When she didn't answer, he released a noisy breath. "I suppose you still want an answer to your question."

"I do."

"I didn't change because there was never time."

It made sense, up to a point. There was always a

war, a fire, crop failure or some other emergency. Good kings barely had a private life, and Arthur had taken his duty to heart. Gwen had never found fault with his care of Camelot's citizens—just with his care for her. She breathed a sigh, but it did nothing to expel the tension jangling inside her. She snatched up the champagne and filled her glass, drinking it down.

"And now?" she asked quietly. "Is there time for us now?"

He turned from the window. "Is that what you want? Time? Passion? Lazy afternoons to share our thoughts?"

Gwen sucked in a breath. "Yes."

He frowned. "What else?"

She set down the glass, pulling her thoughts into order. She might only get one chance to say what she needed to say. "I will not live the way I did before."

He actually looked shocked. "You do not wish to be queen?"

"A queen rules by her husband's side. I can't do that if I'm, um, if I…" She stumbled, wanting to say that she wanted him very much, but that wasn't the sum and total of who and what she was.

"Gwen?"

"I want to matter," she finally said. It sounded selfish, though she didn't mean it that way.

"You do matter. I want you at my side," he said, but she couldn't decipher his tone.

"Do you really? A real queen would be involved with the running of whatever kingdom you establish here. Otherwise, I have no purpose in Camelot."

And if she had no reason to stay, there were other places she could go. All the rules governing women and marriage had changed over the centuries. She finally had choices.

By the look on Arthur's face, he knew that, too. Time seemed to stop. So did Gwen's breath.

"You were indeed very young when we wed," he said.

"I'm old enough now, my lord. I've learned much about the responsibilities of the throne."

Something shifted in his expression. "So you have, my lady."

Was this the reassurance she'd been waiting for? Uncertain, Gwen rose from her chair, her bare feet sinking into the soft carpet. "Then tell me what's going on with the dragon. If you want me at your side, I need to understand what Camelot is facing."

For an instant, Arthur's composure slipped and she saw a flash of unexpected sadness. He turned back to the window before she could fully read his expression. "There is more than one dragon involved. I may well have seen one die today, after I left you and the witch. She was a female of breeding age, I think."

"Where?" Gwen demanded, perplexed. One beast finding its way into the world was an unhappy accident. More than one spelled a plot.

"Are you certain you want to know? It is not a pleasant tale."

"Trust me, I do."

So he told her about what he'd seen at the gas station and about the fight with Rukon Shadow Wing. Gwen listened carefully and didn't interrupt. He was making an effort to restore peace between them.

"There is a fae involved," he said as he finished, "but I'm not certain how."

"There are dragons in the Faery Realms."

"But Rukon Shadow Wing lives in the Crystal Mountains, deep in goblin territory. No fae would dare set foot there."

Guinevere shook her head. "In our time, that was true, but centuries have passed while we slept. Perhaps the fae have made peace with the goblin king."

"That's possible." He rubbed his eyes. "I can't get the image of that unfortunate creature out of my head. I have fought many of her kind, but nothing deserves that suffering. Why are they coming here?"

The sadness in his words moved her. "Perhaps she had no choice."

He reached out, his fingers tracing her cheek until she caught his hand. A spark of angry confusion streaked through her. "How could you sit drinking wine with this fresh in your mind?"

"We needed to talk."

Gwen closed her eyes, exasperated and grateful at the same time. "How can you block something like that out?"

"I don't feel it any less, but there are many terrible things, all wanting attention." He freed his hand from hers, and then ran his fingers down the length of her hair. "I wished to contemplate beauty for a time."

She couldn't help but smile, although it was bittersweet. "Have you borrowed a poet's tongue for the night?"

"I always speak the truth. Once in a long while I do it well."

They were standing close together now, sharing the same breath. Her arms and face tingled as if he gave off an electric charge, but it was just his presence. It was always like this, the anticipation of touch a kind of fire beneath her skin. She lowered her gaze, hoping her need for him didn't appear as naked as it felt. She gave a light sigh, and then met his blue, blue eyes. "Can we make this work?"

Chapter 9

Arthur didn't respond—not in words. Instead, he slid an arm around her waist, stepping into her embrace as smoothly as a dancer. Or a swordsman. He had a deadly grace Gwen had seen in no other man and it left her dry-mouthed and hungry in places no decent woman would name.

Her hands were around his neck, though she did not remember reaching for him, or when they'd started to kiss. When the times were peaceful between them, making love came naturally, needing no thought or will, nothing but instinct. As easy as breathing, and as necessary. Maybe that was why the last years had been so hard—he'd been gone, and in the empty, loveless halls of the castle, she'd been fighting for air.

Her fingers eased beneath his jacket, finding the satin lining warm with his heat. He shrugged off the coat, letting it fall, and pulled her close. His mouth was on her lips, her jaw, the sensitive place just below her ear. Everywhere, and each lingering touch was more inviting than the last. It was like being pulled into the ocean, the current too strong to resist. A reckless part of Gwen yearned to be swept under. Love—or whatever it was Arthur offered when he was in this mood—wasn't about caution. Her response was the hunger of a flower for the sun.

His hands found the bare skin beneath the fall of her hair and caressed it lightly, trailing his fingers down to her waist. Gwen shivered, but kept her attention on the buttons of his shirt. They weren't what she was used to—shirts in her mind pulled over the head, with strings to pull the neckline closed. This was like a puzzle box, each little fastening revealing a few more inches of masculine skin. The process was tantalizing but slow.

And Arthur wouldn't stand still for it. He was kissing down her throat, his tongue leaving hot licks as he progressed toward the low neckline of her dress. Gwen arched into it, feeling the brush of his hair as he bent his head, the beard a coarser sensation against her sensitized skin. Her nipples ached, wanting the hot wetness of his mouth on them. If she could have torn the dress away, she would have, but she'd lost command of her limbs.

He looked up, revealing a man who had abandoned any pretense of civilization. Appetite dominated his gaze, the raw need of possession. These moments were as close as she ever got to reaching his soul. She ran her palms up the delicious planes the open shirt now revealed—the hard stomach, the swell of his chest, the thickness of his shoulders. Finally, Gwen took his face between her hands and kissed him full on the mouth, her tongue meeting his and tasting sweet champagne beneath the richness of the man. He returned her ardor, demanding more. Gwen gasped as he lifted her, the sudden weightlessness adding to her sense of abandon. She hooked her legs around his waist and let him carry her to the bed.

He laid her down with exquisite care, everything in his manner declaring her a rare prize. "You are so beautiful," he rumbled, pressing his lips to the base of her throat. That nearly undid her, right then and there. She had no more will than warm candle wax, ready to be coaxed into any shape he desired.

And she could tell he was eager to do it, the swell of him plain against her belly. Her hands went to his belt, finding a new challenge—but also something passing strange. "My lord, you are vibrating."

Arthur pulled the phone from his pocket with a colorful oath, and tossed it onto the bedside table. That only made the insistent buzzing worse. He snatched it up again, glaring as if looks alone could make the phone burst into flames. He jabbed the screen to silence, only to have it burble a moment later as a text message popped into view.

"By Saint Sebastian's bleeding arrows," he snarled, tossing the phone to the coverlet.

He jammed both hands into his tousled hair. From Gwen's vantage point on the bed, the gesture did interesting things to his chest muscles.

"What is it?" she asked, sitting up.

His eyes were wild. "There's another dragon. It's at the park."

"Medievaland?"

He nodded. "I'm sorry. I need to go."

"Of course you do," she said, and meant it. This was serious.

As she watched, his frantic expression vanished bit by bit, as if a series of walls slammed into place. One moment he was filled with emotion—desire and distress—and the next he was all icy control. Watching the change sobered her faster than any cold shower. She sat up and slid off the bed.

"Wait a moment and I'll change," she said, padding to the closet.

"Why?"

"Because I'm going with you." She pulled out the jeans she'd worn earlier. Surely they'd be practical enough if she had to run or climb.

"No, you're not." His voice was a whip crack.

She spun, all her anger pouncing on his words. "What did you say?"

"Dragons are dangerous, Gwen. I can't let you walk into that." He buttoned up his shirt with brisk movements, erasing all her careful work before retrieving his jacket from the floor. "You're my wife. It's up to me to protect you."

"How can you protect me when I'm here and you're at Medievaland?"

"I'll call for one of the men to guard you. I already told you I'd do that."

If he was reverting to the plans already in place, nothing she'd said that night had mattered. Frustration exploded inside her, a huge and unreasoning beast. She tossed the jeans at him, but they only flopped to the bed in a defeated sprawl. "What happened to having me at your side? What happened to me being a grown woman? Don't you think I have a right to serve our people, too?"

His expression hardened. "I don't have time to argue about this now. We'll talk when I get back."

"If I'm here," she snapped.

Annoyance twisted his features, settling into the angry scowl she knew too well. "That is, of course, entirely your decision." He jammed his phone into his jacket pocket, picked up his sword and strode toward the door.

With that, he left her alone.

Arthur bolted from the hotel, furious with Guinevere. She thought she'd join the dragon hunt? That was pure insanity. The one time he allowed her to march with his army—during a simple, dragon-free engagement—she'd nearly died from a fever that ran through the ranks like wildfire. And she'd caught it because she wouldn't listen to him and keep safe in her tent but insisted on nursing the sick and dying.

How would she fare against a monster that had nearly killed a seasoned warrior like Gawain?

The notion of Gwen anywhere near a fire-breathing monster brought a prickling sweat to his skin. If something happened to her... He couldn't find an end to the statement. There was no room for that possibility. Why couldn't she understand that always, always he'd been doing his best to protect her? Yes, sometimes that meant leaving her behind, but wasn't that better than death?

He pulled out of the hotel parking lot at breakneck speed, sailing down the main drag that would take him out of the downtown. Three blocks later he ran a red light and only after that forced himself to slow down. The witches—mostly Tamsin and Clary's family—had shepherded the knights through the labyrinthine process of establishing fake identification. The last thing he needed to do was risk it all for a traffic violation.

Or at least that was what the reasonable part of his brain insisted. There was a burning pit beneath his breastbone that bubbled with frustrated lust and wounded pride. Anger urged him to be reckless, but he was a king. Royalty didn't have the luxury of emotion— not when they had a realm to protect.

Arthur swung into Medievaland's parking lot and barely stopped the SUV before jumping out and running for the gates. The theme park re-created the Middle Ages, complete with jousts, banquets, artisans and costumed minstrels. There was also a midway and rides guaranteed to curdle the hardiest stomach. For the knights of Camelot, it was the one place they could exist in the modern world without completely abandoning who they were. They couldn't afford to lose it to a dragon.

The workers at the gates knew him by sight and he ran past without comment. The familiar mechanical whirs and bells of the midway assaulted him, while the aromas of fried onions and popcorn were sharp in the chilly air. Jugglers roamed the pathways, tossing clubs that glowed in the dark while far above, lights from the roller coaster swirled through the starlit sky. As it was close to ten o'clock and a half hour away from the winter closing time, the crowd was thinning out.

Arthur charged ahead, seeking any sign of fire or panic, but all seemed normal. He stopped beside the life-size statue of a pink unicorn to get his bearings. The text message that had called him to the theme park had come from Gawain. He dialed the Scottish knight's phone. "I'm here. Where is it?" he demanded the instant Gawain picked up.

"Look above the church."

The Church of the Holy Well was the only truly medieval item in the park. It had once housed the sleeping knights of Camelot and had been transplanted from England decades ago when Medievaland was built. Arthur's gaze found it easily among the theme park's structures and he obediently studied the roofline. "I don't see anything."

"Keep watching."

Impatient, Arthur paced, the phone still to his ear. What was Gwen doing? Was there any chance of returning to her hotel room that night? His anger was still a live thing, flaring if his thoughts touched it, but hers had been just as hot. Would that make a reunion impossible, or delectable?

His reverie lasted only seconds before he saw a dark shape gliding above the whirling lights of the rides. It was as if a scrap of nothingness flitted across the sky, but he knew what that absence of light meant. "I see it."

"It's been circling for the last half hour," said Gawain. "We've gathered at the tourney grounds."

"Ready my gear," Arthur ordered.

He sprinted to the complex where the jousting took place. The games themselves were held in an amphitheater, while the stables and equipment rooms were in low buildings behind. When the white wooden structure came into view, Arthur put on a last burst of speed. Gawain, already clad in his red armor, waited outside the locker-room door. He turned as Arthur approached, silently leading him inside.

The space where they donned their equipment was much like any locker room, with sinks and showers. Beaumains had Arthur's white-and-blue armor already spread out on a bench. This was not the gear they used for jousting, though much of it looked similar. This was battle-scarred and shaped to personal taste, often sacrificing coverage for ease of movement. Jousting was inherently dangerous, but it was nothing compared to true warfare, where speed could save one's life.

"We don't know if the dragon will even land," Gawain said, buckling Arthur's breastplate in place. His fingers flew with the urgency of one well used to donning battle gear on the fly. "This preparation may be for nothing."

"I would rather not meet the beast's teeth unprotected," Arthur replied, "though armor never did much against a dragon's flame." Unhelpfully, his imagination pictured a potato in tinfoil, ready for the barbecue.

"Perhaps there's a modern material that would help," Beaumains suggested, fastening the metal vambraces that protected Arthur's forearms. "Maybe asbestos?"

Gawain gave an eye roll only an older brother could produce. "Perhaps we could put a sprinkler system in our helms and spout like fountains. Go help Owen with the horses."

Beaumains bowed and left, giving a cheeky grin. Arthur took Excalibur from Gawain and fastened the sword belt in place.

"I'm sorry this happened tonight of all nights," said Gawain. "I know you went to see the queen."

No doubt Clary had told him. There was nothing worse than being the object of gossip. Arthur shifted from foot to foot, his armor clanking softly. "The queen understands the urgency," he said in a tone that didn't invite conversation.

Gawain studied him, but said nothing more on the

subject. He simply handed Arthur his shield, with its three golden crowns against a field of blue. These were the great kite-shaped shields rather than the smaller, round bucklers—clumsier, but they offered better protection from flame. Arthur took it, and they marched toward the door. Just as Arthur's mailed fist touched the door handle, he heard the scream of horses.

As the door opened, Rukon Shadow Wing landed at Medievaland's heart in a gout of flame. This time, Arthur knew, the dragon had come to kill them.

Chapter 10

Only the dragon's breath was visible in the unlit amphitheater. Scraps of flame picked out pieces from the shadow it cast—a shoulder, a curl of tail, a flare of amber eyes. In contrast, the men of the Round Table stood in the pool of light cast by the building, their shields defiantly bright with color. Beaumains and Percival had readied their horses and were struggling with their mounts' bridles. The terrified animals were stamping and tossing their heads, nostrils flaring at the unfamiliar scent. They were good, brave mounts, but they weren't trained for dragons.

"Get the horses back in the stables," Arthur ordered. "We're doing this on foot."

"What's your plan?" Gawain asked, as the younger knights hurried to obey.

Arthur heard the blare of sirens—fire and police, no

doubt. This was just getting worse. There was no hiding a flapping, talking dragon from the human authorities. "I've tried polite reason. Now it's time to make our scaly friend leave."

"I'm right beside you," said Gawain. Putting action to words, he drew his sword and stood at Arthur's right.

"I never thought I'd have the chance to fight a dragon." Percival stretched his limbs, hiding his eagerness with a show of preparation.

"I've battled one before," Palomedes replied, sounding less enthusiastic. "I can't say I wanted a rematch, but here we are."

The dragon was moving now, advancing at a steady pace that said it had an agenda. At the same time, Arthur was aware of the other knights clustering around him, shields up to present an unbreakable wall of courage. Every knight who could be was there. With five mighty warriors against one dragon, the odds were almost even. All the same, it was going to be a bloodbath.

Rukon folded his wings and bellowed, the pale underside of his neck a stripe against the inky sky. A second later, a dozen camera flashes bleached the darkness. Reporters, Arthur realized with a sinking stomach. The hidden world would be in the headlines by breakfast—unless Rukon made the press his late-night snack.

If Arthur had been a glory seeker, a horseback charge with lance and shining armor would have set social media aflame—right along with Medievaland. As King of Camelot and protector of the mortal realms, Arthur had to put an end to this drama before it began. "No hashtag for me," he muttered under his breath as he drew Excalibur.

"Stay here," he ordered his men, his voice brooking

no argument. "I go in first. If he attacks, I'll keep him busy while you move in."

"You're buying us a chance," Gawain said darkly.

"A king spends the lives of his men as carefully as he can."

"What about your own?"

"Give my regards to the late-night news. Now, do as I ask."

While he heard armor clank and feet scuffle, the knights knew better than to protest. Discipline had been hard-won among these fighters, but Arthur had enforced his will through respect and occasional bravado. Just the same, when he strode forward their watchfulness prickled along his spine. He was protecting his men, but they had his back. In moments like this, he loved them fiercely.

As always, the prospect of battle heightened his senses. Night robbed the world of color and precise edges—the amphitheater had no lighting for after-dark events. But he could smell the fairground's tapestry of scents—horses, food, exhaust, dust and, over it all, the thick musk of dragon. The last clogged his nose and throat worse than it had in the forest, or maybe his chest was tight because the fight was on his ground now. Here, he had far more to lose.

He stopped halfway down the field. Walking in armor was noisy, and only now could he hear the profound silence surrounding him. No one spoke, no car doors slammed. All attention was fixed on the king and the dragon. As if on cue, the clock tower at the Church of the Holy Well bonged the half hour, confirming that the park had closed. Fewer bystanders would be in the line of fire. Something to be thankful for.

An image of Gwen's face flickered through his mind,

but he shied away from it. Right now, he had to be a king, not a man. Remembering his wife, in all her softness and fiery temper, would undo every scrap of courage.

Arthur's mouth had gone dry, and he had to swallow twice before he could speak—but when he did, he spoke loud enough to make himself heard by everyone present. After all, he'd been trained to address crowds in a time before microphones. "Greetings, Rukon Shadow Wing. To what do I owe the honor of your visit?"

Rukon let another scrap of flame escape his muzzle. The fire floated like ragged scarves around him, giving the impression of something birthed in a painter's conception of hell. Arthur guessed it was a sign of temper, and a dangerous one. If the arena floor hadn't been dirt, the entire place would be in flames.

"I warned you that I would come," Rukon replied, the rumbling voice grim. "I have already explained what I will do to reclaim fame and glory among the human realms. Are these your reporters?" He snaked his neck toward the news vans, blowing a puff of steam.

"Do you really believe renown will come if you eat me on television?" Arthur said wearily.

"It must be seen and commented upon to be of value. Isn't that how this world works?"

"That is hardly the point."

"That is precisely the point." The dragon snorted more fire.

This wasn't telling Arthur anything new. He gambled then, the ache in his chest an indication of how much he feared. "You've given me words. I will think of them whenever I shovel the stable."

Rukon's head swung back, the yellow eyes glowing hot.

Arthur lowered his sword and shield, but just enough to show his intention to talk. "You could have killed me yesterday, but you did not."

"I spared you so that we would meet tonight, in front of your tale-tellers."

"You are here again, but so far you haven't touched a single blade of grass. Meanwhile, I have received threats from an anonymous fae. These are all part of a pattern, and I don't believe you are a willing participant. Nor was the dragon who fell from the sky. She was chained with magic, a pawn in a murderous plan."

At that, Rukon threw back his head and gave another roar. It was filled with sound and flame, bringing screams from the gathered crowd. From the corner of his eye, Arthur saw uniformed men press forward, but the knights rushed to hold them back.

Eventually the bellow subsided, fading from fury to what Arthur had expected to hear—grief. "Her name is Elosta," Rukon said. "Remember her name well, human, and remember it with reverence. There is no telling what befell her. He will not say."

"Who?" Arthur demanded, wondering if Elosta was Rukon's mate. "What is going on?"

"Treachery," Rukon rumbled. "You are the Pendragon, little king. Figure it out."

But Arthur didn't have a clue. "Tell me more."

But Rukon fanned his wings, spreading them wide until they blotted out the stars. Arthur just had time to lift his shield before he was engulfed in flames.

Gwen had all but ripped the hotel-room door open at Clary's tentative knock.

"Sorry I'm back early, but I had a sense that it was

time to come home." The green-eyed witch regarded her closely. "I'm guessing the reunion didn't go so well."

"Ya think?" Gwen snapped, using an expression she'd heard Clary use at least a dozen times that day.

"You're wearing my flannel pajamas."

Gwen looked down at the fuzzy garment, which was covered in prancing pink sheep. "Nothing I bought today felt comforting enough."

Clary finally stepped through the door, closing it behind her. "Do you want to talk about it?"

"No." Gwen said it with finality, but carried on in the next breath. "I thought he was listening. Everything was going so well. He told me about the dragon problem—he actually talked about something important happening in Camelot—and he said he wanted to change. But the moment one of his men called, he left and I had to stay behind. That's not partnership."

"That's pretty patronizing," Clary agreed. "Has he always been like that?"

"He's a king. They're the definition of patronizing." Gwen walked to the bed she'd claimed as her own and sat on the end. "I've never been able to really serve the people of Camelot. Yes, I arranged receptions and banquets and ran the king's household, and that was all necessary, but it wasn't *vital*. And it certainly wasn't anything we could build a relationship over."

"Sounds boring," Clary agreed.

"It was to me. He only let me go to war with him once. Women sometimes did, as laundresses and cooks as well as…other things."

There had been a few wives, but more whores who traveled with the baggage trains. Gwen hadn't considered herself sheltered until she'd seen what went on in the tents at the back of the encampment.

"What happened?" Clary sat down on the opposite bed and kicked off her ankle boots. They fell to the carpet with a thump.

"A fever ran through the camp, and I caught it. I was sick for a long time." There was more to the story, but this wasn't the time for that tale.

"Let me guess. He treated you like a glass ornament after that."

"Exactly. One that can't be chipped or covered in fingerprints. But there's a difference between caring for someone and being careful nothing happens to them."

Clary rose, restlessly pacing the room until she opened a tiny door beneath the television stand. It rattled as she pulled out two small bottles and tossed one to Gwen. "This kind of a talk needs lubricant."

"I already drank the rest of the champagne." There hadn't been much, but it had taken the edge off her hurt for a few minutes.

Clary tossed a bag onto the bed. "Snack food. The secret is to soak up the drink so you can start over."

"It occurs to me that you're what my nurse called a bad influence."

"I'm the terror of mothers everywhere." Clary fell back onto the bed with her own snacks. "Usually I can't afford the minibar, but we still have the king's credit card."

At that, Gwen pulled open the bag and extracted an orange object she recognized. There had been a bowl of the bright orange worms sitting on the table in Arthur's living room. "What is this?"

"Cheese Wizards."

Gwen stared at it, thinking something that orange was possibly lethal, and then popped it in her mouth. Experience never came without risk. The snack was salty and crunchy, although it didn't quite taste like real food. "I don't understand why they call it a wizard."

"Because they're fabulous," Clary said with a shrug. "A wizard is just an extra-special witch, after all."

"Merlin was born a witch?"

"Yeah," said Clary, "I wonder how he feels living in a world with Cheese Wizards. One day, you're the most magical person ever, and the next they name a snack food after you."

"Someone named these after Merlin?"

"Not really. The normal world has no idea real wizards exist. It's just advertising. Magic is sexy."

"Oh." Gwen really didn't want to mingle images of bright orange worms and reproduction. Not one bit.

"But we're not here to talk about Merlin," Clary prompted.

All the same, Gwen didn't mind taking the spotlight off herself. "Have you met him?"

"No," Clary said, flopping back onto her pillow. "Although he came to my hometown to see the high muckety-mucks of witchdom."

"What about?"

"There's been talk about information sharing between the covens. Boring stuff mostly, though it's meant loosening up on some of the rules we live by. More chances to travel outside our own coven. No more arranged marriages, for which I'm grateful."

Clary rolled to face Gwen, propping up her head on one hand. "I would've gone completely fangirl over the Great One. I mean, I've never traveled without my spell kit since I was a little girl. I would have had him autograph it. But I was out of town for work. Even witches have to eat."

Gwen sat up. "You see, that's what I want."

Clary raised her brows. "To eat?"

"No, to live the way you do." Gwen waved a Cheese Wizard for emphasis. "You have a job, places to go, an independent life. That doesn't make you any less of a witch."

Clary's eyes narrowed. "I agree, though the older generation would argue."

"I can be Guinevere the queen and still exercise my mind," Gwen said, sure of herself now. "You told me that the witches where you come from could help if I wanted to start fresh."

"They can forge identity papers," Clary said, sounding less certain.

"You said they could teach me what I need to know so that I can go to school and eventually earn my own keep."

Clary sat up, setting food and drink aside. Her expression was completely serious. "Yes, but I live on the other side of the country. If you come with me…"

"You live by a completely different ocean," Gwen said quickly. "I looked at a map. If I go with you when you return home, I'll be leaving Arthur and Camelot far behind."

"Are you sure?" Clary frowned. "That's a big step, and even if you turn around and come home again, you've made a statement you can't take back. And you just got here."

Gwen didn't have a good answer. She'd tried to get what she wanted tonight. Rather than argue yet again, she'd shared her feelings with her husband and urged him to share his own. She'd been more than willing to hear him out and find a compromise.

But one text message had hurtled them back to where they'd started. Guinevere, Queen of Camelot, would never be a real partner. Gwen, the woman, was an even-lower priority.

"If nothing else, it will give Arthur and I time to decide what we want." Her words were quiet but firm.

"A cooling-off period?" Clary asked in a cautious voice.

"He will never change his mind about me. To him, I'm still the overeager young girl who came to court and made a lot of mistakes."

"Can't he notice that you've grown up?"

"He's too focused on other things. Perhaps it's not his fault. I've tried making things better, but nothing works."

Clary reached across the space between the beds and squeezed Gwen's hand. "The witches of the Shadowring Coven will have you in school in no time."

Gwen squeezed back, incredibly grateful to her new friend. "I am no warrior queen, nor am I a mighty sorceress like Nimueh or Morgan LaFaye. But I have other talents. Even if Arthur doesn't care about them, I do."

Clary gave a slight cough. "For a mighty king, he's a bit of an idiot, isn't he?"

Chapter 11

"Oh. My. Goddess."

Clary's voice was strident with alarm—loud enough that Gwen emerged from the bathroom, hairbrush in hand. "What's wrong?"

Clary sat cross-legged on her bed, remote control in hand. She'd turned it on for a late-night talk show, which had prompted a whole new flood of questions from Gwen. It appeared the modern world had taken gossip to a professional level, a notion guaranteed to horrify a queen with a crumbling marriage.

Clary pointed at the screen. "They interrupted my show for a news bulletin. This is happening at Medievaland."

Gwen moved so that she could see the screen. "That's Palomedes! I know his armor."

The handsome Saracen knight was acting as a human wall so the reporters couldn't pass. Behind him, Gwen could make out flame. This was about the dragons! Transfixed, she slid onto the bed next to Clary.

Some effort had been made to illuminate the scene, but the field was too large for whatever the news vans had on hand. Only the dragon's glowing eyes and fiery nostrils were clearly visible, the rest a winged hulk with patches of shining scales.

"Look!" Clary pointed again. "The firemen are turning on their hoses."

Bursts of water whooshed through the air, arcing toward a black shape shifting in the shadows. A disgusted bellow drowned out every other sound. Gwen felt her mouth drifting open in astonishment.

The jiggling camera swung around to a female reporter with red lips and hair that didn't move despite an obvious breeze. "There is what appears to be a fire-breathing dragon on the field behind me, along with members of the Knights of New Camelot, an entertainment troupe employed here at Medievaland. Most of the entertainers are engaged in crowd control, along with the police. However, the leader of the troupe, Arthur Pendragon, has confronted the monster."

Gwen gasped as the scene cut to an image of Arthur crouched behind his shield while flame flowed over it. "Arthur!" She jumped off the bed, bounding toward the TV before she realized the futility of it.

The camera focus jerked back to show a draconic head, but a mailed fist immediately closed over the lens. Gwen collapsed back onto the bed, tears standing in her eyes. "Is he hurt?" she demanded. "Tell me if he's hurt!"

Clary put a hand on her arm. "Wait and see what they say."

"As you can see," the reporter continued, "it hasn't been easy to get good coverage of this event."

"But, Megan," said the male voice of the announcer, "isn't this all a publicity stunt?"

There was a second's delay while his question made it to the reporter's earpiece. "Undoubtedly, Kevin, but the authorities at Medievaland are denying all responsibility. No doubt this incident is related to the flaming apparition that dropped from the sky. Animal control officers won't confirm that it was actually a live cow or whether it was dead when pushed from some kind of aircraft or whether it was actually a hologram."

"Is Arthur hurt?" Gwen wailed.

Kevin must have heard her. "Megan, have there been any injuries?"

Gwen realized her nails were digging into her palms.

"None that have been reported," said Megan.

Gwen and Clary exhaled together.

"But with uncontrolled fire in play, all we can do is hope for the best."

Someone on TV shouted and the camera did another stomach-turning swing. Gwen leaned forward, trying to see better, but the screen showed only a muddle of shadows.

"It's hard to see, Kevin, but it appears the so-called dragon is getting ready to fly."

"To fly?" the announcer asked incredulously.

There was a rush and a roar and the camera swung upward, following a trajectory of flame and bat-like wings. "Kevin, these animatronics—or holograms or whatever—are incredible."

"Every theme park in America will want to know how this was done," said Kevin.

Clary made a rude choking noise. "It came from an egg, dude."

The cameras followed the dragon until it was swallowed up by the night.

"Well, that appears to end the spectacle," Megan chirped. "I'll have interviews with the entertainers for the morning show."

"Thank you, Megan."

"Thanks, Kevin. This is Megan Dutton, Nighthawk News."

Clary hit the power button, sending the TV into blackness.

"So that's why Arthur had to leave." Gwen drew her knees up, wrapping her arms around them. "It was for an important reason. But then, it always is."

And their marriage never mattered quite as much.

Clary dialed her phone. "Hey, Gawain, is everyone okay?"

Gwen watched her friend's face darken as the conversation went on. Clary said little before finally heaving a sigh and ending the call. "What did he say?" Gwen asked.

"No broken bones. No major burns. He doesn't know more than that."

Still, it was good news. Gwen realized that she could in fact phone Arthur. He'd put his number in her cell phone. Would her call to him be welcome or would it be considered a bother? Why hadn't he called her to put her mind at ease? Gwen put her forehead on her knees, wishing her heart would stop aching.

Clary turned to face her. "What do you think is going on? With the dragons, I mean."

Gwen considered. "I can't say. I only ever knew one

dragon and she was very, very old. She had a cave in the hills near my father's castle. She didn't like humans much and rarely strayed far from her nest, but she'd talk to me sometimes."

"You knew an actual dragon?" Clary sounded impressed.

"I can't say that I actually *knew* her," said Gwen, unfolding herself. "The only ones who are close to the dragons are the goblins in the Crystal Mountains. They live alongside the dragon strongholds beyond the Forest Sauvage."

The Forest Sauvage was a no-man's-land, neither a mortal realm nor part of the Faery Kingdom and beyond the laws of either. Magic dwelled there, as well as the last remnants of demonkind. It was the kind of place young knights went seeking adventure, some never to be seen again.

"You're thinking," Clary said. "I can see it on your face."

"Arthur is asking the same questions we are. He said as much earlier tonight." Gwen slid off the bed to pace. "If he really wanted answers, he'd talk to the goblins."

"And he won't?" Clary asked uncertainly.

"No one talks to the goblins. The court was all politeness to their envoys, of course, but only as far as they had to be."

"You met goblins?" Clary went for more liquor from the tiny fridge.

"Yes. The goblins had mineral resources and came to trade. The Crystal Mountains are filled with gold and all sorts of precious gems, but not common salt, which we had in abundance. I learned all this because I was the one left to entertain the goblin delegation while the knights found urgent business elsewhere."

"Why?"

Gwen waved a hand. "Goblins are repulsive—rude, smelly and unpleasant to look at—but they *are* interesting. They know more about mining gemstones than anyone I know. That's why they live in the Crystal Mountains and consequently know about dragons."

"Which is exactly why Arthur should have you at his side." Clary crumpled up her chip bag and tossed it neatly into the garbage can across the room. "You're the one with the answers."

"No," said Gwen. "I just know who probably has them."

"Then tell Arthur. Tell him to get on it."

"I doubt he'd have much success with the goblins' king. When the ambassador and his retinue came to Camelot, I'm the one who poured their wine and laughed at their jokes. The will to build a relationship counts for much among their kind. I even gave Ambassador Krzak a lock of my hair as a token of regard."

Gwen folded her arms, thinking through what Arthur had told her about Rukon, the female dragon and the fae making threats. One didn't have to be Merlin the Wise to detect the stink of skulduggery and plots. And if she drew that conclusion, Arthur surely had.

But he didn't allow anyone to help bring these enemies to justice. Oh, he'd trust his men to swing a sword on command, but Arthur kept control where it mattered. He'd protect the human realms with his own flesh and bone if necessary—even if that meant facing down Rukon Shadow Wing. That willingness to bear the brunt of sacrifice was the stamp of a good king. But working alone was also Arthur's weakness. It would never occur to him to ask a lowly goblin for aid.

But it had occurred to Guinevere, and only she had a welcome with the goblin king. It was up to her to act.

At that thought, a wave of terror passed through her, strong enough that she had to sit down before her knees gave out. She reached for the tiny bottle of wine and uncapped it, taking a healthy gulp.

"What's wrong?" Clary asked sharply.

"Witches know how to work portals, right?"

"Yes," Clary said suspiciously. "I've been practicing ever since we rediscovered the spell last year."

Gwen's heart leaped at the same moment her stomach sank with a fresh wave of fear. It was a horrible sensation. "I need a portal to the Crystal Mountains."

"Wait." Clary held up her hands. "Why?"

Gwen wanted a lot of things—school, independence, a chance to explore this exciting new world. But she had accepted the role of queen, and that meant putting the mortal realms first. "I can't stand by when there's something I can do, and I'm the only one who actually *can* do it."

"Will Arthur agree?" Clary asked, doubt plain on her face.

"No, but that doesn't matter." Gwen hugged herself, wanting nothing more than to crawl beneath the bedcovers and hide. "I'm not asking for Arthur's permission."

Arthur lay on the bed in Medievaland's infirmary, staring at the cracked ceiling. He could have risen and faced the world five minutes ago, but it was quiet and the ice pack on his head felt good. The lack of sleep last night—not to mention the twin calamities of dragons and Gwen—were catching up with him.

Unfortunately, the peace was short-lived. The door opened and Gawain tiptoed in, forehead creased with worry.

"I'm awake," said Arthur.

"How are you feeling?" Gawain asked, folding his arms.

"Lightly toasted."

"Fortunately, your shield took the brunt of the flame. Your burns aren't serious."

Arthur sat up, swinging his legs over the side of the bed. The room swam, forcing him to brace himself.

"Careful," said Gawain, putting a steadying hand on his shoulder. "You have a concussion. That was a nasty blow you took."

He could have been incinerated, but once again Rukon had held back. Instead, a flick of the dragon's tail had sent Arthur flying. Again. It was the same trick the dragon had pulled in the forest, and it was getting old. Although Arthur had broken no bones, he'd lost consciousness for a minute or two.

Gawain lifted an eyebrow. "Rukon must have hit you with as much force as a truck."

"The beast did it on purpose. A last insult as it flew away." And the dragon had answered none of his questions—just given him nonsense about his family name.

Gawain handed Arthur a clean T-shirt, and he shrugged it on. It was then he noticed his armor piled in the corner. He vaguely remembered the knights helping him from the field and unbuckling the heavy gear so he could rest. The shield was a charred ruin. "Was that on television?" he asked quietly.

"The flames, yes. Your flying lesson, no." Gawain shrugged. "The news reported that no one was seriously injured."

"Good," Arthur replied.

"There will be a lot of questions. The police, the press and even Medievaland's owners have been trying to contact you. Go out the back way. I'll drive you home. We can think up a cover story in the morning."

Arthur grunted his agreement and pulled on his boots while Gawain picked up a call. As he wasn't listening to the one-sided phone conversation, it took a moment before Arthur realized something was wrong.

The knight had gone beet red. "You what?" Gawain demanded, voice rising.

The faint sounds of a female voice emanated from the phone. The words were muffled but the tone was clearly excited. Cold dread began creeping into the room.

"Stay where you are. We'll be right over." Gawain stuffed the phone in his pocket. He rubbed his temples, then turned to Arthur with an apologetic look. "It's about Queen Guinevere."

Arthur rose, Gawain's tone instantly flooding him with tension. "What about her?"

"The queen believes she knows a way to gather information about the dragons' recent behavior."

Arthur frowned. "She does?"

Gawain smiled an apology that looked more like a wince. "You should sit down again. You're not going to like what I'm about to tell you."

Arthur complied, but anger was rapidly eroding his confusion. "Tell me!"

Gawain heaved a sigh. "According to Clary, Queen Guinevere has gone on an adventure."

Chapter 12

Clary had made the portal in the hotel closet, saying it was easier for her to draw the necessary arc of light within a defined space. Gwen, who had no magic whatsoever, couldn't comment. The only time she'd gone through a portal was with Merlin just days ago, and stepping through that had been like walking through a door. The mechanics—whatever they were—had been seamless. A wave of his hand, and time and space parted.

Clary's portal, however, had required almost the entire contents of her spell kit, several more snacks and a quantity of curses. It came together quickly, but the effort involved had made the young witch break into a sweat. Eventually, though, there had been a blur of color and light, like the reflection of torches on water, and then a spinning, gasping tumble. Gwen landed face-first on cold, wet grass. For a panicked instant, she couldn't breathe and flopped over onto her back, willing her chest to inflate. A heartbeat passed, then two, and finally she dragged in a long, rasping heave of air as her lungs remembered how to work. The air was sweet and fresh, tangy with mud and growing things. Gwen rejoiced deep in her soul—this smelled like home, not the city with its motors and garbage and thousands of rushing people. Beyond the sound of her panting, there was the rush of water and a distant cacophony of birds.

Only then did she venture to open her eyes to a blue sky untroubled by clouds. She sat up, feeling a twinge where her elbow had hit the ground during her unceremonious landing, and gazed about her. She was on a gentle mountain slope that rolled into a deep valley. She couldn't see the bottom from where she sat, only steep angles blanketed with pines that turned the warm greens of her meadow to a somber blue black. On the upper edges of the valley, a scattering of deciduous trees showed it was autumn here, as well. Slowly, she got to her feet and turned to see behind her. There, the land rose, eventually giving way to enormous boulders. The peak of her mountain was cloaked in mist, but she could tell it was only one of many. All around her were snowcaps shrouded in mist wrought gold by the sun. A cool breeze kissed Gwen's face as she turned, shading her eyes. In the distance she made out twin mountaintops with a distinctive curve to their peaks— an outline she'd seen many times in tapestries and illuminations about the goblin realms. They were called The Fangs—a deadly pass into troll territory. The sight both frightened and reassured her. Despite her inexperience with portals, Clary had indeed sent Gwen to the Crystal Mountains.

But the mountain range was a large wilderness. She'd asked Clary to set her down near the goblin king's palace but there was no such place in sight. She clutched her hand around the bracelet Clary had given her—a simple leather thong strung with painted wooden beads. It was bespelled to open the portal to return home at a spoken command—an innovation the witches had recently invented. Clary had been inordinately proud of her work, but cautioned her that reopening the portal would only work once and there weren't enough supplies in her kit to create another. So, Gwen wasn't giving up and running home unless she was certain there was no other option. She marked the site carefully with a pile of small rocks and began walking.

To her left was a stream flowing down the mountain, light dancing off the churning water. Gwen followed it up the slope, using it as a guide to keep from wandering in circles. She'd dressed in warm clothes, with the sturdy boots she had bought, and taken along a knapsack filled with the food left in the minibar and the small knife she'd brought with her from Camelot. It wasn't truly a weapon—knives were everyday tools, even for a queen—but it could be used for self-defense.

The rise ended in a steep but brief climb. Gwen had grown up scrambling over hills and made it to the new plateau with no trouble. Here, the view was wider and she went to her hands and knees, crawling to the edge of the rocks for the best possible panorama. She was warm from hiking, and her cheeks welcomed the mountain chill. Although she'd found nothing useful yet, excitement bubbled inside her as if she were made of champagne. This was what she had lacked all along—adventure, a purpose and a way to challenge herself.

Her new viewpoint showed more breathtaking views, but also something that made Gwen give a triumphant cry. There was no castle, but there were signs of habitation on the face of the mountain below. Rings of earthworks were held in place by smoothly sculpted rock. They were cut in half by a steep stair that wound out of sight around the face of the steep cliff. Bridges arched over steep crevasses, miracles of engineering and craftsmanship Gwen longed to study up close. All of it led to a doorway in the face of the mountain, a huge arched maw of blackness surrounded by elaborate geometric carvings. When the goblins had said their king lived in the mountains, they meant literally *inside* the mountains. Gwen had found where she needed to go.

She looked a moment longer, plotting the best route to the stairs, and began to back away from the cliff's edge. She had barely moved when a cold, hard point pricked her neck.

"Have you done spying on our home, human?" came a rough, nasal voice.

Goblin, Gwen thought, remaining absolutely still. No other voices had that same rasping quality, as if the speaker was being slowly strangled. The words were obscured further by the speaker's accent—goblins had their own language, though most could speak at least one human tongue. "I was seeking a way to your door, guardsman. I would ask you to escort me the rest of the way."

"Escort you?" he mocked. "I will *escort* you straight to our dungeons."

Gwen's heart skipped in fright, but she kept her voice level. "I request an audience with your king. I am Guinevere, Queen of Camelot and wife of Arthur of Britain. Ambassador Krzak knows me well."

"Krzak died in my great-great-grandsire's time." Now the guardsman sounded incredulous. "What's a queen doing crawling around the mountains alone? Where is Arthur? Where are your men-at-arms?"

Pulse thundering now, Gwen realized she'd made a terrible mistake. Krzak had been young when she'd known him, but too much time had passed for even a goblin to live so long. "Please," she said. "I'm telling the truth."

The blade poking her neck was removed and rough hands pulled her to her feet. She turned to the guard, catching sight of the stone-tipped spear before finding the guardsman's face. If there had been any doubt what he was, one look dispelled it. Goblins came in every shade of the rainbow, and this one was a mossy green that blended into the vegetation. He was perhaps four and a half feet tall but sturdily built, wearing a leather tunic and cap scrunched down over straggly green hair. But what set goblins apart, besides the earthy, mildewed smell of them, was their lumpiness. Like autumn gourds, they were covered in bumps and warts that in any other species would be a sign of a contagious skin disease. To them, it was a natural hallmark of beauty. Gwen had trained herself to see past it long ago, and so she gave no reaction to the guardsman's irregular face.

"I see you are familiar with our kind," he said with a ferocious grin that showed blocky, crooked teeth.

Gwen remained firm. "I am. I entertained the ambassador many times." And she knew better than to ask the goblin's name. Only public figures like Krzak shared their names with outsiders—which meant anyone not born of goblin kind.

"So history says, human, but that doesn't explain how you're here now."

"Magic," she said simply. "And I came for information only the goblins, with their great wisdom, can provide."

The dollop of flattery must have worked, because the guardsman gave a slow nod. "All right. We'll go to the palace and my captain can decide what to do with you."

"Better to let the tall heads roll than risk those bowed in humility," she said, quoting one of the ambassador's favorite lines.

He gave her a sharp look. "My mother used to say that."

"Then she gave good advice," Gwen said, although she knew her tall head was currently at risk.

With the barest flicker of a smile, the guardsman angled his spear until the point prodded her in the chest. He jerked his head toward the stream Gwen had followed to get there. "Walk."

The route to the stairs was arduous, testing Gwen's endurance to its limit as she scrambled over rock piles and up slippery screes of gravel. The goblin, on the other hand, had no such trouble, skipping like a goat over stone and stream and only occasionally using the butt of his spear like a walking stick. A half-dozen times, he had to help Gwen along.

But once they reached the stair, the real climb began. Ever afterward, Gwen tried to forget that upward slog. She arrived at the top gasping, sweaty and with a fire in her legs that promised excruciating muscle cramps.

She collapsed outside the door while the guardsman

conferred in his own tongue with a blue goblin wearing a steel chain about his thick neck—presumably an officer of some kind. He glanced at Gwen, but didn't bow, and she knew better than to expect it. Even if he did believe she was the Queen of Camelot, goblins barely recognized any royalty besides their own.

When another guard shoved an earthenware cup of water into her hands, she gulped it without question. Only when she caught her breath did she realize the goblin's captain had disappeared, and the others stood watching her with curious eyes.

"What are we waiting for?" she asked, refusing to admit that anything could go wrong after she'd made it this far.

The goblins didn't answer. They were clearly under orders to wait in silence. Gwen settled with her back to the rock and did her best to ignore the chill of her sweat-dampened clothes.

Minutes later, the blue goblin returned and gestured to his men. They stood at attention, spears straight, while Gwen got to her feet. "Come," he ordered, and led the way inside the mountain. Gwen followed, and the guardsman and his companion brought up the rear. Their small procession had the appearance of an honor guard, but she knew very well she was their captive.

The dark cave mouth gave way to a smoothly hollowed tunnel several times her height. Flaming torches sat in stanchions every dozen yards to light their path, but Gwen barely noticed where they were going. The entire tunnel—walls, ceiling and floor—was lined with glittering mosaics depicting scenes from goblin history. Each tiny tile was a chip of glittering, translucent stone set against a field of gold leaf. The torchlight caught the gold, the reflection making the passage shimmer with light. Her steps slowed as she stared openmouthed, her whole being dazzled by the unexpected beauty.

The captain, however, was impatient and soon spear points prodded her back. She was almost trotting by the time the tunnel emptied into a large chamber set with double doors of carved oak. As Gwen was marched closer, a pair of blue goblins opened the doors wide enough to let them pass through.

Beyond was the throne room, packed with citizens come to beg justice or a favor or leniency from taxes. This was daily business for a court, and Gwen had seen thousands of such gatherings before, though none had smelled quite so bad. She was used to unwashed humans, but a room packed with overheated goblins was enough to make her gag.

The king sat beneath yet more mosaics. The alcove was lit from behind and surrounded the king in a halo of sparkling light. Only when Gwen drew near the throne did she see the goblin king clearly.

He was scarlet and lumpier than any goblin Gwen had ever seen. A crown sat on his hairless brow, a cloak of ermine over a tunic of royal purple. The picture wasn't improved by the fact that he was as wide as he was tall. It was like meeting a royal red toad, especially when he gave an unexpected burp.

Gwen's escort stopped, and then stepped aside, leaving her alone before the throne. "Greetings, Your Majesty," she said, sinking into a deep curtsy. "I am grateful to be granted an interview."

"I am Zorath, King of the Goblins and Emperor of the Crystal Mountains, Spear of the Deep and Blade of the Fangs." The king spoke with almost no accent but plenty of attitude. Every syllable of his title rang with pride.

"And I am Guinevere, Queen of Camelot," she said, bowing before him. "I have come seeking Your Majesty's wisdom, so that I may return to my royal husband and help him save the mortal realms."

Without warning, Zorath burst into a raucous laugh, holding his stomach as if to contain his merriment. The outburst finished in another belch. "Is that so?" he asked wryly, wiping his mouth with his sleeve. "If I were you, I'd be asking for mercy. No outsider has left here alive for the last thousand years."

Chapter 13

"Your Majesty," Gwen said with forced calm, "please explain what you mean."

Their eyes met. Zorath's shrewd gaze was as hard as twin black buttons.

Gwen silently panicked. Krzak had never mentioned anything like this. By all reports, the goblins had always been eager to show off the glories of their mines. Something had changed during the centuries of the stone sleep.

"We have riches. Outsiders have armies. No one visits the goblins for the pleasure of our company." Zorath leaned forward, studying her features with keen interest. "Tell me, pretty human, how did you find our stronghold? Was it the fae who told you of it?"

"The fae? Have they troubled your borders?"

"Ever since the end of the demon wars. Now our lands are closed to any but our own tribes."

That explained much. Gwen rose from her bow, dizzy with fear and an urgent need for fresh air. "With your indulgence, sire, I will tell you everything."

"A story!" he exclaimed with obvious delight. He snapped fat fingers. "Bring wine and food."

As servants hurried to obey, he turned back to Gwen. "Before you start your tale, did you bring me any presents?"

Gwen was stumped, realizing she should have anticipated this. Goblins set great store by tribute, but what could she offer a king already wealthy beyond measure? "In my pack," she said, scrambling for ideas. "It is a small gift, sire, barely worthy of your notice, but it is a great delicacy among the humans of my new home."

The green guardsman brought her knapsack forward and watched carefully as she opened the zipper. Gwen was careful not to reach for the knife, but instead plucked out one of the cellophane packets. She went down on one knee, offering up her gift in outstretched hands. "Sire, I offer you Cheese Wizards."

A murmur ran through the crowd as Zorath delicately took the bag between fat fingers tipped in long dark claws. With a frown of concentration, the king wrestled the bag open. As she expected, he gave a cry of pleasure at the bright orange color of the treats. He extracted a curl and chomped it down with relish. The only thing goblins craved more than color was salt.

"More," he demanded, waving at her knapsack. "Show me all your tribute."

Gwen emptied the knapsack of food, laying out the bright packages of snacks at the goblin king's feet. "I hope the variety pleases Your Majesty."

The king now had a huge golden goblet and was al-

ternating slurps of wine with bites of Cheese Wizards.
"It is acceptable," he said with a full mouth. "Now, rise
and tell me your tale."

She did, from Krzak to the stone sleep to the dragons at Medievaland. The story took time, but Zorath's
attention did not waver. Neither did that of the audience in the hall.

"You say that you knew our ambassador to Arthur's
court in Camelot?" Zorath asked after she had at last
finished.

"I did," she agreed. "I knew him well."

"You gave him a lock of your hair?"

"I did."

"We will put your word to the test."

There was a long wait while the king summoned
a historian who trotted off to do the king's bidding.
Then more time passed until the historian reappeared
with a small box on a purple velvet pillow and knelt at
Zorath's feet.

"Your Majesty," the historian said in a wheezing
voice, "Ambassador Krzak placed the lock in a casket bespelled to preserve it from the ravages of time.
That casket has been kept in our treasure stores, for the
memory of Queen Guinevere's respect and kindness has
been a legend among our people."

"Very well." Zorath lifted the lid of the box. "Step
this way, lady."

Gwen obeyed, kneeling at the king's feet. The goblin
king lifted a long golden lock tied with sky blue thread
and held it beside Gwen's fall of hair. "It is a match. This
human woman tells the truth. She is Camelot's Queen."

The assembly of goblins erupted in a cheer, tossing
caps into the air and bowing as she turned her head

to witness the commotion. Zorath broke into a wide grin and offered an unexpectedly graceful bow. "Queen Guinevere is always welcome in these realms. For her, the borders are always open."

Gwen exhaled a long breath, her heart lifting. "Your hospitality is gratefully received, King Zorath."

A herald called for silence as the king replaced the lock of hair in its casket and motioned its keeper away. Zorath turned to Gwen. "There was something you wanted to ask me, my lady?"

Now Gwen wanted to cheer, as well, to stamp her feet and wave her arms in jubilation. She'd done it— she'd won the goblin king over without threats or swords or magic. She'd done it just by being who she was and never forgetting that a queen owed courtesy to everyone who came beneath her roof. And now she would have something to offer in pursuit of keeping the human realms safe.

"No one knows the dragons of these mountains better than the goblins," she began. "Can you tell us why they are leaving their dens to terrorize the new Camelot? It does not make sense. Dragons do not ever stray far from their hoards."

Zorath opened his mouth to answer, but a commotion came from the back of the room. Dismayed by the interruption, Gwen turned to stare as the great doors to the throne room swung open and a knot of goblins appeared, half marching, half trotting after a prisoner who seemed to be in charge of the procession.

"What is the meaning of this interruption?" Zorath demanded.

The goblins parted to reveal a figure with a large

sword. Gwen stared for a moment, disbelief stalling her brain for a beat. "Arthur?"

He was muddy and bruised, and his expression crackled with temper. He fixed Gwen with a look that spoke of relief and fury in equal measure. "You're not hurt?" he demanded.

"No!" she protested. "I'm completely fine. What are you doing here?"

"Kneel before the king!" a blue goblin ordered, prodding Arthur with his spear. Arthur swung around to glare, and the goblin scampered backward.

"Kneel, human," Zorath commanded.

Casting a puzzled glance at the bag of Cheese Wizards, Arthur sheathed his sword and went to one knee. "Greetings, King of Goblins. I am Arthur, King of Camelot and High King of the Britons."

Zorath looked down from his dais with incredulity. "Two outsiders in one day? And one such a mighty warrior of renown."

Arthur glanced up from his bow. "I came in peace to find my wife."

Gwen met his eyes. "Are you trying to rescue me?" she asked.

"Of course. I made Clary send me through her damnable portal as soon as I'd found out where you'd gone."

Gwen huffed in exasperation. It might have been touch and go along the way, but she'd managed to navigate the goblin court on her own. In fact, she'd been about to get the answers she needed before Arthur had interrupted.

Her thoughts must have shown, because Arthur's gaze snapped away. A stubborn angle formed along his jaw. Gwen turned to Zorath. "A thousand pardons for the interruption, Your Majesty. I hope you can find it in your heart to excuse the actions of a protective spouse."

Zorath sank back onto his throne, a hard tone creeping into his words. "Ambassador Krzak wrote of the generous Queen of Camelot. I have no reason to welcome the king."

"Then we shall leave at once," said Gwen, "though I hope you will still give me the answer I seek."

Arthur's brows crooked in question, but he let her speak. It was Zorath who interrupted with a wave of his hand. "No, those who venture here do not return to tell the tale. In honor of past friendship, we will let you leave, Guinevere of Camelot, but only you. The king stays."

Arthur sprang to his feet, his hand on Excalibur's hilt. He could fight his way out, but that would get them nowhere.

"No!" Gwen cried, pushing past the guards to stand at Arthur's side. Her mind scrambled frantically, reviewing in seconds everything she knew about goblins. "No, I beg you to let us go!"

"Gwen!" Arthur interjected.

He got no further. As theatrically as she could, Gwen fell to her knees and held up her hands in supplication. The crowd, who had fallen silent, responded exactly as she'd hoped. A murmur of sympathy and protest rippled through the room. "Please, great King Zorath," she asked, putting a throb of anguish into the words.

She gambled on what she'd seen so far—the shimmering tunnel, the glowing mosaic over the throne and even the fact they'd kept her token of affection as a relic. Goblins loved theater, especially when it elevated their role in the world. How could they resist an honored queen begging for the return of her spouse? "Word of your generosity would be sung among our people."

A crafty expression came over Zorath's features. His gaze moved from Gwen to Arthur and back again while black-clawed fingers rubbed at his warty chin. "You are persuasive, Queen, and I can hear the approval of my citizens in their cries. But law is law, and what ruler can break it without weakening his position? I cannot grant your wish without exacting a price. Will you pay it?"

Arthur's expression was puzzled. "Clearly my wife had a purpose in coming here. If there is a way I can further her mission without dishonor to either Your Majesty or the good name of Camelot, I will assist you. And, yes, I would like to go home without the need to battle my way to freedom."

"Spoken like a noble man." Zorath sounded unimpressed. "But a public hall is not the proper place to speak of bargains."

"Do you fear so many witnesses?" Arthur asked coolly.

"I fear your clever wife, King of Camelot. She has them wrapped around her dainty fingers. We will adjourn to my conference rooms."

Zorath rose and stumped his way down from the dais. The guards gestured with their spears for Gwen and Arthur to follow as he led the way to a side passage, ermine cape flapping around his crimson knees. The walk was short, ending in a smaller chamber with many maps pinned to the walls.

"Clear the room," Zorath said to the guards.

The guardsmen looked hesitant, but Zorath shooed them away. The goblin king roamed the room, arms folded, his expression thoughtful. "You are carrying Excalibur, I see."

Arthur's hand went to its hilt. "I am."

"I know your reputation," said Zorath. "You could have killed my men. You let yourself be taken."

"It was the fastest way to find out if you had Guinevere." Arthur's tone was firm, but not challenging. "And I have no wish to start a war with you, King Zorath. There is enough turmoil among the realms."

"We have a common enemy in the fae, it is true." The goblin jabbed at one of the maps. "The fae realms are at our back door. There are those among them who hunger for the treasures in our mines."

"Is that your price? Do you require protection of your lands?"

"Yes, but it has nothing to do with the fae." Zorath slapped a different map. "There is another who plagues us. Here."

Gwen and Arthur drew closer to inspect the map. It appeared to be a network of tunnels with a large red *X* over the entrance to a nest of twisting lines. Arthur frowned. "Something has blocked access to a subsection of your mines?"

Zorath nodded. "Mines, living units, surface access and vaults. Miles of treasure and territory stolen and hundreds of lives lost. We sent our soldiers, but they never came back."

Gwen took a step back, as if the red mark on the map might suddenly come to life. "What is it?"

The crafty look was back in Zorath's eyes. "A troll. Only a charmed weapon like Excalibur will kill it. You'll get your freedom and all the information I can

give you about your dragon problem once you bring
me the troll's head."

"A troll!" Gwen wasn't even sure what a troll looked
like, but she knew their reputation. There was little
wonder Zorath needed a warrior of Arthur's caliber
to defeat it.

The goblin king nodded. "It has taken our livelihood
bit by bit, tunnel by tunnel. There is no family who has
not lost a son, a brother or a husband to its ravages.
None of my workers will report for their duties. We lose
trade, and soon we will begin to fade. It is devouring us
in more ways than one. We have been desperate for a
solution." Zorath turned to Arthur. "And here you are."

Too worried to stand on ceremony, Gwen grabbed
Arthur's sleeve and dragged him to the other side of
the room. He followed willingly enough, but his mouth
was set in a hard line.

"Can you kill a troll?" she asked under her breath.

Arthur's eyes were dark with temper, but his answer
was calm. "They're deadly, but not smart."

She squeezed his arm, feeling the hard muscle beneath
his sleeve. "That doesn't answer my question." There was
much wrong between them, and she knew the risks every
warrior accepted as part of their mission. But she suddenly wanted guarantees, a word, a hint of safety to cling
to. She needed to believe this adventure would end well.

"In the stories I've heard, trolls are conquered more
often by wit than brute force."

Gwen nodded slowly, remembering that she'd seen
dragon flame dousing Arthur's shield only hours ago.
She reached up, and cupped his cheek. She wished she
could rewind time until they were back in the hotel,
drinking champagne and unbuttoning each other's

clothes. How did they go from that to goblins and trolls in a single night?

"Have you ever done it before?" she asked quietly. "Killed a troll, I mean."

He shook his head. "I've never seen one. They stay in mountains like these, far from Camelot."

She didn't like that answer. Experience would have been better. She leaned closer. "Why does it have to be a charmed blade that kills it?"

"Ordinary weapons won't pierce their hide."

Her stomach dropped. "Oh, Arthur."

He studied her face, and something in his expression softened. "This is what I do, Gwen. My job is to keep people safe. That includes goblins."

"You're agreeing to this?" She tightened her fingers, holding him fast. She could feel his heat in the cool air of the room. She wanted to press closer, to soak it up and claim it for herself. It wasn't her fault that he was here—he had come of his own accord—but reason couldn't erase the ache in her heart.

Unexpectedly, a faint smile curved his lips. "You paved the way for this exchange of information for my services. Now I'll do my part to close the bargain." He turned to Zorath and gave a sharp nod.

And it was done. Her husband was committed to hunting a deadly, iron-hided troll that had already devastated hundreds. His only advantage would be in a game of wits.

That was her department. She wasn't letting him do this alone. "We're both going," Gwen said suddenly. "Or the deal's off."

Chapter 14

"Under no circumstances!"

The only surprise in Arthur's response was the look in his eyes. She'd expected irritation or pride or resignation that they must retread an argument they'd had so many times. He was the warrior. Even as king, fighting monsters was his stock-in-trade. She was a woman with no such skills.

What she saw was real fear. On some level, she'd assumed he was simply fulfilling a role—the protective male to a hopefully submissive wife. But perhaps the strangeness of the situation had caught him off guard, because the wall he kept between his thoughts and the world was missing and Gwen saw what was in his heart. He truly cared.

An ache settled in her chest as she reached up, cupping his face in her hands. He was hot to the touch, the pulse in his temple throbbing. "Don't leave me behind again," she pleaded.

She wasn't a warrior. She could manage a bow—everyone in Camelot's court knew how to hunt and hawk—but more important, she was another set of eyes. Someone had to watch Arthur's back, even if it was just her.

Gwen could see him weighing his answer and prepared herself to be stubborn. Arthur rarely changed his mind, especially about the things that mattered to him.

"You leave me a poor choice, my lady." His voice was soft, but angry. "If I leave you here, you will curse me. If I take you with me and you come to harm, I will never forgive myself."

As if on a single instinct, they both turned to Zorath, who held up his hands as if to shield himself. "I have three wives and know better than to say a word."

Arthur pulled Gwen's hands from his face. "Promise that if you come, you will obey my every word. Both our lives might depend on it."

He was giving in! Joy and trepidation both stopped her breath—she'd been so focused on changing his mind, she'd barely thought beyond the moment. "I promise," she said, barely managing more than a whisper.

When she kissed him, his eyes were angry, but they were also sad.

In less than an hour, they set off. Gwen watched the stiff line of Arthur's back as he disappeared down the tunnel. Although he'd given her permission to come, he was not happy about it. With grim determination, she hoisted her knapsack and charged after him, breaking into a trot to keep up.

The goblin tunnels were surprisingly comfortable.

They were as wide as any castle corridor and high enough for even a tall man to walk without bumping his head. A complex system of crossbeams and bracing kept the tunnels stable and provided an anchor for an ingenious system of pulleys used to move buckets of ore and unpolished stones. Frequent ventilation shafts brought in fresh mountain air, and storage chambers with food, water and other supplies were dotted throughout the tunnel network. The only drawback was the miles of rock over Gwen's head. All that stone weighed on her imagination, making it wonder what it would be like to be buried alive.

And she disliked the darkness. The miners had to carry their own light—either a candle stuck to one of their helmets or a metal lantern. Gwen had opted for the lantern, which squeaked as it swung from its wire handle and cast crazy shadows as it moved. The sounds in the flickering gloom were disturbing—trickles and echoes and mutterings of air in the deep shafts. Since the troll had come, the goblins had deserted the mines, leaving the mountain with only its own voice for company.

Oh, yes, the troll. That had her imagination scrambling, and she desperately needed a distraction. She quickened her pace until she was at Arthur's elbow. "Are you going to refuse to speak to me throughout this entire journey?"

Arthur stopped and turned. He had his sword in one hand and a scowl on his face. "This is not the time for witty conversation, my lady. Too often the hunters turn into the hunted on these quests."

"I saw the map. We're nowhere near the troll's lair."

He made a face. "As Clary would say, color me cautious."

She stilled. "Cautious, or are you still angry?"

"Believe me, if there had been any chance that I might leave you in Zorath's care, I would have." His eyes bored into her. "You left me no choice."

She bridled. "I will pull my weight. You'll be glad of me before the end."

"Slaying a troll is not a Maypole dance. Trust me, Gwen, the penalty for losing on this hunt is death. You should not be here."

"I'm not playing a game." She poked him in the chest, tired of his judgment. "You should be glad I'm here. I got us this far."

"That's no excuse for behaving in a reckless fashion."

"Reckless? Reckless is confronting a dragon single-handed!" Gwen suddenly felt short of air and struggled to catch her breath. "I was watching the television. I saw what happened. Why didn't you call me? You might have reassured me that you were all right!"

He stalked away, making it three or four steps before he turned again. "By the time I was in a fit state to call, you had left for this realm. I followed as soon as I could."

"In a fit state?"

"I was unconscious," he mumbled.

She buried her face in her hands. "By all the saints, Arthur. The knights might have attacked as a group. Why did you face Rukon alone?"

His expression grew opaque, closing her out. It was worse than his anger. It was like she wasn't even there.

"How can I ask anyone else to risk what I am not willing to give?" he said in a low voice. "Acting as shield and champion for the human realms is my responsibility."

"Others want to help, Arthur," she said softly. "They deserve the chance."

She wanted to reach out, reassure herself with touch, but he turned away and silently resumed his march into the tunnels. The only change was that now he slowed his pace enough for her to walk by his side. It was little enough, but it was something.

Their quiet passage gave her time to think as she stole glances at his rigid profile. If she had to guess, she thought he was cursing himself for imperfections only he could see. But why? There was so much she didn't know about her own husband, and what she did know was more legend than man. He never spoke of his childhood, and it was little wonder. His parents had been murdered when he was still a baby. It had been Merlin who'd rescued him from slaughter and smuggled him to Sir Hector, who raised him as his own son. Every time Gwen heard the story, it turned her blood to ice.

They kept on walking for what seemed like hours, but time was deceptive in the lightless silence. One tunnel looked much like the next. Their only guides were the clay tablets screwed to the support beams and marked with the goblins' system of wedges and slashes.

"We're at the twenty-ninth tunnel," Gwen said, running a finger over the indented clay.

"You can read their tongue?" Arthur asked in surprise.

"Only the numbers, but someday I'll learn more. Ambassador Krzak said their written language is sophisticated, containing many dialects and a long history of epic verse."

Arthur gave her a sharp look, but this time it wasn't critical. "You really did spend a lot of time with the goblin delegation in Camelot, didn't you?"

"I liked him. He said what he thought, and that wasn't easy to find at court."

Arthur gave a wry laugh. "True enough."

"Most of the delegations from other courts were fascinating." There had been humans from other countries, and once elves from far, far away. Her favorites had been the fae, but that had been before the demon wars, when they were still in full possession of their souls. "I made many friends among them."

Arthur was watching her, a furrow in his brow. "I didn't know you found them so interesting. Many look on entertaining the castle guests as a chore."

"Sometimes it was dull, but there's usually at least one intriguing thing about any person. I just looked for that."

They kept walking, falling back into silence, but it was a different quiet. They were both deep in thought.

"I'm sorry I trusted the Mercian prince," she said suddenly. It came out before she even knew she was thinking it. *Impulsive as always, Gwen.* "He made me feel important. I didn't know any better."

It had been a disaster. He'd flattered her, danced with her, was always there to hold her horse or play a game of chess. And then he'd drawn her into political discussions—about this treaty or that. She'd divulged too much, and the damage was done.

Arthur nodded. "I bear some responsibility for that. I should have been at home more."

"And I should have known better." Gwen's stomach twinged at the confession. She'd blamed Arthur for leaving her alone, but it was true—she should never have mixed business with flirtation. The truth made her feel small.

"Our instinct is to trust," Arthur said gently. "Knowing when we can't is a bitter lesson."

As they turned down the tunnel, he put a hand on the small of her back as he had in the cocktail lounge. The memory, so out of place, jarred her.

He glanced down, his eyes sad. *Our instinct is to trust.* The one time he'd formed a significant alliance was during the demon wars, and that had ended with the fae swearing vengeance against Camelot and humankind. It was a war they were still fighting.

"I understand why a king doesn't trust, but how can you live with that as a person?" she asked.

"Should I point out that when hunting monsters, it's best to keep your mind on the job?"

"I understand," she said, wincing a little. "But just tell me, was it the incident with the prince that made you question my judgment?"

"It gave me pause, but you misunderstand me."

He stopped, holding up a hand as he edged toward an intersection of tunnels and listened intently before waving her forward. Gwen quickly obeyed, aware that they were nearing the *X* on Zorath's map—the troll's lair. It was time to stop talking, but she couldn't help herself. This was an answer she'd waited years to learn. "How do I misunderstand?"

"All my life, I've been surrounded by assassins. Mordred, Morgan LaFaye and a hundred others. That puts everyone around me in danger. Often it seems better to work alone than expose others to that risk, especially those I love."

Gwen blinked, suddenly understanding much. She wasn't the only one that Arthur shut out. At times he'd distanced himself from Merlin and even his foster father, Sir Hector. On other occasions, it had been his friends—Lancelot or Gawain. She'd assumed Arthur had suspected them all of disloyalty, but perhaps she had it wrong. Maybe it had been a wrongheaded expression of love.

"Family shares your danger, whether you like it or not," she said.

"I know," he replied, his tone grim. "And a king is expected to marry."

He made it sound like a prison sentence, and Gwen recoiled in hurt. "It is that much of a burden, my lord?"

His look was unreadable. "When the enemy knows what's precious, it becomes a weapon in their hands."

"Precious?" she whispered, but he had already moved on. It suddenly made sense—his distance, his temper and his solitude. Arthur believed he was protecting everyone around him, but he was also protecting himself. Love for him was a perilous risk.

How did I not see this? Gwen cursed herself as she hurried along behind him. She'd known him six years. At first she'd had too little experience to fathom such a complex man, and most of their marriage he'd been away at war. But at some point... She gave up, letting the past slide through her fingers. They'd done a good job of nursing their anger with one another, of making a mess of every attempt to truly connect. The real question was what they would do next.

Arthur interrupted her roiling thoughts with a sharp gesture. Gwen froze, reading the urgency in his stance. Her senses stretched wide, trying to find whatever it was he had detected. For a moment, she was baffled, but she heard it—footfalls, far ahead. They were slow—

not just unhurried, but as if the stride itself was long. If that was the troll, it was disturbingly large.

Arthur's glance went to the lantern. Gwen guessed his meaning and slid the lantern's shutter all but closed. In the sliver of light that remained, the blackness around them seemed absolute. The troll's footfalls were silent, but still Arthur didn't move. They waited, Gwen's knees unsteady, for a long time before Arthur advanced again. When they did, he leaned close and spoke in a voice that was nearly a whisper. "When we find its lair, we'll study the beast for weakness. I'll have one chance to strike. Even with a charmed blade, I'll need to hit a vulnerable point."

The prospect of killing the creature became far too real. Gwen's mouth went dry as she all but glued herself to Arthur's side, hurrying into the next corridor. There, the tunnel ended in a dark, cave-like chamber. The map had indicated a series of such rooms, one leading to another. They'd reached their destination. "The map said this is a storeroom," she said softly.

Arthur took her hand in his, his mailed glove rough but welcome against her skin. He pulled her close as they stepped through the arched doorway. Gwen gasped as the faint lantern light swept over the walls.

"By the saints," Arthur breathed. This was no stash of picks and shovels; it was a treasure room worthy of a dragon's hoard. There had been shelves and chests, but the troll had scattered it all. Heaps of gold dishes, coin and jewelry spilled over the floor in drifts, mixing with the gems that gave the Crystal Mountains their name. The lantern picked sparks from the treasure as the light flashed on facets of precious stones. To Gwen, it looked like a scattering of stars in the darkness. She wasn't normally swayed by wealth, but it did leave her a little breathless.

"Is this where I steal the silverware?" Arthur asked, his lips all but touching her ear.

"I feel underdressed."

He bent and picked up a long dagger set with gems. He handed it to her, the gesture almost courtly. "Sometimes the best accessory is a blade."

She took it, not bothering to point out she'd brought her own knife. This one was bigger, and right now she was fine with that. They kept moving, placing their feet as silently as possible on the sea of shifting coins. It was no mystery why Zorath wanted to regain access to this room. The contents were a king's ransom—enough to buy all of Medievaland, perhaps all of Carlyle.

They emerged into a broad empty space, and then into another cave. The scene here was as awful as the treasury had been wondrous. Gwen clamped her mouth shut, swallowing hard. A thick, meaty smell hung in the air and sent a surge of panic through her gut. Every primitive instinct screamed to run, but her legs refused to move. Arthur stepped close, urging her back.

"You don't need to see this," he said, his arm slipping around her shoulders.

But she already had, and she sidestepped his protective gesture. A cool detachment slid over her, freezing the panic into a numbing fog. Her heart beat a little too fast, but she gave no voice to the incessant screaming at the back of her mind.

There were torches burning in the next room, shoved into black iron stanchions along the walls. They gave a clear view of what had become of the missing goblins. What Gwen saw answered the question of what a troll wanted in the goblins' mines. Not gold, but meat. Goblin meat. This was the troll's larder, and it was a messy eater. Most of the torn and bloody limbs strewn over the floor still had clothing attached. Scraps of uniform said some were the soldiers Zorath had sent.

Arthur stood rooted to the spot, his eyes incandescent with rage. But there was something else in his expression—fear. The *thud-thud* of the troll's footfalls was back, and they were loud.

"Run," he said softly. "Run and hide."

Slowly, as if in a dream, he closed both hands around Excalibur's long hilt and took a deep breath. In that moment, he shifted from the man she knew—king and husband—to a warrior she had never met up close. It sent a zing of shock through her bewildered mind.

"Now," he ordered in the voice of command.

Her body obeyed out of reflex, making her back away from the scene of carnage. A protest rose in her— she'd come to help, to use her wits to help Arthur—and yet what could she do against a creature who'd turned the mine into a butchery? There had been more bodies and parts of bodies than she could count. It was hopeless. She was useless. Terror for Arthur choked her, as if her lungs were suddenly gone.

She wasn't sure if panic or despair claimed her first, but she stopped moving. She'd made it as far as the treasure chamber. Here, she was hidden from view but still close enough to see past where Arthur stood and into the larder. It wasn't a good enough hiding place. As soon as she could gather her wits, she would run, but she couldn't remember how.

Then the troll lurched through the door where Arthur stood. Gwen bolted.

Chapter 15

The troll was massive, scraping the high doorway as it lurched forward. Its gait was top-heavy, unbalanced by its barrel chest and massive shoulders. It was wrapped in a kind of kilt made of hides, the long tail of the motley garment flung over one shoulder. What the hides had once been, Gwen didn't want to know.

Her feet moved of their own will, scampering backward until her shoulders hit a towering stack of treasure chests. She spun around with a squeak, flailing out to smack the cold, brass-bound boxes. Her lantern swung, making crazy patterns on the walls. With a curse, she dived behind the chests and sank to the ground, panting and trembling. She'd faced danger before, but a charging bull was nothing compared to this. She wiped her face with her sleeve, mopping away sweat and tears of fright, and then made herself peer around the corner to see Arthur standing firm as the creature charged.

Black lips peeled back from the troll's fangs as it gave a grunting roar and rushed forward with a rolling, side-to-side gait. For all its awkwardness, it was fast, closing in on Arthur in a blur. Arthur swung Excalibur, the blade ringing as it struck the creature's leathery hide. The troll lashed out, its arms seeming far too long for the rest of it. Arthur spun lightly away, sword poised high. The beast grabbed again, sharp claws screeching against the stone walls, but Arthur smacked its knuckles before dancing away. Gwen could see the concentration in every line and angle of his movements. It was a game of cat and mouse, with the mouse the smarter of the two.

Unfortunately, the cat was especially deadly. The shredded bodies in the next room made that clear. All the heat seemed to leave Gwen's body as a fresh wave of fear overtook her. The troll's head thrust forward, its prominent jaw jutting with annoyance as it swung toward Arthur one more time. The dance between monster and warrior could go on and on, ending when the loser made just one mistake.

Arthur launched into a flurry of thrusts and slashes, aiming for eyes and throat, but the troll's long reach made it all but impossible to get inside its guard. The beast hammered its fist, but Arthur dived and rolled, escaping the pulverizing force by an inch. As he rolled to his feet, he swept the sword low in a move that should have crippled the beast.

Excalibur rang against the troll's hide, achieving nothing.

Gwen sprang to her feet, her own fear forgotten in her worry for Arthur. He couldn't keep the fight up forever. Something had to change, and she was the only one with enough breathing space to do it. She jammed the jeweled knife through her belt and left the lantern on the ground. With her hands free, she tore through the treasure room, picking things up and tossing them aside. If she'd had a slingshot, there were plenty of jewels and coins to hurl at the monster. There were dishes and crowns and scepters of fine goblin workmanship, stockpiled and ready to trade at the unearthly markets where the realms met on Midsummer's Day. All those riches were useless to her now.

She kicked a pile of coins in frustration, causing a glittering avalanche. And then she saw what she needed, flung down in panic by some unlucky goblin in flight— a plain ash bow and quiver of arrows. She snatched it up, testing the string. The bow was made for a goblin man and so a good height for her, but the draw was stiffer than she liked. *Too bad*, she thought, slinging the strap of the quiver over one shoulder and climbing onto a chest to get a clear shot. She'd just have to manage.

Gwen was a good shot and the troll made a huge target. All she needed to do was distract it long enough for Arthur to strike. She notched an arrow with trembling fingers and drew the bow, panic giving her the extra strength she needed. The battle was still in progress, a spinning flurry of sword and claw. She aimed, forcing herself to gauge the rhythm of the fight, to anticipate where her target would be. She loosed, snatched another arrow and loosed again.

The first hit the troll between the shoulder blades, the second smacked its forehead when it turned to howl in protest. Arthur didn't miss his chance, driving Excalibur upward at the underside of the troll's chin. The sword tore through flesh, the point sinking deep, but not deep enough. A trickle of black blood coursed down the troll's neck and chest, but it barely seemed to feel the wound.

The troll caught sight of Gwen and charged. Fright stabbed through her and she leaped from her perch, bow in hand. She landed lightly and dodged around a tall golden statue, finding speed she didn't know she had. The troll swung its huge head from side to side, peering among the treasure while she circled the room and dashed behind the beast. In a dozen strides, she was at Arthur's side. With a look of fierce pride she'd never seen before, he grabbed her hand, and they ran.

The only place they could go was through the scene of slaughter. Gwen quailed—though her feet kept flying. Behind them, the troll turned and roared its fury. Gwen kept her eyes fixed forward, refusing to look at the carnage on either side. She didn't see the slick of blood in her path until she skidded, falling to one knee and coming face-to-face with a limbless torso, the rib cage cracked open like a walnut robbed of its meat. She made a gurgling shriek as Arthur hauled her up and dragged her stumbling forward.

Gwen's mind blanked for an instant, surrendering as Arthur led her from the scene of slaughter and into the tunnels beyond. There were torches here, too, but they were farther apart, at times providing only the faintest glow. The troll was behind them, each step a mighty thump, but it was slowing. Fatigue or blood loss was finally taking its toll.

Arthur pulled her down one of the smaller side passages, finding a dark chamber filled with miners' gear. Panting, they squeezed behind a huge wooden cart on wheels.

"Did we lose it?" she asked.

"I don't know."

They sank to their knees, Arthur's arms around her. Gwen buried her face in his shoulder, breathing in the familiar scent of him. Like a frightened animal, she needed his warmth and the comfort of his touch while she steadied her thundering heart.

"Gwen," he whispered. "My brave Gwen."

She couldn't read his tone well enough to tell if it held sorrow or laughter or both. As long as he kept holding her, she wasn't sure she cared. "I couldn't leave you there," she murmured.

His lips pressed against her hair, the sigh of his breath hot as his arms curled more tightly around her. "Thank you."

They were two simple words, but there was an ocean of feeling in them, a bridge between them that she'd longed for. Gwen squeezed her eyes shut, reliving the last minutes. He'd lifted her out of the blood. If he hadn't, she might have died of despair. She dug her fingers into his coat, holding him tight.

"Are you recovered?" Arthur asked softly. "We need to keep moving."

It was then that she heard the troll's footsteps coming down the corridor, each slithering slap of bare sole oddly stealthy. It paused, snuffling the air. Gwen cringed with revulsion as she realized her pant legs were soaked in blood. The stench would surely betray them.

Arthur released her, his hand silently gripping Excalibur's hilt. There was no room behind the cart for Gwen to draw her bow, so she forced herself to stillness, her muscles coiled with fierce tension. The only possible way to survive was to outsmart the beast. Gwen had thought herself so clever as she'd barged her way into this expedition, but her mind was as blank as fresh parchment. The frustration of it burned.

The *slap-slap* of the troll's feet started again and stopped, then resumed. All the while, it sniffed the air like a bloodhound, steadily growing closer. Arthur made a low sound that was nearly a growl, lifting his sword and balancing his weight in readiness to spring. Gwen willed the troll to keep moving past their door, but it lingered outside, the steps dwindling to a shuffle as if choosing a new direction. Gwen shrank down another inch, hope crumbling. The scant light in the room dimmed as the troll's hulking shape blotted everything else from view.

Arthur sprang with a mighty battle cry, but the troll was too quick. A huge, clawed hand scooped Gwen up as if she were no more than a doll. An outraged shriek flew from her lips and she snatched for her bow, but it was lost behind the cart. The troll clutched her to its chest, the thick, hairy arm pinning her despite her desperate squirming. Wheeling in a two-handed strike, Arthur stabbed his sword straight down, driving the point into the troll's bare toe.

This time, the troll felt the sword. With a weirdly high-pitched yelp, it hopped in a circle, one foot in the air. Gwen flailed at the dizzying movement, arms and legs flying. The quiver emptied of arrows and they hit the ground with a clatter, snapping as the troll crushed them in its dance. Arthur stabbed again, aiming for the other foot. The troll howled, tossing Gwen aside to clutch at its feet. She smacked into the stone wall, skull ringing with the impact before she slithered to the ground. Stomach churning, Gwen struggled to her hands and knees. Dizziness made her falter, but Arthur's strong hands were suddenly there, setting her back on her feet. She blinked frantically, clearing her head.

Then her thoughts came into focus. She spun, stumbling a little as she searched for the troll. "Where is it?"

"Gone." Arthur looked down the corridor. Gwen followed his gaze and caught a glimpse of the creature loping away, whimpers fading as it retreated to nurse its hurt. "I doubt it's felt true pain before."

"How did you know to attack its feet?" she asked. "No other blow seemed to damage it."

"Fingers and toes always hurt the most, even when the wound is slight." Arthur gave a faint smile. "I gambled that was true for trolls."

The brief reprieve from danger left her in a strange free fall. She sagged against him, every limb tingling as her panic drained away. Arthur pulled her close, dipping his head to kiss her brow. But that wasn't enough, and he cupped her face, pressing his lips to hers. His skin was salty with sweat and dust. All at once, Gwen hungered for his touch, as if his kiss was the last breath of air before she drowned in endless dark. She returned the embrace, letting that need remind her she was still alive. Arthur's breath caught with a ragged noise. They pulled apart, panting a little.

"Will it be back?" she asked, regret thick in her voice.

Arthur's mouth turned down. "We've shamed it. It will want revenge."

And their luck wouldn't last. "What do we do?"

His gaze darted toward the tunnel where the troll had vanished. "Retreat until we have a better plan and more swords."

"I'm going to strangle Zorath for sending us here

alone," she said darkly, scanning the ground for usable arrows. Every one was broken. She tossed the empty quiver aside in frustration. "I understand the goblins are afraid, but these are their mines. He could have mustered some backup."

"I agree." Arthur sighed. "In the meantime, can you run?"

Her whole body ached, but her brief moment as a troll's plaything had been worse. "I can run."

Arthur held out his hand. He'd made the gesture often at dances and during ceremonies, but here it was different. This wasn't protocol. He was offering her his protection when she needed it most. Gwen accepted it, squeezing his fingers, and they set out at a gliding trot.

They retraced their steps to the main corridor, careful to end up in no more dead ends. Gwen hadn't noticed what was in the broad tunnel before, but now she saw carts piled with ore as well as winches and scaffolding. The goblins had been mining a vein near the ceiling, and they had hauled a huge bucket up by ropes. There were still picks and water bottles on the high catwalk, and the bucket brimmed with ore destined for the furnace. Judging from the abandoned worksite, the troll's initial attack had been sudden.

Farther along there was a pool of standing water to her left and what looked like an abandoned pumping station. More personal items were scattered along the path—a pipe, a hat and a pair of boots tied together by their laces. Gwen tried not to think about the fate of their owners. Their retreat led through the cavern littered with bodies.

They had nearly made it when she heard the troll's roar. She started, disoriented. "It's ahead of us!"

Arthur was already pulling her the other way, pelting back the way they had come. Somewhere, there was another parallel route the troll had used to cut them off. Clearly, it was not as witless as they had assumed. And it was fast, so fast. Gwen sped with the desperation of prey, lengthening her stride to keep up with Arthur.

They passed the lake again, bursting into the part of the tunnel lined by scaffolding. Arthur dragged her toward it. "Climb!" he ordered, grabbing her by the hips and heaving her upward.

Gwen grasped the rough wood, scrabbling with her feet to find purchase. The spaces between crossbars were at odd intervals, making her wonder how goblins climbed—and then she was too busy to think. Arthur let go the moment she was secure, leaving her bereft of his comforting touch. A moment later, she heard Excalibur hiss from its scabbard. The urgency of the sound gave her strength and she hauled herself up the wooden structure. When she finally crawled onto the platform, she was far above the stone floor.

The walkway was narrow enough that she knelt, gripping the sides with both hands. She had to twist her neck to see the troll bearing down on Arthur. Her husband stood braced for attack, his chosen ground below Gwen's perch. It was clear he would defend her to the death.

Chapter 16

Gwen screamed as the troll leaped toward Arthur, slashing the air with its claws. The king ducked and rolled, dodging behind one of the carts only to wheel behind the beast and deliver a two-handed blow. Delivered with such force, the strike should have cleaved the troll's legs from beneath him. Excalibur rang with the sound, but the blow had little effect.

Gwen cursed, using a word no lady should even know. She'd seen this battle before—they were right back to where they'd been when the troll first appeared. She knew all Arthur's heroism would avail nothing. She looked around, hoping for another bow and arrow or pot of miraculously boiling oil. What she had was a winch and a bucket of rocks.

That made her sit up, forgetting how delicately she was balanced. She'd seen enough siege engines to understand the principles of the machine. The rope that held the bucket arched over an iron wheel barely a foot from the platform. The bucket was balanced by a counterweight, making the business of raising and lowering the load of ore more easily controlled. If the rope were cut, the full container would smash to the ground.

Surely that much crushing weight would stop a monster? She glanced down, seeing Arthur aim for the troll's feet one more time, but the creature was wiser now and evaded the flashing blade. Gwen choked on a gasp as one clawed hand streaked out, ripping through Arthur's chain mail shirt. Arthur spun away, links pinging as they hit the ground.

Gwen anxiously forced her mind back to her task. If she cut the rope, the massive stone block that balanced the bucket would drop. That was expected, but parts of the winch were torqued. With no tension to keep the weight in line, it looked poised to crash into the scaffolding's supports. If the platform fell, she fell, possibly into the troll's clutches. Or she might just break her neck.

Another glance at the fight made her decision. She'd just have to take the chance. She drew the jeweled dagger from her belt and inched toward the spot where the rope was easy to reach. It was a matter of waiting for the absolute right time.

For the briefest moment she caught Arthur's eye, and made a frantic gesture.

Arthur saw Gwen waving, but he was fully occupied with the troll, who had picked up a boulder in one hand and heaved it like a toddler learning to throw a ball. Arthur jerked aside, feeling the rush of air as it sailed past. Apparently pleased with this new tactic, the troll bent to pick up another projectile.

It was then Arthur looked up to see Gwen pointing down, and then mimicking a hammer squashing something flat. With a leap of excitement, he understood. A deadly simple plan, but it had a certain elegance. Despite exhaustion, he grinned. He'd all but lost hope, but Gwen—all the saints bless her—had just changed everything.

He ran beneath the bucket, turning and raising Excalibur as if ready to make a final, desperate stand. With a grunt of satisfaction, the troll charged with fangs bared. There was a creak as weight shifted, then a snapping noise. The troll looked up in surprise, but by the time it bellowed in shock, Arthur had leaped away, hitting the ground and rolling as an avalanche of rock crashed down. Wood splintered and dust flew, creating a choking cloud that blotted most of the cavern from sight.

Arthur coughed, scrambling to his feet. "Gwen!" There was no reply. He blinked and sneezed, still blind to anything but dust. "Gwen?"

Rock shifted, and he heard a low growl. The troll was still alive! He groped for Excalibur and prowled into the cloud. It was then he saw her, lying full-length on a beam that tilted at a crazy angle. His heart dropped, and for an instant he forgot everything else. She was dirty and pale, but her eyes were defiant. When a faint smile curled her lips, Arthur forgot to breathe. *She is so brave.*

And she had given him such a gift. He turned to the half-conscious troll, poised Excalibur over its vulnerable throat and swung the mighty sword. The troll's head rolled free.

It was over.

The walk back to the goblin castle was slow and weary, Gwen leaning on Arthur's arm. All the same, there was grim satisfaction to be had as they marched into Zorath's dining hall. All conversation stopped and the crimson-skinned goblin rose to his feet.

"You have returned!" King Zorath exclaimed.

"We have returned victorious." Arthur dropped a miner's sack containing the troll's head before the king. "There is all the evidence you need. Your mines and treasure are safe once more."

The goblin king's expression moved from stunned incredulity to joy. Zorath snatched up a goblet and raised it into the air. "All hail King Arthur and Queen Guinevere, saviors of the goblin tribes!"

There was a general roar and pounding of fists. It went on and on until Arthur raised his hand. "We have fulfilled your quest, and now claim your promise."

"The King and Queen of Camelot are granted freedom to come and go from the Crystal Mountains for as long as they shall live," Zorath declared.

The cheering and pounding resumed for a full minute. It might have gone on longer, but a fresh barrel of ale was borne in by servants, distracting the diners. Zorath sat and beckoned Arthur and Gwen to approach.

"You sense trouble among the dragons," the goblin king said. He kept his voice low, indicating the discussion was not for all to hear.

"Yes," said Gwen, speaking for the first time. "I think they're in trouble."

The observation surprised Arthur. He wouldn't have stated things that way, but she was completely right. "There is a fae involved," he added.

Zorath nodded. "The fae's name is Talvaric. You

know well that our borders are closed to outsiders, but he has roamed these parts for centuries and knows how to come and go undetected. He is also a magic user and skilled with portals. It is not easy to bar someone with such skills."

"What is his business here?" asked Arthur.

"Until recently, we believed he simply liked the mountains. Fae walk in wild places."

Arthur shook his head. "That might have been true once, but fae lost their love of beauty along with their souls. He was here for another purpose."

"I know." The goblin king's expression grew crafty. "As time went on, I began to ask questions. And then I sent eyes and ears to verify what I heard."

Arthur gave a slow nod. Every king had his spies.

Zorath leaned closer. "He came to the Crystal Mountains in search of magical beasts. He takes them prisoner for his own ends. When we tried to put an end to his raids, our trouble with the troll began."

That made a horrible kind of sense. "Is that all you know of this Talvaric?"

The goblin shook his head. "As you well know, the Lady of the Lake has imprisoned Morgan LaFaye. That leaves the Kingdom of Faery without a ruler. Most are not bold enough to risk Morgan's wrath if she should break free, but Talvaric wants to claim the crown."

"How does he hope to achieve this?" Arthur asked incredulously. "He is not one of the high lords of the fae. I've never even heard of him."

"He hopes to win support by proving to the world he can beat the great Arthur of Camelot. You wield Excalibur, the one sword that can kill Morgan LaFaye and cleave through the darkest of fae magics. If he can defeat you, then he will be worthy of their allegiance. Or so he would have them believe."

"How does he hope to achieve this?" Arthur demanded. "And what does that have to do with these mountains?"

"Dragons," Gwen said. "You said Rukon Shadow Wing dwells here."

"His weapon is dragons. Beasts. That's why he takes them." Arthur said it aloud, finding it hard to believe. Dragons couldn't be tamed, and yet the ones who'd come to the mortal realm had behaved strangely. It all fit together.

Gwen made a disgusted noise. "Talvaric needs proof of his victory, so he will use the dragons in the most public way possible, in full view of the human media. Haven't you noticed all the TV cameras?"

Arthur's temper flared. It was bad enough the fae yearned to defeat him, but dragging the hidden world into the full view of mortal eyes was utterly unforgivable. "This Talvaric has a short and undignified future. Where can we find him?"

"We do not know," said Zorath.

"Is there anything else you can tell us?" Arthur asked.

"Unfortunately, no," said Zorath. "Believe that if I knew more I would share it, for you have done us a great service."

"And you have given me the name of the villain who threatens my realm," Arthur replied. "That is also a service of great worth."

The goblin king rose, a wide smile on his ugly red face, and spoke so that all could hear. "King of Camelot, my new friend and ally, you have earned a place at my table, as has the lovely Queen Guinevere. This is an occasion to celebrate, so let us speak no more of dark things tonight."

Arthur bowed, recognizing the honor for its full worth, while Gwen leaned forward and left a kiss on Zorath's cheek. The goblin beamed and called for wine and food, as well as water and towels so they could wash before they ate. Arthur suddenly realized that he was starving. By the way Gwen fell on the many dishes set before them, so was she. And the food was well worth a hearty appetite—tender greens, bowls of delicately seasoned grains, fresh berries and lamb in a rich, spiced sauce. Almost everything came from the mountains, but the spices were hardly local. The goblins had a vast trading network, and Arthur realized the value of an alliance with their kind. Much had been achieved during this adventure.

And without Gwen, he never would have had it. He watched her eat, fascinated by her swift, precise bites and the delicacy of her hands. She wiped her fingers often, for there were few utensils. The goblins used triangles of a nut-flavored flatbread to scoop up their food, sometimes slathering it in a cool, herbed sauce. It was messy but very good, and Gwen gave in to the temptation to lick her fingers like a child. She caught Arthur's gaze, her eyes bright.

"Food tastes good after you've been frightened half to death," she explained.

"I know." He wanted to say more, but his throat ached too much. On any other occasion, he would have been planning, calculating and moving pieces around his mental chessboard to find a path through the future. Now all he could do was relish being next to his wife, grateful they were safe and together. For once, the present was enough.

The feast went long into the night, and Zorath offered them a bed. But Gwen and Arthur both wanted the free air outside the mountain, so they took their leave. The night was clear and cold, thick dew sparkling on the grass. Arthur sucked the freshness into his lungs, clearing them of the peculiar scent of goblins. The air was like iced wine after a mouthful of greasy stew.

Zorath sent a guide to lead them back to the place where Gwen had been captured, and from there she easily found her way to the meadow where the gate had been. Arthur followed in her wake, oddly content to let her take charge of getting them home.

It wasn't hard to locate the gate itself, because there was a queen-size bed sitting in the meadow, along with a collection of coat hangers, bathrobes, extra blankets, the minibar and a nightstand. None of it was neatly arranged, but scattered as if hurled from a catapult, a few of the lighter items stuck in the lower branches of a pine tree. The bed at least was upright, although the covers were strewn everywhere.

"I think Clary's portal has developed a mind of its own," Gwen said, sitting down on the edge of the bed with a sigh. "I wonder if it's actually safe to use it."

Arthur wandered through the meadow, picking up items as he went. Some things had been there awhile, judging by the heavy layer of dew. Others weren't damp at all. He picked out the driest items and carried them to the bed. He stood for a moment, looking down into Gwen's face. The moon was bright, picking out her features in a wash of silver. He'd always thought her delicate, which was true. Her bones were fine and graceful, and every part of her spoke of an artist's love of harmony. But she was also incredibly strong. Perhaps that wasn't a matter of muscle, but character. He'd seen it expressed in her stubbornness, but now he understood there was more to it than that. She had something the best of his knights had: a willingness to accept their own fear and fight past it.

Arthur sat down beside her, lacing his fingers through hers. "Today I've been roasted by a dragon, captured by goblins and attacked by a troll. I'd rather not face a temperamental portal through time and space. Are you okay if we stay here tonight?"

A laugh bubbled out of Gwen and she tipped her face up to the sky, showing the long line of her throat. "Am I okay? Yes. All I want to do is fall over." And she did, flopping backward with her slender arms spread wide.

Arthur lay down beside her. The stars above were dimmed by the moon's full radiance, but even so they spread into a full canopy of lights. It made him feel tiny, a mote of dust clinging to the high mountains in one of countless realities. It was peaceful.

"There are no people here," said Gwen in a soft voice. "No cars, nothing electronic, no huge buildings to hem a person in. It feels like home."

Arthur turned to look at her profile, but became distracted by the strip of bare flesh where her neck curved into her shoulder. He kissed her there, nuzzling her warmth. "Camelot is in a different world now."

"I know. And there are so many opportunities for me there."

He heard it then—a note of hesitancy in her voice. She was expressing a desire she thought he wouldn't ap-

prove of. It made him wonder how she really saw him.
"Is that what you want—opportunity?"

She turned toward him, eyes catching the moonlight.
"I think I want to go to school."

It wasn't what he'd envisioned for her, but every instinct told him to change course. Gwen was smart—wasn't it her quick thinking that had felled the troll, just as much as his sword?—and the desire to fulfill that potential was simply part of her intelligence. "If you want school, then you shall have it."

She raised herself on one elbow, the shadow of her form filling his vision. Moonlight turned her fair hair into a halo, as if Gwen were as much angel as woman. "Thank you." And her breath sighed out, as if in profound relief.

Arthur's heart stopped for a delicious beat, hearing the truth of her gratitude. He'd finally touched something essential in her—not the superficial place that could be pleased with jewels or clothes or even one of Gwen's beloved hounds, but something deeper. He'd recognized something about who she was.

He reached up, burying his fingers in the silk of her hair, and kissed her deeply.

Chapter 17

Gwen caught her breath, lost for a moment in the pure sensation of his lips on hers. His breath was hot compared to the cold night around them, and she drank in the kiss as if eager to pull his warmth into her. She cupped her hands around his face, the feel of skin and beard and bone her anchor in the starlit dark.

The kiss ended, but she remained kneeling above him, unwilling to release the intensity between them. A breeze stirred the trees, whispering icy secrets. She kissed him again, the sigh of his breath mingling with the wind.

She shivered, and he pulled her down, wrapping his arms around her. She turned into his chest, feeling the hard, hot solidity of him. All the strangeness of the past few days battered at her, and a sense of spiritual vertigo made her cling yet closer. As if sensing her need for comfort, Arthur sat up and reached for the thick pile of blankets that were still free of dew.

"Wait." Gwen kicked off her boots and shrugged out of her clothes. She'd cleaned up as best she could before entering the feast hall, but she felt a thousand times better without the soiled garments. When she was done, Arthur settled the covers around her as he stripped down to his skin. Gwen watched him while his back was turned, letting her gaze play over the planes and shadows of his form. The moonlight turned his skin to marble whiteness, showing every curve and valley of hard muscle. Gwen knew swordplay had as much to do with speed and balance as it did brute force, and Arthur was perfectly proportioned, every muscle honed by training from childhood. Her pulse skipped as a sweet ache filled her belly.

When he lay down and put his hands on her skin, she gasped at his cold touch. "Sorry," he murmured, kissing her brow. "I'm afraid we'll have to keep close to stay warm."

His voice held teasing regret. Gwen had no words to respond. Desire pushed sore muscles and fatigue aside, but it couldn't restore her wit. Instead, she kissed him again, nibbling at the strong muscles of his throat. He released a pleased groan, rolling her so that she lay on her back. She was warming up now, their cozy nest all the sweeter for the crystalline night around them. This was stolen time, an unexpected gift of intimacy.

Arthur knew how to make use of it. He pulled the covers over their heads to trap the warmth around them, and then set about exploring her form. His hands were rough, but his touch was a caress, arching over her ribs with a firm but gentle pressure. Gwen pushed into it,

ing a wooden frame together. She'd stopped to suck at a splinter in her thumb when she realized someone was watching her.

It was that young man again, the one named Arthur. Everyone said he was the king, but she found that hard to believe. Kings were crusty and ancient and prone to chopping off heads. So far, Arthur had betrayed no signs of any such flaws. All the same, she scrambled to her feet and managed a curtsy, holding her dress in a way she hoped hid her dirty, bare feet.

"What are you doing?" he asked. He looked at the scraps of wood scattered around her feet, his eyebrows furrowing in an intense frown.

"I'm building a trap."

"Really?" he replied. "What for?"

"Foxes. They've been bothering the chickens."

A speckled hen approached, picking at the frame and prancing around it with bobs of her head. Gwen picked her up, tucking her in the crook of an arm before the silly bird could scatter the nails. The hen gave a squawk of protest but settled in happily enough. Gwen could see Arthur trying to assemble the pieces of her trap in his head, but she doubted he could. This was her own design, and not even the gamekeeper believed it would work.

Gwen kept looking at Arthur—he was handsome enough to look at for hours at a time—but couldn't help wondering why he was there, in her barn. She knew plenty of men-at-arms, but he was different. His clothes were never stained with ale or worn through at the elbows and knees. He stood straighter, his shoulders squared as if in constant combat. It clashed oddly with his tendency to stare at her. If she were honest, she found their encounters rather uncomfortable. But she tended to ignore the honest part of herself when confronted with a gorgeous young man who was supposedly a king greater even than her own father.

He looked up from the frame with an amused frown. "A bow and arrow is less work than nailing all this together and then having to cut their throats."

"I don't kill the foxes!" she said in horror. "I take them out to the woods."

He gave a surprised laugh. "You know they'll just come back?"

"No, they don't," Gwen said defiantly. "I give them a stern talking-to. I tell them to stay away or they'll end up lining my father's cloak."

"And do the foxes listen to you?"

"Yes."

His blue eyes shone with hilarity. "Really?"

"Really," she said with annoyance. "I can tell you don't believe me."

"I am devastated to say it, but I'm afraid I don't."

In her fury, Gwen clutched the hen hard enough that it began to flap. Gwen tossed the bird away, and it settled on one of the low rafters. "I know it's the truth. Not one of the foxes has returned."

"How do you know that?" Arthur asked, a little less certain now.

Gwen shook her skirts back into place, ignoring the dust that billowed from their folds. "Because otherwise the foxes are dead and all I'm left with is heartbreak. I won't accept that."

His slow smile was the first real one she'd seen from him. "I think I understand. You have to try."

The dream ended abruptly when the heavy insulation of the bedcovers was jerked from Gwen's head. Her eyes flew open at Arthur's yell and the rattle of Excalibur's sheath. Cold air slapped her face and she clutched the blankets close—only to see Merlin's astonished face. Excalibur's point was all but tickling his nose, but his eyes were flicking from Arthur to Gwen and back again. She burst out laughing at his mix of embarrassment and amused curiosity—and then realized she was naked. She sank back beneath the blankets, feeling blood rush up her cheeks.

"Did I startle you?" Merlin asked drily.

Arthur lowered his sword, fury fading to annoyance. "The least you might have done was bring coffee."

"Tea," said Gwen, refusing to be cowed. "I like tea better."

Merlin tossed bathrobes marked with the hotel crest onto the bed. "I suggest you get up and follow me back through the portal. I've got it stabilized, but I don't know how long that will last."

He turned his back, and stalked toward a shimmering doorway that rose out of the long grass. Gwen grabbed a robe and pulled it on, her arms disappearing into the oversize terry-towel sleeves. She noticed the sun was high and the air was only slightly cool. They must have slept for a long time.

Arthur offered his hand with a gallant bow. "Your escort awaits, my queen."

Gwen took it, rising on her toes to give him a kiss. She should have felt foolish, standing in bare feet and a robe, her unbrushed hair falling in a tangle, but she felt more herself than she had since childhood. By the light in Arthur's eyes, he was happy, too.

Merlin kept his expression blandly neutral and held

out a hand toward the portal. "If Your Majesties would care to step through, I shall return the meadow to its pristine state. I doubt the squirrels have a use for the minibar."

"Hard to say," replied Arthur, retrieving Excalibur. "The bottles are about the right size."

Merlin gave him a withering look. "Not even you can look regal in a hotel bathrobe."

A moment later, they were back in the hotel. Clary jumped up from where she sat on the floor, her expression wild with concern. "Are you all right? You aren't hurt, are you?" She bowed to Arthur, then clasped Gwen's hands and finally gave her a rib-crushing hug.

"I'm fine. We're both fine," Gwen squeaked, realizing her ribs hurt from hitting the wall during their fight with the troll. She probably had bruises.

Clary let go, looking her up and down with a raised brow. "So it seems. I take it the trip was a success."

"Yes." Gwen might have said more, but was distracted by the state of the room. There was a dusty patch on the floor where her bed had been, and the nightstand that had stood beside it was missing. Her gaze went quickly to the pile of shopping bags that held her beautiful new clothes, the black dress tossed carelessly on top. At least the portal had left those alone.

"I met Merlin," Clary whispered in Gwen's ear. "And I'm devastated. He's *horrible*."

There was a flare of light and Merlin emerged from the hotel closet, dusting off his hands. "Next time you want a portal, call a professional." He gave Clary a dark look.

"Hey," the witch protested. "I got the job done."

"And I'm certain the hotel proprietor appreciated the

bull moose who traded places with the bed. Somebody needs to review their homework on the principles of portal stabilization."

"I was in a hurry," Clary protested.

Merlin folded his arms. "Get the spell right, unless you want to keep swapping furniture for livestock."

"Nobody died."

"Tell that to the breakfast buffet."

Clary folded her arms and stuck out her chin. "Moose like waffles. Who knew?"

Gwen and Arthur exchanged a look. "Everybody likes waffles," Arthur suggested. "I'll call room service."

Gawain picked that moment to come through the door. His gaze flicked from one face to another, finally settling on Arthur. "I hope you got some rest."

Gwen saw Arthur's expression shift, face settling into hard lines. It was as if an artist had erased and re-drawn his features in a single heartbeat, deleting the man who'd slept at her side. She yearned to cry foul, to turn the clock back and bar Gawain from the room. In-stead, she took Arthur's hand and squeezed hard.

"What's happened?" he asked, returning the pres-sure of her fingers.

"Rukon Shadow Wing has been sighted in the woods near where we first encountered him. This time we ride as a company and finish this once and for all."

"No," said Arthur.

Gawain scowled. "Why not? We've tried being nice. We've tried single combat. This is no time to send a basket of home-baked cookies."

"The dragons are under the influence of a fae named Talvaric," said Arthur. "He's the quarry we want."

"And in the meantime?" Gawain demanded. "Sir Hot and Smoky has to be dealt with."

"The dragon is our connection to the fae."

Merlin gave an evil grin. "You're going to use the dragon to draw Talvaric out."

Arthur shrugged. "Or at least provide information on him."

Gawain appeared less than convinced. "One does not simply interrogate a dragon."

"Sure you can," Merlin said helpfully. "You just have to catch it first."

Arthur's expression said everything Gwen was thinking. This wasn't the dragon's fault, and punishing it was unfair—and yet somehow they had to stop it before innocent people were hurt.

"I have an idea," Gwen said before she could stop herself. Last night's dream was fresh in her mind, as if a hidden part of her was already working on the problem. "We could build a trap."

Arthur turned to her, his eyes narrowing. She expected him to tell her to be silent, but he paused a moment before speaking, speculation in his gaze. "Explain."

Chapter 18

Once in a while, it was good to be king.

Arthur, freshly showered, lay on the remaining bed in the hotel room, his hands behind his head and Excalibur propped against the nightstand. Clary had changed to a different room, and Merlin was running interference with the hotel staff. Opening an interdimensional portal in a hotel closet probably wasn't covered by guest-room policy, and even though the portal had now been closed, it would take wizardry to dispel awkward questions. Everyone else was off tracking the dragon in an effort to locate its lair in the woods outside town.

Normally, Arthur would have been in charge of the search party, but not today. They had too little information about their fae enemy, and Talvaric had made a veiled threat against the queen. Arthur's self-appointed job was to watch over Guinevere, who sat at the desk sketching furiously on hotel notepaper. Like him, she was still in a bathrobe, her hair pinned up in a knot that left her neck bare. Arthur was transfixed by the curve of her spine as she bent to her task.

The notion of trapping a dragon seemed ludicrous to Arthur, but he was curious to hear her idea. Their adventure in the Crystal Mountains had reminded him just how much Gwen could surprise him.

She'd been dancing when he'd first seen her. It was hot, even for July, with the sky a merciless sapphire. Arthur was on horseback, Merlin at his side and a company of men behind him. They were near the castle of King Leodegranz when he looked down from the road and spied a hollow of cool grass shaded by elms. There she was, leading a mob of children in a round dance. The children ranged from babies to ten or twelve years, but she was at the threshold of womanhood. Flowers wove a drunken crown around the spill of her gold hair and her skirts were knotted up to display coltish, grass-stained shins. She was hardly elegant, but she drew his eye. How could she not, with so much joy shining from her face?

"Who is that?" he asked Merlin.

"I don't know," the sorcerer replied without much interest. "Some servant's daughter, I expect."

And yet Arthur stared, watching her as his column of men wound up the hill and between the castle gates. That year had been nothing but war, and his soul echoed with the clash of steel. He'd forgotten what innocence looked like, and he'd forgotten about dancing. Now he yearned to bound across the soft green grass to join them, shedding pieces of his armor as he ran.

"She's a pretty thing," Merlin said, amused.

Arthur tore his eyes away, suddenly uncomfortable. "The children look happy, that's all. It's a pleasant change from battle."

A thoughtful look crossed Merlin's face. "Indeed."

Much of that year's war had been with Leodegranz. Eventually the old wolf had surrendered his sword and agreed to a treaty, which was why Arthur and Merlin had come. Arthur's goal was to unite the petty kingdoms of Britain into a single political force, and Leodegranz was the fifth to swear allegiance to Arthur of Camelot as high king. Earlier that month, Arthur had turned twenty-three.

They were received with every courtesy, and a banquet was prepared. To Arthur's surprise, it was no page who filled his wine cup that night, but the dancing girl. She was dressed in a gown of soft gray, the sleeves lined with cloth of silver and her shining hair bound in a fillet of gold. Clearly, she was no servant's child, but a maiden of rank.

"Do you like her?" asked King Leodegranz, eyeing the girl with the same assessment he might show a prize hound. "That's my daughter, Guinevere."

She lowered her eyes as she poured the wine, tawny lashes hiding her thoughts. In the dark and smoky feast hall, the pale dress made her shine like a piece of lost moonlight. "She is very beautiful," Arthur said, fascinated by the graceful curve of her long neck.

Her gaze flicked to his before she moved away, her slim back spear-straight. Furtive though it was, there had been a dare in that look. Guinevere was bold, for all that she was young.

Merlin leaned close. "You know it's no accident that she's here. Leodegranz wants a marriage as part of the treaty. His grandson will be high king, if he has his way."

Arthur watched Guinevere and remembered her joy. If he was her husband, he could protect that bright spirit, or that's what he told himself. In truth, he needed that happiness as a balm to his soul. Happiness and beauty and innocence. Guinevere held the promise of them all the way a new flame holds light.

Arthur lifted his goblet, touching it to Merlin's. "Make it happen."

And Merlin had. Almost two years later, after a long and complicated negotiation, they were wed.

Back on the bed in the present day, Arthur opened his eyes. He'd been drowsing and yawned with the drugged lethargy of daytime sleep. Gwen was sitting on the edge of the bed, the pad of notepaper in one hand.

"I have the door figured out," she said. "The other parts may need magic."

Arthur took the drawing from her and studied it, recognizing a sophisticated and yet simple device of counterweights and pulleys inspired by what they'd seen in the mines. "I wish I'd had this for the drawbridge at Camelot."

"Do you think it will work?" she asked, her fingers twisting the bedcovers.

"Yes," he said. Gwen had a natural talent. She'd already provided a list of materials so the others could get started gathering them, and from the look of it her estimates had been sound. "You're good at this."

Her smile was shaky. "Thank you."

He understood why she was hesitant. There had been some understandable doubt from the knights. None of them knew this side of the queen, but that was only the beginning of their objections. Even if Gwen's unusual plan worked, a caged dragon would be an angry one. There would be consequences. However, Arthur had overruled his men. The trap might give the knights the upper hand for a brief window of time, and maybe that was all they'd need.

Gwen put a hand on his knee. "We must find out how to help your dragon."

With a twist of regret, he remembered her fox trap, and how she'd lectured the bewildered animals. A dragon wouldn't be so easy to ignore if he came slinking back. "We can try. I can promise that much."

"And if you can't?"

Arthur set the drawing aside and sat up to slip an arm around Gwen's waist. He pulled her close, kissing her hair. It smelled of the sweet hotel shampoo. "Your trap will buy us time. That will save lives."

She nodded, her expression tight, and tapped the notepad. "I won't know how to finish the design until Gawain comes back with a description of its lair."

"You're going to build the trap where it sleeps?"

"If I can. Owen says dragons prefer caves or other rock formations for their home. We can take advantage of the surrounding landscape to provide some of the walls of the cage."

"That makes sense." Arthur was finding it increasingly hard to pay attention. Her lips had taken over his imagination—their shape and softness and his memory of their taste.

She stopped talking and gave him a look of fond exasperation. "I can explain all this later."

"I'm listening," he protested.

"No, you're not." But she smiled, and everything was all right.

He lifted a hand to her cheek, stroking the silken skin with his thumb. "I can't stop feasting my eyes on you."

She caught his hand. "One would think I'd be a commonplace sight by now."

"Never commonplace."

"Then what, my lord?" Her gaze searched his face. Now that the aftermath from their time in the mines was fading, uncertainty had crept back into her expression.

His first instinct was to say she was his wife, his queen, but he stopped himself. Guinevere belonged to herself. It was one thing to claim a woman, but first he had to respect her. Arthur took her hand and kissed it. "You are exquisite."

She glanced down at the hotel robe, which was made for someone with much longer arms. "I am simply Gwen."

"That is precisely the point."

Her smile managed to be wry and flirtatious at once. She *was* exquisite, the golden goddess poets and painters adored. And yet that was just surface, like the gilt decoration of a jewel chest. The real riches were beneath, where so few cared to look. Where he had failed to look for so long.

Shame speared him and he bowed his head, searching for a plea of forgiveness. She brushed his hair back with a soft hand, prompting him to raise his eyes. "What is it?"

She truly didn't understand the ache of regret inside him. It wasn't just remorse for leaving her behind, or even a wish that their marriage had thrived sooner. He should have been a better man, one unbroken by the path his life had taken. She deserved so much more.

He'd tried to let her go. Now he didn't think he could. He was far too selfish, too possessive to attempt that sacrifice again. The collar of her robe had slipped, leaving one shoulder bare. His lips found it, delighting in the smooth, pale flesh.

Her warm breath tickled his ear. "You're distracting me from my design."

"I'm concentrating on mine," he replied.

"You have a design?" Her tone was arch.

"Of course. A good king always does." He slipped the tie of her robe loose and slid his hand inside the folds of cloth. He palmed her hip, pulling her tight against him. The throbbing low in his body drowned out every other idea. He was only dimly aware of his course of logic—that his men were hunting a deadly beast, that he was guarding Gwen from harm, that he was king and ultimately responsible for them all. Instead, all he wanted was warmth and relief. He wanted to hear his wife laugh and cry out in pleasure. He wanted what any man did—that simple peace that kings rarely enjoyed.

Gwen leaned into him, letting him take her weight. "Then perhaps you ought to show me what you have in mind."

"I am all obedience, my queen."

He pulled her down onto the bed, sinking into the soft covers. She threaded her arms around him, rolling so that she balanced lightly on top of him, her hands on his shoulders and her knees straddling his waist. Eyes dancing with expectation, she gave a feline smile. "What should I choose as my first command?"

Her kiss was deep and filled with a sweet, unconscious lust. Arthur wove his fingers through the long curtain of her hair, glorying in its soft caress. She sat up, shrugging off her robe and letting it fall. The pale afternoon light bathed her skin, showing off flawless, slender limbs and breasts soft as silk.

Arthur suddenly felt far less obedient. He raised himself up until they were nose to nose, their breath mingling. Gwen's neck corded as she arched back, refusing to give ground. "I am queen here," she whispered, voice dark with need.

He shifted, freeing his legs so he could trap her between his knees, but still she met him, skin to delicious skin. She grasped the lapels of his robe and pushed it off his shoulders. He was breathing hard now, almost panting. It was all he could do not to shudder as her nails traced down his chest and belly with sharp, exquisite strokes.

Then she took possession of him in her hands, and he groaned with the hot, throbbing pleasure of it. He suddenly doubted the wisdom of letting Gwen take charge. He might not survive her regal commands. She bent, her lips brushing his tip before she slid her body upward, giving him the full benefit of the soft friction.

"Take me," she whispered. "I'm ready for you."

Arthur was all too happy to oblige. He took her by the waist, lifting her. She settled over him in a tight, wet heat, her wordless cry vibrating through him. They began to move as one, and his mind slid from thought to sensation. All that remained was color and heat and a kaleidoscope of imagery—a slender shoulder, the translucent curl of an ear or the rosebud perfection of a breast. And the mindless, heartless need to possess it all. When it came to Guinevere, he had always been mad with greed.

To keep her had meant putting her in danger. To release her had meant tearing out his heart. And now he was once again the bridegroom drunk on the scent of her skin. He had lost his willpower. Perhaps his mind. He didn't care.

At last they fell apart, sweat slicked and boneless side by side. His limbs were leaden, but his head felt light, as if he'd drunk too deeply of a strong wine. With the last of his strength, Arthur took her hand in his. This was what he wanted, to be man and wife in full enjoyment of each other. She was bold, clever, demanding and his.

"Is Your Majesty satisfied?" he asked, turning to stare into her eyes.

Her pupils were dark, swallowing the blue. Her features were flushed and soft with relaxation. "That was very, um, majestic."

They laughed like drunkards until Arthur's cell phone cut them off with an emphatic buzz. He turned to glare at it, hating the way it turned his stomach hard with the anticipation of trouble. With fae and dragons on the loose, what else could it be?

He snatched it up, fully alert now. "Hello?" He realized too late his greeting was a growl.

"My pardon, Your Majesty." It was Sir Owen's voice, the Welsh accent unmistakable. "We've located the dragon's lair. We thought you would want to know at once."

"Of course." Arthur cleared his throat. "Where is it?"

Gwen stirred as the knight gave directions. By the time Arthur ended the call, she had slipped back into her robe. "The dragon?"

"They found its nest five miles west of town." Arthur tossed the phone aside, too aware his respite from duty was over.

"So what do we do next?" she asked, sitting on the edge of the bed.

The innocent question struck hard. He asked himself again if he should ignore the misgivings of the knights and trust Gwen's design. The chance for success seemed slim, and then there was the question of how to help the creature once it was confined—or even if it wanted help. If it got loose, its vengeance would be deadly.

"Arthur?" Gwen said, prompting him when he didn't answer.

The alternative was to forget the trap and battle the beast until it fled back to its home or died. In all probability, at least one knight would not survive.

And what of Gwen? Did he insist she remain behind, when every path he could see ended in peril? And yet he needed no imagination to foresee how *that* conversation would unfold.

"Arthur?" She put her hand over his.

Ultimately, his word would shape the events to come. This was what he hated most about rulership— the knowledge that a bad decision could end in pain and death. Whatever happened would be his fault.

Some days it sucked to be king.

He squeezed her hand. "We go investigate the lair."

Chapter 19

For the first time ever, Gwen became a partner in one of Arthur's adventures without the need to threaten, cajole, blackmail or sneak her way onto the team. She should have been delighted. Instead, she clutched her notebook to her stomach like an improvised piece of armor as she stood beside him in the elevator, watching the numbers count down to the lobby. She'd been given a chance to prove herself, but by extension she'd also been given the opportunity to fail. It was all part of the same package.

The fact pressed on her like an anvil crushing her skull. It was actually hard to breathe past the knowledge that her failure—a flaw in the design or getting in the way at just the wrong moment—could cost the life of someone she knew. Owen. Percival. *Arthur.*

Shying away from that thought, she put on her most

queenly face and hoped that confidence would find its way to her roiling stomach. In the past, she'd guessed at the kind of pressure Arthur was under, day after day, but this was as close as she'd ever come to that much responsibility. How could he stand it? Then again, what choice did he have?

Gawain was waiting for them in the hotel lobby, his usual scowl in place. They'd never liked one another, and his expression said nothing had changed. "Arthur," he said, with a nod that added the implied "Your Majesty."

Then he turned to her. "My lady, did you get the photos I sent?"

Gwen handed him the notepad. "I used them to complete the design."

The knight flipped from page to page, rapidly scanning what she'd drawn. Then he looked up, still scowling, but with something in his eyes she'd never seen before—approval. "This should do the job. It's better than anything I've seen from a master builder."

Gwen kept her face still, but she knew she'd hoard that brief moment as carefully as any dragon. Impressing Gawain wasn't easy. "I'm glad. I know better than to expect empty compliments from you."

The knight gave a wry grin as he led the way to the front doors. Arthur stayed at her side, a hand resting on the small of her back. Gwen looked up at him, and he dropped a quick kiss against her lips before giving a smile of his own.

"What's so amusing?" she asked.

"You two. Your endless arguments."

Some of those had been spectacular. Gawain had a temper equal to hers and was deeply loyal to Arthur.

The Scottish knight had gone ahead far enough to be out of earshot, so Gwen ventured a complaint. "He used to shout at my greyhounds."

Arthur made a face. "You spoiled them until they were impossibly ill behaved."

"Well, so was he."

That made Arthur laugh, a rich sound that turned every head in the lobby. Gwen noticed people smiling. No doubt they looked like a couple in love and on holiday, about to head out to enjoy the outdoors. It was a good feeling, and Gwen was so absorbed in it that she barely noticed when Gawain came to a dead stop as the automatic glass doors to the lobby whooshed open.

The hotel driveway curved from the main road to the doors and back again, giving easy access for tour buses and taxis to load passengers and luggage. Camelot's large black Escalade waited among the vehicles, with Clary leaning on the front bumper and typing on her smartphone. Merlin stood a few steps away, for once looking concerned.

And so he might have been, because three news vans crowded the drive, along with their cameramen, reporters and a swelling mob of onlookers. Red-jacketed hotel staff were trying to wave them off, but all they'd managed to do was keep the cameras out of the lobby.

One of the reporters caught sight of Arthur and visibly brightened. She charged forward, but was blocked by a wall named Gawain.

"What do they want?" Gwen asked, letting Arthur drag her back to the safety of the lobby. "Do they still think the dragon was your fault?"

"Right now they believe it was a machine or some

other construct the theme park invented to draw more visitors."

That fit with what Gwen had seen on television, though she didn't fully understand how anyone could imagine the dragon was a fake. Many things about the modern world still confused her, and the media was right at the top. "And they think it was a dangerous invention because of the fire? Why not tell them the truth?"

"The shadow world is secret here."

"I know that, but—"

"That secret is the only thing that keeps frightened humans from turning against anyone different."

"Why?" she protested. "In our time—"

"Times have changed," Arthur explained. "Once all the peoples lived side by side, but after the demon wars that's no longer true."

Gwen realized that he was right. Almost everyone she saw was human, and she felt the loss of the others like a missing limb, or a feast reduced to a single, uniform dish. "What happened?"

"There is no time for a history lesson," he said, speaking quickly. "But in short, the witches were nearly wiped from the earth, thousands burned at the stake, and they wouldn't thank us for dragging them back into the public eye. And that doesn't begin to describe what would happen to those like the sprites, dryads or merfolk, who don't even appear human. We keep the shadow world secret for their safety. Even the fae—or most of them—respect that."

Gwen rubbed her forehead, feeling the start of a headache. "And so we have to find a way to put the media off the scent of dragons."

Their conversation had taken no more than a minute, but it had been long enough for the crowd outside the doors to muster their forces. The hotel staff wouldn't hold them off much longer. Gawain returned to Arthur's side. "Should we find a back way out of the hotel?" the knight asked.

Arthur shook his head. "Giving them a chase will only sharpen their hunger for blood."

"Please tell me that's metaphorical," Gwen muttered.

Arthur shook his head. "We will face the lions head-on, and let the good people of this establishment continue their day in peace."

Gwen linked her arm through his as he started forward. She hadn't come this far to be left behind now.

Camera flashes exploded in her face as they stepped outside, and several mics thrust forward. Gwen raised a hand to shield her eyes, and Arthur drew her closer, making it clear Gwen was his to protect.

"Mr. Pendragon, how do you explain the phenomenon everyone is calling the Dragon of Carlyle?" said one reporter.

"Care to comment on the accusations of public endangerment?" asked another.

"This story is beginning to spread to the national media. Was that your intention all along?"

"How do you feel about your increasing celebrity?"

The questions weren't so much asked as hurled. Arthur stopped, drawing himself up as if delivering a speech from the stone balcony of Camelot's tower. An instant hush fell over the crowd, and when he began to speak, he sounded every inch the king.

"I assure you my only desire has been to ensure the

safety of the public. This has been in no way a design to increase my own reputation."

Through the forest of cameras, Gwen saw Clary advancing through the crowd. The young witch's eyes were snapping with annoyance.

"Mr. Pendragon has no additional comments," Clary said firmly.

"Who are you?" asked a reporter Gwen recognized as Megan Dutton.

"I'm his social media advisor," Clary announced, sounding rather like Camelot's old court chancellor about to order an execution. "Anything that needs to be said will be said under the Pendragon hashtag. Keep your eyes on Camelot's feed."

She took Gwen's arm while Merlin took the king's. Clearly, the two were working together to get them safely through the crowd.

"And who are you?" The cameras swung toward Merlin.

One corner of the enchanter's mouth turned up. "I'm special effects."

That started a murmur of speculation, and they managed to inch toward the Escalade before the cameras closed in again, halting all progress. Would they never make it out of here? Even with two magic users, the trap wasn't going to build itself, and every hour that passed was another opportunity for the fae to use Rukon Shadow Wing against them.

She glanced at her notepad of sketches, firmly gripped in Gawain's hand, and made a decision. She took a diagonal step that intercepted Megan Dutton. "And I'm Arthur's wife."

Every mic and camera swarmed her way. Gwen gave

her best smile. "Didn't you know the celebrated leader of Medievaland's tourneys was married?"

She'd offered the reporters fresh meat, and they obligingly pounced on it. "Why is this the first time we've seen you in public?" Megan asked.

"Of course, my husband is athletic and handsome, not to mention an excellent administrator, but he is also a very private man," Gwen replied.

"For all the danger and excitement of the tourneys, half the attraction is the male eye candy. Did Arthur maintain the illusion of bachelor status to attract female fans?"

Gwen forced a merry laugh. "A truly determined woman would hardly notice my existence."

"Are you sure? I've heard Arthur receives daily offers of marriage from his fan base."

Oh, really? Something with fangs rose up in Gwen's spirit, but she kept her smile in place. From the corner of her eye, she saw the men slipping into the Escalade while Clary remained firmly at her side.

"So tell us more about your romance," another reporter asked.

Gwen's smile grew genuine as she changed the topic from serious accusations to the romantic chatter village gossips would enjoy. It was something she'd always been good at, and people hadn't changed all that much. They still liked a good love story.

"Have you seen your husband fight?" somebody asked.

"I've seen him fight," Gwen replied. If only they knew about the troll.

"What about children?" asked Megan Dutton.

Gwen opened her mouth, but for a nightmarish instant, nothing came out. It was the one thing she never spoke about, and for reasons no one suspected.

The only time she'd followed Arthur to war, they had begun to settle into their marriage. By then, Arthur had united the kingdom and turned his mind to other things, including Gwen.

War in Camelot wasn't like the images Gwen saw of modern battles. Most people walked to the battlefield, so progress was dependent on the weather. Supplies, including medical support, whores, laundry facilities and family members traveled in the baggage trains that followed the main body of the forces. That summer, the Queen of Camelot had followed with the other spouses.

Gwen had begged to accompany the army because she had a passion to understand Arthur's world. The fight—a border dispute, really—wasn't expected to last long or be particularly bloody. They would march, wave their swords, have a picnic and be home by Midsummer Day. But then halfway to their destination, it had begun to rain, and that lasted until the fields were lakes of standing water. Fever broke out in the ranks.

Arthur forbade her to go near the tents where the sick were tended. Gwen was supposed to do what she did at home—sit with her ladies, read poetry and entertain whatever guests Arthur sent her way. But the friars tending the ailing soldiers needed all the helping hands they could get. Besides, she had learned how to mix herbs and medicines, like any good mistress of a noble household. That included a knowledge of how to preserve her own health—an easy task when she was strong and fit and not yet twenty. She waved goodbye as Arthur and the healthy soldiers went on ahead, and remained behind to do whatever she pleased.

At first, she'd spared a few hours at a time tending the sick, but as the disease spread, she devoted every waking moment to her task. The fever touched all the mortals, both witch and human. Among Gwen's charges were the three sons of the witch-born blacksmith, all of them black-haired, stocky lads. The eldest was just big enough to swing his father's hammer.

The blacksmith stayed away, but their mother came. Every day she thanked Gwen for her care. "They're all I have," she'd say when she rose to leave each night. "Don't let them leave me."

"I won't," promised Gwen each night, for the woman's plea broke her heart.

The youngest boy died first, and then the middle child. Gwen wept with the mother, sharing her grief, but tears could not bring back the dead. The eldest boy died last; his still, cold face a silent accusation when Gwen crept into the tent as dawn broke the sky.

"You swore you would not let them die!" wailed his mother. "Now all my sons have left me."

"I'm sorry," Gwen said, smoothing the woman's hair and patting her back.

"Sorry? Is that all a great lady can say to a poor blacksmith's wife?"

"I can't presume to know how you feel."

"No, you can't," the woman snarled. "Not yet, but you will. There is only one fit punishment for breaking your promise to keep my sons alive. You will never have a child of your own!"

Though all who heard the woman speak cried out in shock and fury, Gwen would not punish her, not even for speaking so to a queen. But the painful emotion behind those words carried weight, especially when they came from a witch. Not long after, Gwen fell ill herself, and in the fever dream the woman spoke to her again.

"As year after year passes by with no babe in your arms, you will come to understand my grief," the woman said. "I'll take from you what you took from me, and you will die unloved and alone."

That night, Gwen nearly perished from the fever burning in her blood, and she almost died twice more before the illness ran its course. The blacksmith's wife went to her grave soon after. That was just as well, for cursing the queen was treason in most men's eyes, even though the woman was crazed with pain.

Gwen floundered, her spirit languishing although her body healed. Her guilt was indescribable, but she sat through Arthur's scolding as he pointed out how he'd forbidden her to nurse the sick, and how that disobedience had nearly cost Gwen her life. He spoke like she was a willful child, which was true, but never mentioned the lives she'd saved at great cost to herself. It was that lecture that had made her decide to keep the tale of the curse to herself. And it sowed the seeds of the unhappiness that drove them apart, because in her moment of grief, he had judged her. That made it impossible to build trust.

She'd never followed him to war again, at first by her own choice, and then by his. She understood that he was afraid for her, but locking her away only gave her more time for regret.

And not once had she conceived a child.

Chapter 20

Hours later, Gwen found Arthur and slumped down on the rough ground next to him.

"Hello." Arthur looked up with a smile. "My thanks for saving me from the slavering fiends."

Silently, she took in the landscape with a frown. The bite of the ocean wind was cool as the late afternoon sun retreated from the sky. Arthur's perch was high above the slash of valley that led down to Rukon's nest. It would be possible to see the dragon coming for miles. It was perfect, except for one detail.

"I don't see the cage," Gwen replied without preamble. She was still rattled from the reporters, and her tone came out sharper than she intended. Her next words were softer. "I mean, did anyone work on it?"

"It's done," Arthur replied. "The men built the gate as soon as we gave them your drawings. It was elegantly simple, after all, and your instructions were clear. Merlin put it in place and reinforced the rest of the nest to form the sides and roof."

Gwen took a second look. The dragon had chosen a deep hollow sheltered by a tangle of trees for its nighttime resting place. She could make out red-barked arbutus trees and the bright splash of rowanberries, but nothing else. She knew the others were supposed to be concealed in pairs around the woods. The scene looked deserted.

"Where is the gate?" She should have seen a frame of wood and steel balanced over the mouth of the cave, ready to drop once the dragon was inside.

Arthur sounded slightly smug. "Merlin's hidden it with magic, erasing even our scent. All we need to do is watch and wait."

It made sense, but it felt as if the trap had become Merlin's accomplishment and not hers. Or maybe that was just the memory of her father claiming her design for the Round Table. It shouldn't have mattered, and the trap might not work, anyhow. That didn't make Gwen any less unhappy. Or defensive.

"What's wrong?" Arthur asked, taking her hand.

Gwen forced herself to be honest. "I'm unsettled."

"Because of the reporters?"

"Yes." They had kept her for over an hour. Afterward, Clary had taken her to a distant tea shop and fed her cups of chamomile and lemon until she was calm again. "The questions they asked were too personal."

Arthur pulled her close until her head rested in the crook of his shoulder. "I'm extremely grateful to you. Your quick thinking made it possible for the rest of us to get away."

"I'm glad it worked." She wasn't sure if she could endure another session like that. She turned her face into his chest, needing to feel his warmth. "They asked things no one has the right to know."

His hand cupped her head, stroking her as he would a cat. "I'm sorry. That's what they do."

"If I'd been any less startled, I think I would have punched Megan Dutton."

"I should have left Gawain there. He could have pinned her arms for you."

She sniffed, trying not to laugh. "Clary was there for that. She wouldn't let me answer some things."

"Good." He kept stroking her hair. It was hypnotic, and she began to relax. "Clary understands the media far better than the rest of us."

"You should talk Medievaland into hiring her. Perhaps we really need a social media advisor."

"Maybe I will. We could use another witch around."

That was true, but not even magic could assuage the ache inside Gwen. The horrible memory of the blacksmith's wife gnawed like an open wound. She'd wanted children, and not just because it was every queen's duty to provide an heir. There were places in her heart waiting for small, young lives. She closed her eyes, forcing back tears.

She'd tried hard to put the memory behind her and move on. Despite her sadness, she'd had to continue living. And so she did, for years, although her marriage had slowly crumbled. Much was due to Arthur's increasing preoccupation with the coming war against the demons, but she had to admit she'd withdrawn as well, crushed by what had happened and too afraid to share her pain.

But since the Crystal Mountains, everything between her and Arthur had improved. It had barely been any time at all, but it was enough to make her hope. Arthur had wanted her, and she'd almost trusted the happiness that brought. She couldn't allow Megan Dutton's curiosity to ruin it all.

"What did they ask you?" Arthur stopped petting her and looked down, clearly worried by her silence.

"How do you take the pressure of looking after a whole kingdom?" she asked, changing the subject. "How do you face it day after day?"

"I was raised to it," he replied, the words flat. "I had a destiny, or so everyone said."

"You were just a baby. An orphan." Demons had murdered his parents. How could anyone consider that a destiny?

"Merlin took me to Hector, who lived far from anything or anyone. I grew up knowing the moment I left home I'd be a hunted man. And yet somehow I was meant to unite Britain and free it from the threat of the demonic overlords. Until I did, everyone I loved was in peril."

Gwen sat back, studying him. Once in a very rare while, he'd spoken about the small things of his childhood—fighting with Kay, his foster brother, and all the usual pranks and spills of boyhood. He'd never spoken of this.

"My father, the great Uther Pendragon, couldn't keep his family safe," Arthur said, reaching over to brush a strand of hair from her eyes. "So how could I do better? It's always been on my mind, especially after what happened to the fae. I thought the demon wars would fulfill whatever the fates had planned, but I only created more enemies. I'm sorry, Gwen. I pulled you into a life I cannot control."

His words made her want to weep, and that made her glad of the gathering darkness. "But beyond a certain point, it's not possible to control what happens. I don't believe in destiny."

"Then explain my life." His eyes were shadowed with unhappiness. "Explain a sword in a stone that would come to only my hand. Then explain how my reign went so wrong I ended up here. Was one fated, and the other bad luck? Or am I simply doomed?"

He sounded lost, and she folded his hand in hers. "All I know is that you're not responsible for everything that happens. Not to yourself, nor to those around you. We're not puppets."

"I've struggled all my life to figure this out." He shook his head. "I truly believed you were better off if I was far away."

She finally understood the conversation. "I accept your apology for leaving me behind."

He smiled, but it was weary. "I'm glad. I'm not particularly good at saying how sorry I am."

She used his hand to fold herself back into his embrace. When she settled, her back was to his chest, the top of her head beneath his chin. He wrapped his other arm around her and they waited silently as the stars came out, pricking the indigo sky.

When she finally saw the dragon, she nearly mistook it for a shooting star. It skimmed the hilltops, a speeding scrap of red flame. The bulk of its body revealed itself as it drew closer and she saw the fire was the glow of its breath.

She straightened to get a better view. "Look."

Her focus should have been on the monster hurtling through the sky, but Arthur was there, right behind her, and his presence muted everything else. His breath stirred her hair as he sat forward, too. "I see it."

Her gaze followed the dragon as it circled far above, no doubt checking for danger. She could see the long neck and tail snaking through the air, the wings working in a slow, lazy flap. There was no sense of urgency in its flight. She hoped that was a good sign.

It made a last turn and banked, sliding into a long and gradual dive. The rush of air over its wings reminded her of thunder, or wind filling a ship's canvas. Branches snapped as it brushed them and the trees seemed to shudder as it pushed through the canopy. In another moment, it landed with a muffled crunch.

And now came the part where her skills were put to the test. Gwen tensed despite Arthur's reassuring touch, and she moved to stand. Arthur pulled her down. "Wait," he murmured.

Keeping still, she peered down, trying to match sight to the sound of something slithering over rock and brush. Was that the dragon crawling into its cave?

A white flash of magic filled the sky, the afterimage resolving into the gate perched over the mouth of the cave. Gwen heard the telltale click of the gate's release and the bars dropped with a mighty thump. The instant they hit the earth, magic flared up the steel rods, turning them into bars strong enough to hold the great lizard. Merlin had done his work, and done it well but, she thought with pride, it had been her idea that had given his magic form.

Their handiwork was instantly put to the test. Rukon hurled himself against the bars with an outraged roar.

Power flared, turning the forest into a phantasm of glowing light and dark, twisting branches. Arthur jumped to his feet, his gaze riveted to the scene.

"The cage is holding." Merlin's voice came out of the dark forest, making Gwen jump with surprise. "Magic works best with a physical shape to support it. Thanks to the queen, we might just survive this."

"My compliments," said Arthur. "To both of you."

Merlin stepped forward, arms folded. His smile was grim. "Who knew that you and I would make a team, my lady?"

Certainly not Gwen. She said nothing, too transfixed by the outraged dragon throwing himself against the bars once more. A hollow pit was forming in her stomach. She had designed the cage for a good reason, but she still hated it. She was sure this wasn't the dragon's fault, and no creature should ever be trapped like this.

Arthur was already descending the path to the lair, Merlin a step behind. Gwen knew she was meant to stay where she was, safely out of sight, but she was responsible for the creature's captivity. It only seemed right to look her prisoner in the eye. She descended a few steps behind Merlin, trusting her feet to find their way despite the darkness.

When they reached the floor of the valley, she could see Arthur's men emerging from the trees. Some had flashlights, but a few carried candle lanterns, as if they still found old-fashioned firelight more comfortable than modern convenience. They barely needed illumination however, for the dragon itself glowed with rage, its nostrils burning like hot coals. Sir Owen stood to one side, his face tight with sorrow. Gwen knew precisely how he felt.

The dragon's head could barely move in the tight space, but it scanned the group with its glittering eyes. "So this is your doing, little king," Rukon said in a quiet voice that was somehow worse than any roar. "I will roast you for this indignity."

"Do your worst." Merlin stood directly before the cage, hands on his hips and an arrogant tilt to his head. "Your fire won't make it past the bars."

Rukon's response was to peel back his lips, showing fangs like swords. "Then one day when you least expect it, wizard, I will eat you for dessert."

Merlin laughed, as if the threat had genuinely amused him. "I hope you have antacids."

Arthur stepped forward to stand beside Merlin, and executed a respectful bow. "I hope someday you can forgive this practical necessity, Rukon Shadow Wing, but I desire conversation with you and have no wish to fight."

"Because you'd lose."

"Perhaps," he said frankly, "but I don't think the real fight is between you and me."

Rukon's response was an insolent puff of smoke that slid past Merlin's barrier and made them cough.

Arthur cleared the smoke around him with an irritated wave. "King Zorath named Talvaric of the fae as the true enemy of us both."

That got a reaction. Rukon growled, gathering his feet beneath him as if readying for another spring. "The goblin king risks much by revealing that name."

"He had a troll problem like I have a dragon problem. I was able to get rid of the nuisance troubling his mines."

"By slaughter," Rukon said darkly.

"It was a sad necessity." Arthur took a step forward,

his hand on Excalibur's hilt. "You're smarter than any troll. There is no need for your death."

"Yet," Merlin muttered under his breath.

"Is Talvaric forcing you to be here?" Arthur asked Rukon. "Is that the treachery you spoke of?"

Gwen had seen Arthur like this before. It was how he dealt justice from his throne—respectful, but firm and always searching for the real issues beneath a problem.

"It's Talvaric's name that the minstrels are supposed to sing, not yours," Arthur said. "Your boasting was a sham. Talvaric wants the other fae to know how powerful he is and how worthy he would be to sit on the throne of Faery. You're just his weapon."

"That is the truth." Rukon bowed his head, both in acknowledgment and defeat. "He took my choices from me."

A ripple went around the gathered men, Owen's outraged voice carrying above the others. Gwen drew closer to Arthur, proud of him for uncovering the facts.

"You are the Pendragon," said the creature, sounding lost.

"What does that name mean to you?" Arthur asked, his voice solemn.

"It is not a name," the dragon said. "It is a responsibility. The first Pendragon was our protector in a time of dire need, and his line was sworn to do the same. But that duty has been forgotten."

"My father died and never had the chance to tell me of it," Arthur said. "You can."

"It is too late. Talvaric knows how to ensnare the beasts of the Forest Sauvage, the Crystal Mountains and the enchanted realms beyond."

"The enchantment over you is not enough to force

your every move," said Merlin. "How does Talvaric bend your will?"

The dragon exhaled another angry breath of smoke and steam, causing Merlin to fall back a step. "He came for me first among my kin."

Gwen had been silent, letting the facts unfold, but the pieces were falling into place now. "He came for you first, and you hesitated to kill without cause. So, he went to the other dragon next. The one you call Elosta. But it sounds as if she struggled to escape his snare and fell from the sky."

Rukon bellowed in rage, shaking branches from the trees. Flocks of birds filled the night sky with frantic caws and whistles.

"She is my mate, and Talvaric has our young."

Chapter 21

Talvaric pushed branches aside, ignoring the rake of thorns against his skin. Something was in his trap—the slight spell he'd woven to signal success had drawn him at once to this distant corner of his lands.

The site was ideally situated near a stream where the beasts came to drink. He used the illusion of a struggling bird as bait, but the trap itself was iron. He could have used something magical to actually hold his prey, but that lacked visceral satisfaction. Metal teeth sunk into a creature's flesh left no doubt who was in charge.

He emerged into the small clearing where the trap lay. His first reaction was disappointment when he saw the struggling fox, one of its dainty, black-stockinged legs caught and bloody. Only a fox? He'd hoped for something better. Another dryad, perhaps. They were about as entertaining as potted ferns, but he needed more slaves to clean the cages of his collection.

The fox's desperation was plain—which was some compensation—as it bit and worried at the iron, at the ground, even at its own paw. Left to itself, it would probably chew off a limb. He was tempted to let it, but then saw the splash of green at the tip of its tail. This wasn't an ordinary fox, but a Charmed Beast of the Forest Sauvage.

Talvaric drew near. He saw the fox's ears prick, and then its head turned to reveal wide amber eyes. With a yelp of fright, it started digging with its one good fore-leg, as if it could burrow out of sight. Talvaric grabbed it by the scruff.

"Well, aren't you a surprise?" he said, turning the animal so he could get a view of its face. The fox, how-ever, tried to duck away. He gave it a hard shake.

"Please," the fox begged, tucking its tail as low as it could go. "Please."

"Please what?" Talvaric asked, because he could.

"Let me go." The fox started panting with panic. "I need to go, master."

"I don't agree."

Talvaric released the trap with a single word of power. The mechanism clicked open and fell to the dirt. Instantly, the fox's feet began flailing as it wriggled to break free. Talvaric saw with satisfaction that the crea-ture's leg was not actually broken, even though the flesh was torn. A broken bone would have made it less useful.

"Stop struggling!" Talvaric gave the fox another shake. "Be still."

The fox froze. "I want to go home."

"We all want something, vermin."

Talvaric sat on a fallen log and held the beast in his lap. Beside him, the stream bubbled past, autumn leaves spinning in the current. Once, before his soul had been ripped away by Merlin's spells, he would have been transfixed by the natural beauty of the place. Talvaric recalled his wonder, but it was an impression, nothing more. He couldn't recapture the feelings behind those images. The memory was haunting, like listening to a language he no longer understood.

Arthur and his pet enchanter would pay for what had happened to the fae. Talvaric's people remembered what they had been, and that was enough to serve as a springboard to power. He would prove his worth by crushing the enemy. He would rise and Camelot would suffer.

Talvaric let his dreams go and came back to the present to find the fox staring him in the face. The black nose twitched with anxiety. This creature would be disappointingly simple to bend to his will.

"What is your name?" he asked.

"S-senec, if it please you, master," the thing sputtered in its clear tenor. Why was it that the foxes always had such fine voices?

"Tell me about yourself. Do you have a mate?"

"Not yet."

Too bad. It was so easy to control a creature by stealing its mate or its young. That had worked perfectly with the dragons. He had a clutch of eggs that someday would give him the power to conquer entire realms.

"So you're young," Talvaric mused. "That has its advantages. I can train you the way I like."

The fox's response was another, shorter bout of struggling. That was brought to a quick end with a single blow to its hindquarters.

"You're mine now, Senec," Talvaric said. "Whatever I tell you to do, you will do it. You will do it when and how I say. You will *not* attempt to find a loophole in my instructions but carry out my wishes in both spirit and letter. Furthermore, you will not attempt to escape."

"Y-yes, master," the fox replied.

Talvaric knew foxes. Their reputation for craftiness was deserved. He turned Senec so the fox had a good view of the clearing. "There is something you need to know about this place. I cover it with a glamor that cloaks what is truly here from all the senses—sight, smell and touch included. I do that so creatures like you will wander into my trap."

The glamor hiding the clearing fell away, and Senec gave a terrified whine. As Talvaric withdrew his spell, carnage became visible. Pieces of flesh scattered the ground, the bushes and even the lower branches of the trees. White bone protruded from some. Black-and-white fur clung to many. "The last animal I caught in my trap was a Charmed Beast like you. A badger. He didn't want to obey."

"P-please, master," the fox whined.

"I gave this disobedient badger to one of my trolls to play with," he said. "He lasted longer than you might think."

Senec began to shudder, making faint, piteous sounds. It couldn't have been easy to shake that hard when standing on only three paws, but Talvaric still had a firm grip on his scruff. He turned the fox around again.

"Are you going to obey me?"

The fox cringed into a puddle of rusty fur. It seemed to have lost its ability to talk.

"Good." Talvaric curved his mouth into a smile. "I'm glad we understand one another. That will make it so much less inconvenient for us both."

Perhaps this fox wasn't the disappointment he'd originally thought, but a stroke of luck. His plans with the dragons hadn't unfolded the way he had expected—sometimes ambitious leaps fell short. Senec would be so much easier to control. Reliable. Useful.

And if Talvaric's original scheme had unraveled, there had been unexpected developments in his favor. Who could have expected Queen Guinevere's appearance on the scene? Morgan had tried and tried to find Arthur's weakness to no avail. A foolish mistake, in Talvaric's opinion. If any man had a soft side, it would be vulnerable to the human queen's golden beauty.

"In a handful of hours," he said to the fox. "I will have a message for you to deliver. I trust you will be prompt to obey."

Talvaric petted the soft red fur as the animal shivered in mindless terror.

"We have to let him go," Gwen said, shedding her coat.

There hadn't been much more to Rukon's story, as the dragon knew little of Talvaric's actual plans. They'd returned to the hotel room after Arthur and Merlin had deemed it safe to watch the dragon in shifts, with someone skilled in magic there at all times. Merlin, Gawain and Owen were on first watch.

Arthur paced to the window. "I don't think releasing him is wise."

The light from the desk lamp cast odd shadows that made him look tired beyond his years. Or maybe that had just been the day.

Gwen rose to join him, cupping his face between her hands. "But the mystery is over. We know about

Talvaric. We know why Rukon's caught up in this, and we know what he's suffered."

"And is still suffering." Arthur stepped out of her grasp and pulled off his jacket, leaving only a long-sleeved T-shirt. He'd pushed up the sleeves, and every motion showed off strong forearms, honed from years of wielding a blade. "If we open the cage, we have no protection and Rukon is still in Talvaric's power."

"But he doesn't want to be. He hasn't hurt anyone yet."

"Yet." Arthur's gaze caught hers. "Talvaric has his young, and his mate is missing or dead. There will be no more eggs for Rukon. Dragons mate for life."

"So he's going to do whatever Talvaric says, because his children are hostage."

"Exactly."

That made everything worse. "But we can't keep him trapped forever. He'll die."

"I know." Arthur gave a weary sigh and sank onto the couch. "However, I can't let him go until I'm certain he won't kill us all."

It was hard to argue with that, but she did, anyway. "You're the Pendragon. You're supposed to protect their kind." She sat beside him and took his hand in both of hers.

"And I will, by killing Talvaric as quickly as possible."

That was a plan she could get behind. Gwen tilted her head so she could kiss his jaw. His clothes still smelled of wind and pine, and the image of the brilliant, starry night filled her mind. Arthur slipped his arm around her and they stayed that way for a long moment. His shirt was soft beneath her cheek, the steady thump of his heart hypnotic. The night air had left her sleepy and exhilarated at the same time. Every sense was heightened and yet relaxed, as if she were humming with life.

He hadn't pushed the issue of returning to his apartment, and she was grateful. The hotel was a safe space and neutral ground. Whatever they had started to build wasn't ready for the larger expectations of his personal territory. Here, Gwen had a claim, too.

He kissed the top of her head. It was a fond gesture, and it quickly led to more. They tasted one another, tongues tangling. Arthur's breath was hot and urgent as he explored her, claiming her kiss with the thorough determination of a general. His hand found the comb that held her hair, pulling it free so he could run his fingers through the long tresses. Gwen felt the weight of it fall down her back, uncoiling as it went.

Desire flared so easily between them now, as if just waiting for an excuse. She ran her hands down his shirt, glorying in the hard muscle beneath. Then she slid onto his lap, straddling his legs. Her core ached with the anticipation of what would surely happen next, and she settled carefully, winding her arms around his neck and leaning in until he took her weight. He wouldn't stay trapped beneath her unless he wanted to, but it was the surest way to claim his attention.

"How can I help with Talvaric?" she asked.

The question seemed to startle him, chasing the gathering languor from his eyes. "You've done enough."

"Until Talvaric is dead and the dragons are safe, no one has done enough."

Arthur's jaw set. "I don't want to be Rukon, mourning my mate."

That wasn't the right argument. "We don't know exactly what happened to Elosta, but it's clear she was reluctant to be bound by an outside will. She fought until her wings tangled in that net. I admire her defiance."

"Even so," Arthur said, "I think—"

"I don't want to be bound, either," Gwen interrupted.

They locked gazes, and his only grew more stubborn. She slid off his lap, rising to pace the room. Old anger bubbled inside her. Despite everything, it seemed they had to have this argument one more time. She prayed it was the last.

"What's wrong?" he asked with a touch of impatience. It was interesting how he always took that tone when he didn't know what to say.

She spun to look at him. "I've been part of this, at your side, and for once I feel as if we're working together."

He stood, brows drawn together. "I feel the same way."

"Good. Then learn from the experience. You don't have to bear your destiny alone. You have your men and Merlin, and you have me. You especially have me."

She'd never used this snappish tone with him before. He was her husband, but he was also a king. At the moment, she didn't care that she was supposed to be reverent or even polite. After six years of marriage, she'd run out of patience.

"Guinevere," he said, her name an admonishment.

That only made her temper flare hotter. "If you don't want me by your side, doing my part, say so now. I can build a life here for myself that has nothing to do with Camelot."

It was then she saw his anger rise in a slow flush up his cheeks. "Or me."

"That's your choice." She swallowed, taking a breath

to rein in her words, to make them true instead of just angry. "I have an idea of the burden you bear, and it staggers me. But if you trust the people who love you, we can share the load. And look at what happens when you do—we caught a dragon and found the truth. Take heart from that. Let me be your asset."

"You are. You provided the trap's design." Arthur's jaw worked, but he made a visible effort at control. "I realize how badly I've underestimated what you can do."

Gwen took a breath, because suddenly she could. They'd turned a corner. There was a glimmer of something better for the two of them. Suddenly even the room felt warmer and more welcoming.

"I want you to go to school and learn everything you can," Arthur said, his voice rough. "You deserve it, and I know it will make you happy. And that makes me happy."

Her eyes stung with tears of hope, but she stood her ground. "No guards dogging my tracks."

"Not unless there's an active threat." He nodded, emphasizing his promise. "And if it matters to you, Camelot needs your skills. You can make a solid contribution to whatever we do."

He was giving her everything she'd asked for when they'd met for cocktails. That night felt as if it had been years ago now—and it was, in terms of experience. Then, she'd been content to build a life alongside Arthur's. But now? Now she wanted to be part of his. "So why is that acceptable, and yet you won't let me help now?"

"Sitting at a desk drawing a design for a cage is sensible. It's not the same as running headlong into danger."

"I don't *want* to run headlong into danger. I'm capable of judgment, and there's a wide patch of ground between real danger and being an involved partner. You saw what I did in the Crystal Mountains."

"You nearly got squashed by a troll."

"Not that part." She flicked a hand. "The part where I talked Zorath into speaking with Camelot in the first place."

"That was useful," Arthur admitted.

Gwen gave an unladylike snort. "Thanks."

"But you never know when to take a step back for your own good." He took a step forward, blue eyes intent, and took hold of her shoulder. "You were sick for months after you went with the army to Wales. It broke my heart."

"And you don't think it broke mine?" The memory slammed her, too painful at the best of times, but worse when she was already stinging from the reporter's questions earlier that day.

And she couldn't face it now, when her defenses were crumbling. She jerked back, away from his touch. "I lost every chance of having a child!"

Arthur fell utterly silent, his face a blank mask. "You what?"

Chapter 22

By the blessed angels! Gwen had blurted out the words without thinking, and she panted now, her pulse thundering in her ears. She put her palms to her face, feeling wetness and the heat of her flushed cheeks. There was no point in trying to bury the truth now. "I was cursed. There was a witch. I nursed her sons, but they died."

Gwen suddenly lost all the strength that had sustained her. She swayed where she stood, feeling stranded far from help.

"You never told me," said Arthur, his face drained with shock. "For years, you never told me."

"I'm sorry." The words were a whisper.

He opened his arms to reach for her, but she backed away. She felt soiled, as if finally dragging the secret into the open had exposed a seeping wound. "I disappointed you. Giving you an heir was the one thing I was supposed to do."

"That's not true," he said. "Honestly, you're enough for me."

But Gwen knew better. "Every king has the right to expect an heir."

"That's what we're told, but my heart is yours, Gwen. I want you most of all."

His kindness only made her feel worse. She'd failed because she'd disobeyed him. If she'd been obedient, none of this sorrow would have come to pass. The words rang in her head, but even now she couldn't bear to give them voice. There were tears standing in Arthur's eyes, and each one pierced her like a blade made of glass. *This was his tragedy, too.* And she hated herself still more.

"I love you," he said, saying the words slowly as if to reassure her. "And I'm sorry. I knew you were sick, but I had no idea you were grieving about this, as well."

But she had been, and he'd ordered complete bed rest. Only calming music, only pleasant visitors. No books, no news, no gossip that might unsettle her mood. He'd meant it with kindness, but it was like being stuffed in a box with no air. *You don't understand me at all.* But she couldn't say that. It would only be selfish to hurt him that much more.

"You didn't trust me," he finally said, sorrow hardening to resentment. "Or you would have told me. We could have asked for Merlin's help, or Nimueh's. They might have broken the curse."

She folded her arms, bracing herself. "How could I tell you? By the time I recovered, I wasn't welcome in the council chamber or your private discussions about affairs of state or anywhere that mattered. I was no longer queen, whatever title you gave me."

"I would not risk your health. You were fragile."

"You were barring the door because I dared to make my own decision when I offered comfort to the sick." She gulped air, refusing to cry. "I was wrong, but it was my risk to take. You had no right to punish me, and you're still doing it every time you leave me behind."

"Is that how you see me?" His eyes were wide with frank surprise. "And you say that *I* don't trust *you*. You never told me anything about how you felt!"

"I disappointed you, and you lectured me! What could I expect?"

Silence simmered between them. They'd backed away from each other until they stood on opposite sides of the puddle of lamplight. The distance was a physical pain to Gwen, a twist of desire's knife. She still wanted Arthur, even though she could barely look at him right then.

And why were they arguing now? They'd just begun to build something fresh—or was that true? Hadn't the same mistakes just been waiting like bandits in their path? Or perhaps she'd had to feel confident enough to tell him what had truly hurt her?

She'd finally been honest, but did it even matter now?

"Well," Gwen said, staring at the floor. "There we are."

"There we are."

She forced herself to raise her chin, but it was hard, her neck almost throbbing in protest. Meeting his cold blue gaze was even worse. "Is there a road forward from here?"

A heartbeat passed. All she could see was destruction, an avalanche begun by a few careless words. She felt hollow, as if all her insides had vanished.

With a sudden, startling motion, Arthur snatched

up his coat. "I don't know. I don't know anything anymore."

"Where are you going?" Gwen demanded.

"I don't know that, either."

He stormed out, slamming the door. She froze, listening to his steps stomp down the hallway. When they'd finally faded, she let out a shuddering breath. She felt calm, but it was the calm of devastation. They'd fought before, but this was different. This was falling off a cliff.

Because they'd finally bared their souls. That was supposed to be healing, but it felt like death.

She sank to one of the chairs, staring at the spot where she'd been sitting with Arthur just minutes before. The drastic change wrought by so little time stunned her. And yet? And yet a piece of her felt different. Not relieved, but maybe unburdened. She had no hidden resentments now—they were in the open for all to see.

Sadness overcame her in a sudden wave, and with that came tears—messy, hot, angry sobbing. She gave in to it, letting herself cry in a way she hadn't since her mother's death. There was nothing to hide anymore. She wept for the child she'd never have, wishing she'd been able to hold it and say how much love there was in her heart. She wept for Arthur, who didn't know how to be anything but a king. Finally, she let loose the private griefs, the voices that said no one should be punished for wanting to make their own reasonable choices. There was compromise and sacrifice, and she was more than willing to make them, but as an equal partner. She would not be pushed away like an impertinent kitten, or left behind like someone who doesn't know her proper place.

When the tears stopped at last, loneliness moved in. It was crushing, but when Gwen picked up her phone, she immediately threw it back down. She was heartsick, and there wasn't anything she was ready to share, not even with Clary. She went to the bathroom and washed her face, doing her best to avoid the mirror. She idly considered the freshly stocked minibar, but set the notion aside. These emotions, difficult though they were, held importance. Dulling them would get her nowhere.

But when she left the bathroom, she paused. Something was wrong. At first she thought her nerves were simply raw, but when her gaze swept the room, she saw her instincts were on point. There was a stranger standing beside the couch, a satisfied smile on his lips. An involuntary cry left her lips when she took in his silver hair, olive skin and the bright, predatory green of his eyes. The man was a fae.

"Queen Guinevere, I presume," he said. "My name is Talvaric."

Gwen stood her ground. She was afraid, but she was also a queen, and this creature had interrupted a very private moment. "What are you doing here?" she demanded.

"Tonight, I am here to see you." Talvaric gave a smile, but it was a movement of lips, no more. "The legend of your beauty was not a lie."

Given her red eyes and tear-blotched face, he had to be insane or lying. "What do you want?" she snapped.

"You shall be of use to me."

Like the smile, his words held no emotion. She'd heard the fae had been stripped of their souls, but she'd never quite understood what that meant. She saw it now in the fae's flat, almost-reptilian expression. There was life there—cold, calculating and hungry—but it was vile. Horror rose until Gwen thought she might be sick. Once the fae had been poets and painters, noble warriors and creators of great beauty. Some had even been her friends. Now they were monsters.

"I'm not yours to use," she said evenly, hiding her nerves with a cutting tone. "I am the Queen of Camelot."

"So you are." Talvaric took a step toward her. "You will be coming with me. It's up to you whether you struggle."

Gwen calculated the distance to her cell phone. It was on the bed, too far away to do her any good. She was nearer the door to the hallway, but fae were fast. Instead, she shot backward into the bathroom and slammed the door shut.

Or tried to. Talvaric's boot wedged itself into the gap just in time. Gwen put her shoulder to the door and heaved. There was a grunt of pain, but the foot didn't budge. Gwen shoved for all she was worth, but fingers appeared in the gap, using the door frame to brace against her weight. Slowly, her feet began to slide across the bathroom tile. She was losing the fight.

This was not the moment to be proud. Gwen screamed every curse word she'd learned from Camelot's soldiers, then ones she'd learned from all the ambassadors to Arthur's court. Desperately, she hoped someone would hear and pound on the hotel-room door to complain. Talvaric was going to use her as a weapon against Arthur, holding her life in the balance as cruelly as he'd used Rukon's family against the dragon.

Or he'd try to. Gwen wasn't having any of it. She would battle to the end.

But then the bathroom door burst open and she flew

backward, crashing against the shower door. Her skull pounded, ears ringing as she rebounded, bracing herself against the sink. She'd hit her head already when the troll had tossed her against the wall, and this hurt even more. Her stomach rolled with the pain, but she kept screaming insults.

"Be quiet, human!" Talvaric grabbed a handful of her hair and pushed her down until her cheek squashed against the countertop, muffling her cries. Suddenly, she could barely breathe. His weight bore down on her, an elbow digging into her spine. The hold was impersonal, as if she were no more than a sheep to be sheared. Methodically, he jerked her arms behind her and heavy rope bit into her wrists. Gwen had given every ounce of her strength, but the fight was over in the matter of a minute.

"Arthur will be back at any time," she snarled, wondering if that were true.

"How unfortunate that he'll miss us." Talvaric pulled her upright, his grip back in her hair.

She kicked backward, aiming for his shin, but he shoved her out of the bathroom, letting her stumble before he snatched her back to her feet. Moving was surprisingly awkward with her hands tied behind her.

"Be still," he growled, his lips close enough to her ear that the warning was almost intimate.

"How did you get in here?" she demanded. Her stomach was a cold ball of fear. She was forced to pant around it, her pulse a quick, dizzying beat.

"Someone conveniently built a portal," he observed, opening the closet door with one hand while he gripped her bound hands with the other. "I sense Merlin's hand in it, though he was not the only maker."

"How can you tell?"

"How can you distinguish one painter from another? Every magic user has his own distinctive style. Merlin's is unmistakable."

He said it bitterly, and she remembered it was Merlin's spell that had damaged the fae so completely. She'd even heard they feasted on mortal souls in an attempt to rekindle their dead emotions. The high didn't last, but it turned the fae into desperate addicts.

For a moment, she was at a loss for a retort. It didn't matter—Talvaric kept talking. "I hope the hotel gave you a discount for a room with a breach like this."

"Merlin sealed it."

Talvaric's green eyes glittered. "A portal can be sealed, but it never completely disappears. A competent sorcerer can find a way just as a thief finds an open window. He can also alter its destination."

"You're kidnapping me?"

"Thank you for pointing out the obvious."

When would Arthur come back? Or would he? Their argument hadn't been the kind that would heal quickly. She clenched her jaw, wishing she had one tiny shred of magic that would let Arthur know how badly she needed him now.

As if he could sense her distress, Talvaric was watching her almost eagerly, his pupils large and dark. His nostrils twitched as if scenting her fear. "It will be a brief trip. The portal now leads directly to my front hall."

When she drew breath to scream again, he slammed her head against the door frame of the closet. Her head swam, and time slid away as she desperately gathered her wits again. By the time her eyes focused, it was too late. The portal was open.

The fae's magic burned icy blue, licking like a flame around a hole between realities. Gwen tried one more time to pull away, but there was no hope. When Talvaric spoke a word, the portal flashed so bright Gwen squeezed her eyes shut and twisted her head away. Even then, bright spots danced behind her eyelids.

"Let me go!" she screamed one last time.

Talvaric's reply was a push between her shoulder blades. With a stomach-churning lurch, she fell through an ocean of space and magic.

Chapter 23

Dawn seeped into the sky through cracks between the clouds. To Arthur's eyes, it looked as if the heavens were bleeding. He was taking his turn at watching the dragon, but there was not much to see. The grays and blues of the early morning sparkled with heavy dew, stirred only by a fitful breeze. Rukon was immobile as a large green stone.

Merlin and Owen were also on watch, hidden so well in the trees that Arthur couldn't see their still forms. He alone was restless. He'd chosen a perch on the opposite side of the valley from where he'd sat with Guinevere, not wanting to trigger memories of their temporary truce. The tactic was pointless—thoughts of her permeated everything.

And *complicated* didn't begin to describe his feelings. A chill, heartsick pain seeped through him. In truth, they'd both wanted children, but he'd meant what he'd said about loving her above all things. Discovering that she'd been cursed and kept it secret was an unfamiliar, awkward ache. They should have been able to face the problem together. She hadn't given them that chance.

He should have suspected something had happened when she'd lingered so long in her sickbed. They'd had a stormy marriage, but after that time, they'd begun to drift apart. There were demands of state—Arthur was busy and often away—but Gwen had turned inward, as well. Now he knew she'd been dealing with a terrible loss.

Arthur picked up a pebble, working the cold, hard shape between his fingers before tossing it down the hillside. Had Gwen really believed he would blame her? In truth, he *was* angry about that. They'd fought, but had he really made her think so poorly of him?

He shied away from answering that. Perhaps he was reluctant to share his burdens, but how could he ask such a young woman to take on such a crushing task? True, she was the same young woman who sweet-talked a goblin king, helped him kill a troll and figured out how to cage a dragon. *Utterly helpless. Obviously.*

Arthur cursed, rubbing his sleep-deprived eyes. He'd done everything wrong. He'd protected her more than she liked—she'd made that perfectly clear these last few days. And she'd been afraid of disappointing him. *Disappointed?* That made him sound like an old, cranky father.

The father he'd never be. A grim sorrow surged through him. In modern parlance, a painful bandage had been ripped off. Beneath it was grief, anger and lack of trust. At least he finally understood the wound. That meant there was a chance to heal, even if it was a slender thing.

The silent dawn magnified the crack and rustle of footsteps coming up the slope toward him. It was Merlin, his hands stuffed in his jacket pockets. His breath steamed faintly, as if he'd borrowed some of Rukon's fire. He crouched beside Arthur.

"You're brooding," said the enchanter. "I can hear it clear across the forest."

"Gwen and I disagreed."

Merlin lifted his eyebrows in question. "Do tell."

Arthur tossed another rock. "Have you begun a career as a marriage counselor?"

"I would sooner teach a pit of demons how to crochet." Merlin turned his gaze toward the dragon's cage. "I suggest you put your differences aside for the moment. This is not the time to be distracted."

"It never is," Arthur replied. "Maybe that's the problem."

Merlin was silent, but gave Arthur a significant look.

"There is no such thing as work-life balance for kings," Arthur snapped. "She wants to solve the problem by involving herself in everything I do."

"Seriously?"

Arthur stopped and rubbed his temples. "I'm exaggerating, and I'm tired. Forgive me."

"When you were a boy, you didn't think it was fair that you had to rule Camelot all by yourself. Now you're complaining that someone wants to help you." Merlin sounded amused. "If anyone should share your burden, it's your wife."

Arthur studied the enchanter. Although he looked

about Arthur's age, he was centuries older. He probably did remember whatever it was Arthur said when he was five, but that wasn't the point. "You think I'm shutting her out?"

"I'm merely pointing out an inconsistency."

It sounded more like a character flaw to Arthur. "You told me once good men don't make good kings."

Merlin shrugged. "There will always be sacrifices. Sometimes kingship leaves no room for the heart."

Arthur didn't want to hear more. He rose. "I'm going to check on Rukon."

"I think if he was digging his way out of the cage, we'd know it," Merlin grumbled, but he followed him down the hill.

Owen was sitting on a fallen tree near the dragon's lair, hands on his knees and his expression almost meditative. The only sound emerging from the cave was a slow, rhythmic rumble Arthur guessed was the dragon snoring. A glance inside the lair revealed a haunch and the tip of its tail, but the rest was lost to shadow.

"Report?" Arthur asked Owen.

The Welsh knight was instantly alert and on his feet. "All is quiet, Your Majesty."

There was a snort from the dragon and one baleful yellow eye peered out of the dark for a moment before closing again. Arthur wasn't fooled by the outward show of quietude. He'd already asked Merlin how long he could maintain the spell that kept the cage secure, and all indicators said they needed to make a plan quickly.

Arthur gestured for Owen to relax. The knight sat again, while Merlin lounged against a tree. Arthur paced, forcing his thoughts to the topic of dragons and away from the fight with his wife. It should have been easy. It wasn't, and his head began to pound.

A rustle in the brush broke his concentration. He spun toward the sound, scanning the trees but seeing nothing. His gaze worked downward until he saw a black nose poking from the bushes. It was followed by a long, delicate snout and a pair of upright ears. Arthur stared at the red fox. He had seen hundreds roaming the woods of Camelot, and not one of them had ever approached humans willingly—yet this one was.

There was blood matting its coat. It was also limping, one black-furred leg obviously lame and his bright brush of a tail so low it dragged through the dirt. A tuft of green fur colored the end of its tail, marking it as a Charmed Beast. Arthur remained still, transfixed as it hobbled up to him and sat, trembling and staring up with intelligent eyes. Slowly, Arthur crouched, cautiously aware this was no ordinary creature.

The fox's nose lowered as Arthur went to one knee. "You are the Pendragon?" the beast asked in a clear voice that was firm despite its piteous shaking.

"I am," Arthur replied.

"He is," Rukon rumbled.

The dragon was awake and watching the fox intently. The fox turned, his ears swiveling toward Rukon before he bowed his head in a gesture of respect.

"I am sorry to see you here, little brother," said the dragon in a voice that was almost gentle.

Out of the corner of his eye, Arthur noticed Merlin and Owen approaching. Merlin appeared fascinated, Owen frowning with concern. Their presence made the animal tremble even more. "What can I do for you?" Arthur asked the fox.

"I bear a message from Talvaric of the fae," said the fox.

The name made Rukon snort fire. The two creatures exchanged a look of mutual commiseration. Arthur's fists clenched, hating their shared pain. "And what does he want?" Arthur said in a strained voice.

The fox cringed then, licking his injured leg. "I did not want any part of this," he said plaintively. "You cannot think I call him master out of my own free will!"

Arthur remembered Gwen lecturing the foxes she caught, warning them away from her father's chickens. She'd loved them. Sadness and anger mixed in a volatile brew until Arthur ground his teeth in frustration.

"I understand. You have nothing to fear from me." *No, these creatures need a protector. They need my sword as much as any human.* He reached out, letting the fox sniff his hand. "What is the message you have been sent to deliver?"

"He wants—demands—that you present yourself at the front gates of your theme park in two hours. He wants re-por-ters." The fox said the word carefully, as if it was unfamiliar.

Arthur cursed, thinking of Gwen's unhappy experience with the press. She had been so upset, so in need of comfort. He cursed again. "To what end?"

The poor creature shook with dread. "You are to surrender yourself to him."

Both Merlin and Owen made sounds of outrage, but Arthur felt a cold hand grip deep inside him. "And if I don't?"

The fox's ears flattened, its chin drooping to the ground. Furry eyebrows bunched in a plaintive expres-

sion. "He said by the time you hear this message, he
will have Queen Guinevere."

Gwen landed on her knees, unable to catch herself
with her hands bound behind her back. On this side
of the portal, the floor was marble, and the shock was
enough to send spikes of pain through her hips. Talvaric
was behind her, his light footfalls scuffing as he spun to
seal the portal—and every chance of retreat—closed.

It took him a second, but that was all Gwen needed
to scramble to her feet and run. Talvaric shouted something in his own language. It sounded like a curse, but
it was just words and she kept sprinting at top speed.
At first, she was only aware of where a door was open
and whether it led to a dead end. Her experience with
the troll had made that hazard painfully clear.

A few turnings later, she realized she'd actually left
the fae behind, at least for a few seconds. She ducked
behind a curtain, finding a wide window embrasure
looking onto a starlit forest. It was too dark outside to
see more than trees and grass. No chance of bolting into
some public place and screaming for help. Worse, there
was no way to open the window and escape.

She had to think, not just react. This was Talvaric's
territory, and simply running wouldn't help her. Gwen
made herself small, perching in a ball on the window
ledge. It was awkward without the use of her hands,
but it gave her the chance to calm her pounding heart.

The respite only lasted for moments. She heard
him—or someone—moving, and he wasn't alone. Toe-
nails clicked past. An animal. A dog, she guessed—
Gwen missed her greyhounds with a physical ache and
knew the sound of their feet on the palace floors—but

this one was large, given the length of its stride. Then she heard it snuffling.

She was being hunted. She was prey.

Her whole body tingled with fright. She wanted to jump up and run so badly, her toes cramped inside her boots. But running wouldn't help. Run where and do what? Her hands were numb and useless. Even if she found a doorway into the woods outside this house, she couldn't turn the knob. All the same, remaining still and quiet was an act of will.

I'm trapped. She could hear the rasping breath of whatever it was coming closer. It didn't whine or bark like a normal dog on a scent and that made the suspense worse. *Help!* She pleaded silently, wishing Arthur could hear her thoughts. *Help!*

But he wasn't a mind reader, and he was far away in the mortal realm. Worse than that, he probably hated her. She was lost.

A snout poked through the curtains. It was black, pointed and huge. Gwen cringed back from it, watching a trail of drool dangling from the chops of the enormous animal. It smelled like a battlefield a week after the war. A second later, the curtain jerked aside, revealing Talvaric and a massive red-eyed creature.

"Meet my barguest," said Talvaric.

A barguest. They were creatures of moors and lonely places, and they were the reason no one wandered the roads alone after dark. She'd never expected to see one inside a home—even a fae's home. The incongruity of it broke the spell of terror.

"Is he your pet?" she asked incredulously.

The barguest gave her a withering stare from those fire-red eyes. Gwen held its gaze just long enough to see its defiance fade to something more painful. Monster or not, it was miserable.

"He is your guarantee of good behavior." Talvaric grabbed her arm and dragged her off the windowsill.

She moved awkwardly, her knees stiff from her earlier bad landing. "Where are you taking me?" she demanded.

"To your cage. You will join my other curiosities." He gave her a savage shove, and she stumbled but kept her feet. He snatched her shoulder hard enough a cry escaped her clenched teeth. "If you try to escape again, my barguest will hunt you down and make you his dinner. I never feed him quite enough, you see. That's the best way to deal with picky eaters."

All the same, Gwen did her best to memorize the route through the sprawling residence. It was mostly bare and white, as if decorating it had been too much effort. Not surprising, if the fae had lost their ability to perceive beauty, but it made it hard to find landmarks to anchor the route.

That all changed when they reached his collection. Gwen stopped cold, digging in her heels at the unforgettable sight. This corridor was all of stone and had a series of tiny rooms on either side. The walls that looked into the hallway were plain metal bars, each door fitted with a heavy padlock. There was straw on the floor of the cells, but no furniture.

He really meant to put her in a cage. A literal cage. Gwen's knees went weak as her ability to breathe deserted her.

Talvaric jerked her forward. "Say hello to your compatriots."

She made an involuntary cry when she saw a huge snake curled in the straw of the first room. It had glistening green scales and the head of a woman. In the next was a deerlike creature with a single spiral horn. In the one after that was a bird with feathers made of flame. There was no straw in that cell.

Talvaric all but tossed her into the next, and followed her inside. He held her down with one hand and cut her bonds with a knife he had strapped to his belt. It was rough, but impersonal. The second Gwen's hands parted, he retreated and slammed the barred door shut.

Her shoulders sang with pain, but she spun around to face Talvaric. He stood on the other side of the door, arms folded, with a speculative look on his face.

"You're mine now," he said. "Just like all the others."

All Gwen's rage screamed in her head, but she was too appalled to speak a single word.

Chapter 24

As soon as the sun rose, Talvaric strolled into the cells to admire his newest acquisition.

"I brought you something to wear," he said, motioning to the silent servants who shuffled behind him.

They drew close, unlocking the door and opening it wide enough for two of their number to slip into Gwen's cell. Gwen backed away, unsure what to expect. She'd glimpsed green-skinned beings like this in the Forest Sauvage. They were dryads, creatures who shifted at will into trees. How Talvaric had trapped them and made them his slaves was beyond her comprehension, but it had to be with cruelty. Such beings did not belong anywhere but under open skies.

The scent of fresh leaves surrounded them. Their features were strange—humanlike without following the same rules of proportion. Nevertheless, they were beautiful, with long green hair and graceful limbs. One bore a pitcher of water and basin for washing, the other carried garments. Gwen noted their fingers had too many joints, or perhaps it was too many fingers. Nothing seemed completely fixed, but shifted every time she looked.

"I don't want your clothes," she said, although she silently wished for a bath.

His response was terse. "You are a queen. You will dress appropriately."

"Why? Is your collection diminished if I choose to remain as I am?"

He refused to show annoyance. "You will diminish if I choose to withhold your food. The rules here are simple—do as I bid you, or suffer the consequences."

At his sign, the dryads set down their burdens and left the cell, locking the door behind them. "Thank you," Gwen said to the pair, but the green-skinned creatures remained silent, their eyes downcast.

"Don't bother," Talvaric said. "Plants are terrible conversationalists."

Gwen glanced down at the dress he'd given her. It was a long court gown, full-skirted and jeweled and very much like her clothes from Camelot. It reminded her of all the things at stake besides her own life. "Is there a regent on the throne of Faery while Morgan is away?"

To her surprise, he answered the question. "There is a council of nobles. No one person dares to take Morgan's place."

She heard the derision in his tone. He thought them cowards. "What do they think of my capture?"

Silence. That meant he hadn't told them, and pos-

sibly didn't intend to. She risked going one step more.
"You intend to take the throne for yourself."

"Why not? They are a fractured, leaderless court
with no ambition and less courage. Whoever dazzles
them enough will hold them like flies in honey. I intend
to demonstrate how Arthur and his magic sword are
clay dragons, frightening to behold but easily smashed."

This confirmed what Gwen already knew. Still, her
stomach plummeted. "I'm bait to bring him here."

"Precisely." His smile was icy.

She wanted to scream that Arthur wouldn't come,
that this was all foolishness because he didn't love her,
but there was no point. Likewise, begging for Arthur's
life would be a waste of time. Nothing would convince
the fae to spare their deadliest foe.

And if Talvaric was telling her his plans, he had no
intention of ever letting her go, either.

"Are you certain you want a throne?" she asked bitterly. "I've never seen that much power bring anyone joy."

Talvaric's expression didn't change. "I don't feel joy.
Not any longer."

"Then why bother?"

He shrugged, the gesture stiff with unease. Perhaps he
did feel something, after all—she'd heard some of the fae
had recovered pieces of their soul. Did he want revenge?
Or hunger for recognition? Or was he simply deranged?

"I shall sweep away the unworthy," he said after a
long pause.

She waited for more, but it didn't come. Irritation
overcame her fear. "As a plan, it lacks detail."

His smile was feline. "And yet I know what I am
worth. I will rise by my own merit. That is more than
you can claim."

"I am Queen of Camelot."

"You are a mortal woman, unloved by her husband and cursed to a barren womb. You are worth nothing."

The cold certainty of his words felled Gwen as if they were a physical slap. She dropped to her knees, the shock of violation wrenching a gasp from her throat. "How did you know?" she whispered. *How does he know about the blacksmith's wife and her curse?*

"Please," he purred. "I am a fae enchanter. Your secrets are pebbles on a beach, waiting to be gathered as I please."

The idea of his mind—or any part of Talvaric—leafing through her secrets brought bile burning up her throat. She covered her face with her hands, pushing the image away. But he had stirred something—the aching, scorching disappointment in her own life.

She'd accused Arthur of disregarding her, but was that actually a reflection of her own opinion? Did she blame him for what she felt about herself? The idea sickened her, and yet it felt true—at least in part. She was her own worst enemy.

Talvaric turned away then, the force of his attention shifting like a great weight. It was a relief, and yet she felt obliterated, as if she'd ceased to exist. As if she deserved nothing more.

Talvaric began to walk through the clutch of dryads, returning the way he had come, but then stopped. "I can already feel that this is going to be a momentous day. One worth remembering as a vivid experience." He spun to face Gwen, walking backward. "You've been asleep for many years. How much do you understand about today's fae?"

She had no idea what he meant, so merely shook her head.

He grabbed one of the dryads, holding her face between his hands. The creature, mute until now, shrieked. It was not a human sound, but like the rending of green branches and bark. Gwen flinched, knowing terror when she heard it. Talvaric didn't slow, but brought his face close to the dryad's, almost as if he would kiss her. Horribly, Gwen understood what he meant to do, and a rush of panic prickled over her skin. Arthur had mentioned the fae's hunger for mortal souls, and dryads were long-lived, but as mortal as the trees they called home.

"Stop!" Gwen was on her feet, grabbing the door to the cage and wrenching it. The lock clattered, but would not budge. "Stop it!"

The dryad's eyes, dark brown in her pale green face, had gone wide. She seemed to be screaming, but silently now. She tried to push away, back bowed so far that Talvaric was forced to crouch over her, but there was no escape. Slowly, a mist rose from her lips to his. He was taking her life essence, her spark, and all the emotions that went with truly living.

"Help her!" Gwen reached between the bars, her fingers just brushing the sleeve of the closest dryad. They were all just standing there, faces blank. "She's your sister! Save her!"

At last, Gwen caught hold of the sleeve, winding her fingers in the cloth and pulling for all she was worth. The owner of the sleeve stumbled and turned to look Gwen in the eyes. Then she saw. The other dryads knew exactly what was going on, but he had some hold over them that prevented the slightest interference. That helplessness shamed them beyond anything Gwen could fathom. *Magic. He's holding them helpless with a spell!*

The creature in Talvaric's arms began to shudder as the last of her life was consumed. When the struggle ended, her entire frame went limp. The fae released her, and she toppled like a sapling under the woodsman's ax. Talvaric sucked in a long, noisy breath. As long as the dryad's life essence lasted, he would regain his ability to feel.

"I understand why this is addictive," he said to Gwen, stretching his arms as if waking from a long nap.

Suddenly, there was a leer in his voice that hadn't been there before. If she'd felt vulnerable before, this was much worse. Something inside her curled into a tiny ball.

"You look terrified," he added, obviously amused.

"I've been told that drinking souls eventually destroys your kind."

Talvaric laughed, the sound harsh and hoarse. Clearly, he didn't get much practice. "Don't think I'm that weak."

"Remorse is an emotion," Gwen said, hating this new Talvaric even more than before. "What will happen when you realize what you've become?"

This time, Talvaric's smile held layers of malice. "Moralists always make one mistake. They assume the fae were universally good to begin with. My old self would applaud what my present self is finally able to achieve."

Gwen's heart dropped. He was right. She'd never considered evil fae. "You were already a nightmare. Merlin's magic simply dulled your enjoyment of it."

"And now I am my own true self, at least for today."

Talvaric stirred the dead dryad with his foot, then spared a glance for the other servants. "Clean this up."

"What are you going to do?" Gwen demanded.

"I'm going to have a word with your dear husband." He stepped toward her cage, and she instinctively backed up. "Do put on the dress. If Arthur truly is a heroic fool, he'll give himself up for you. I think you owe it to him to look your best."

With that, Talvaric walked away, leaving the dryads to gather up their fallen friend. As he went, he sang an old and lyrical melody Gwen knew from her first days at Camelot. Sung with such malevolence, the tune made her weep.

Medievaland was in full swing, tourists streaming in and out of the gates. The appearance of dragons—whether or not anyone believed in them—had spurred public interest. During Arthur's brief conversation with management, it was clear they were less concerned about potential bad press than they were sales at the gate. Furthermore, Gwen's interview had turned the conversation to a more manageable direction. On this one front, at least, news was good.

Or it would have been. Despite the fox's message, Arthur hadn't called the media but as he approached the arched entryway to the park, Arthur saw news vans circling the parking lot. Talvaric had been busy.

"I believe there is a movie where two warriors fight at high noon," Owen observed.

The Welsh knight walked at Arthur's side, gaze roving over the crowds. He had a patient stillness that made him excellent security, and Arthur valued his presence. He wasn't so sure about his taste in entertainment.

"I don't know that story," he replied.

"It is a hero tale not so unlike our own."

Arthur would rather have skipped heroism for something involving fewer casualties. Arthur and Owen were dressed in full armor, as were Palomedes and Beaumains, who brought up the rear. Gawain was inside the park, watching for trouble there.

The autumn day had grown sunny and light shone on the polished weapons, drawing the attention of the crowd milling at the gate. Cameras flashed and a few approached for autographs, but the younger knights gently sent the fans on their way. The reporters were less easy to deter.

"Arthur, where's Guinevere? Why do we never see her at Medievaland?"

"Arthur, hashtag Iseedragons is one of the top-trending topics in North America. Care to comment?"

Arthur kept walking, allowing the eternally cheerful Beaumains to deal with the questions. As King of Camelot, he had one purpose, and that was to rid the mortal realms—make that all the realms—of the fae named Talvaric.

"There," Owen said, "by the information kiosk."

A man stood with his back to the knights. He was tall and well built, but slender. A long pale braid escaped a baseball cap to trail down his back. As soon as Arthur saw him, he turned. In spite of the sunglasses, it was clear he was a fae. By the way he moved, Arthur could tell he'd recently consumed someone's life. It was a subtle difference, but he'd learned to spot it—the nervous twitch of the hands, the eagerness in the step. Cold dread weighed in Arthur's gut. Who had died so that this villain could enjoy the pain he caused?

Arthur approached the fae with only Owen to watch his back. For his part, Talvaric strolled to a neutral territory between the kiosk and a photo booth. It was a well-chosen meeting place, public but away from listening ears. Arthur came to a stop a few feet away, leaving distance between them. Neither man bowed.

Talvaric pulled off his glasses, narrowing his eyes against the bright sun. "I see my messenger performed his duty. Where is the vermin?"

Senec was curled up in the back of Owen's truck, sleeping in a nest made of an old sweatshirt. The fox and the knight had bonded at once. "Safe."

"The fox is mine."

"Not anymore."

Talvaric shrugged. "We shall see. For now, there are more important concerns, such as who owns your wife."

Arthur didn't reply, letting the silence speak his contempt.

"I will trade your life for hers," Talvaric said. "Come quietly, and the exchange will be made without fuss or bother to these good people."

Arthur followed the fae's gesture toward the crowd. There were children with balloons, grandparents using walkers, and baby carriages. A sense of nightmare seeped into him, as if Talvaric had literally spread a cloud of horror. Somehow, Arthur had to keep these people safe, but what was the best way to do that? Not by following Talvaric's rules. There was no way Arthur could allow the fae the upper hand.

"Do you truly believe I'm going to give in and hope for the best?" Arthur widened his stance, ready for a fight.

"You don't care what happens to your Gwen?" Talvaric chided. "I took you for the heroic type."

Fury speared Arthur, and his hand flew to Excalibur's hilt. "Do not hasten your death with meaningless chatter."

"I'll take that as a maybe?"

"Touch her and I'll use your guts to lace my boots."

"Then come with me, king of mortals, and I will let her go."

Arthur didn't move. Gwen was foremost in his thoughts, his heart and in the yearning of his body—but he was king and responsible for all the mortal realms. Giving Talvaric control meant condemning everything. He had to—he *would*—save Gwen *and* the girl in the stroller by the ticket booth, her mother *and* her grandfather, who was purchasing a pink balloon with a dancing unicorn. The only way he could save everyone was by destroying the fae here and now.

That was fine. Cutting Talvaric to pieces was going to be a pleasure. "I'll save time and kill you here."

Surprise flickered over Talvaric's face, followed swiftly by derision. "You can't. There are laws here about murder, and I will fight back. You'll never expose the hidden realm to the curiosity of all these mortals. All this press."

Arthur smiled. "I have one advantage you don't."

Talvaric raised a brow. "What?"

"Friends." Arthur held up a hand to signal the figure who stood hidden beside the photo booth.

Talvaric caught the gesture and spun to see who it was. "Merlin!" he snarled.

Merlin gave a finger wave. "The mortals won't see us chopping you to bits. I promise."

"Then see if they'll notice *this*!" Talvaric released a storm of magic.

Chapter 25

The world around him jolted. Arthur fell into a crouch, sword in hand. He didn't need to look at the blade to know it was glowing with a faint iridescent light. Excalibur detected magic and reflected it away from Arthur, saving both sword and man from the effects of any spell. That was why Morgan LaFaye feared it—even her darkest enchantments couldn't keep her safe from its edge.

But Excalibur could only do so much, and the sky was cracking open like a shattered egg, revealing a visible split in the sunny autumn blue. The next moment, Merlin was at his side, chanting a spell under his breath and weaving intricate shapes in the air.

"Not even you can hide this forever, Merlin," Talvaric jeered, and made a tearing motion with his hands.

The crack leaked brilliant flames of light, and then another sky beyond. They were looking through a portal. Was this where Gwen was being held? Heart pounding, Arthur sprang to his feet, ready to run and leap through. Any chance of finding her was better than none.

As if reading his thoughts, Merlin grabbed his arm. "No! It's not stable."

Arthur understood the enchanter's plea a moment later. Another jolt shook the ground, rumbling like a small earthquake. The babble of the crowd rose in alarm.

"Portals aren't meant to be so large," Merlin muttered.

And neither were they meant to release a Noah's ark of fantastic beasts into the mortal realms. All at once, they spilled out of the air, falling where the bottom lip of the portal sat a dozen feet from the ground. Some were naturally airborne: gargoyles and griffins and birds with fabulous plumage. Others ran on hoofs or paws or claw-tipped feet, bearing the green-tipped tails of the Charmed Beasts. Still others slithered and swam, floating in bubbles of water that bobbed and rolled in the air, seeking a lake or a stream to deposit their cargo. There had to be hundreds of strange beasts, each one a scrap of the hidden world just waiting to be revealed.

So many creatures were impossible to contain, even for Merlin. The enchanter grew red faced from weaving an increasingly complex spell. It forced some of the creatures back through the breach, but just as many streamed past. With a sinking stomach, Arthur saw the television cameras fasten on a griffin wheeling in the sky.

He rounded on Talvaric. "Call them back!"

The fae raised his hands in a mock-helpless gesture.

"They're yours to protect, Pendragon. They're all part of the mortal realms, even if they are magical."

Arthur ignored the statement. The attack was meant to overwhelm their defenses, and it was doing a good job. He had to stop the onslaught of creatures, and the fastest way to close the portal was to cut off its supply of power. Excalibur in hand, he rushed Talvaric.

Swords sang as they clashed, the fae's saber snaking through the air to meet Excalibur. Arthur had battled fae before and knew their fighting style, but Talvaric was quick and strong. Arthur's focus narrowed until nothing else mattered but blade and pattern. He had to move faster than with any mortal swordsman, and one misstep would cost blood. At any other time, such an opponent would be a gift, but too much was at stake now. Gwen's life depended on victory.

The saber slashed the air and he ducked, feeling wind kiss his cheek. He parried, Excalibur shedding sparks as blades scraped together. Arthur forced the fae's blade away and circled the tip with his own, following with a thrust that could have skewered an ox. Talvaric stumbled back, falling into a roll that returned him to his feet yards away.

"Well done," the fae said with a panting grin.

His eyes gleamed with excitement, but there was fear, as well. They were evenly matched and Arthur guessed he wasn't used to that. Then Arthur's instincts flared when he saw a flash of deviltry flicker in Talvaric's gaze.

"Look out!" Merlin cried from behind Arthur.

Arthur ducked, and it saved his life. Fangs snapped the air where his head had been moments before. Arthur spun, lifting Excalibur in both hands. He nearly dropped it from sheer surprise.

He'd never seen a manticore outside paintings, but there was no question what the thing before him was. It was the size of a lion, with reddish fur, but a scorpion's barbed tail curled above its back. Black bat wings flared from its shoulders, beating hard to keep it aloft. The noise was like a steady roll of thunder broken only by its blaring, cawing cry. The worst feature was its face, which might have once been human. Whatever had made the manticore—surely it wasn't natural?—had bent and stretched the features into a muzzle crammed with multiple rows of sharklike teeth.

The manticore dived, slashing with claws unsheathed. A spear would have been a better weapon against such an enemy, but Arthur used what he had, leaping into the air to deliver his blow. The tip caught the creature's belly, sending it bolting into the sky. That gave Arthur just enough time to spin back to Talvaric, sure there would be another attack from the fae. Instead, Arthur saw the fae dive into his own portal.

Talvaric had Gwen, and he was getting away. Furious, Arthur bounded forward, hand outstretched to grab him. The two men regarded each other for a fraction of a second, one will testing the other. Arthur expected mockery, or a wild grin, but there was none of that. Talvaric's expression held the cool calculation of a mathematician working out his figures. He was certain everything would end according to his plan.

That he was correct, this time. He grasped both edges of the portal as if they were curtains and drew them together with a flick of his wrists. The portal stitched itself shut in a blaze of light, leaving Arthur behind. Simple grass and pavement took the place of shimmering magic. Arthur spun, dark rage crawling through him.

The manticore swooped, bellowing its trumpeting call. Arthur charged, using the momentum to power his blade. Luck was against him this time, the clack of claws against steel the only contact. He turned the motion into another upward swipe, this time catching the deadly barbed tail. Screaming, the manticore swerved in midair, the damaged appendage spraying blood. The beast rolled in the air, doubling back to make good its revenge.

Arthur readied himself, wishing one more time for a spear's extra reach. But this time the manticore dodged toward Merlin, lashing its injured tail. As the tip swung the enchanter's way, barbs flew as if ejected from a crossbow. One stuck in Merlin's side. He stiffened and fell, shaking as a seizure swept over him. *Poison!*

Fury drowned Arthur in a red haze. This time Excalibur sliced all the way through the creature's tail and the beast screamed in agony. It stooped like an owl, claws extended, but Arthur's armor saved him as the hind legs kicked with razor claws. But where the steel kept his skin whole, it couldn't stop the impact. Arthur skidded to the pavement before the manticore flapped skyward, trumpeting its pain. It banked awkwardly, the missing tail skewing its ability to steer, and disappeared over the midway.

Arthur scrambled to Merlin, placing a hand on the enchanter's chest to feel for breaths. It was there, but faint. With a savage curse, Arthur pulled the barb from his friend's side. The wound wasn't deep, though it released a trickle of blood. "Merlin?"

There was no response. The enchanter's skin was clammy and his eyes were closed. Meanwhile, screams rose from the crowd as a flock of gargoyles tormented a tour group. One man was swinging at the bat-like creatures with his selfie stick. Arthur swore long and hard. The glamor Merlin cast had vanished.

Owen skidded to a stop beside them. "What can I do?" the knight asked. There was a long scratch on his forehead, but otherwise he looked unhurt.

"Call Clary. We need a witch's healing powers."

It was then Arthur saw the manticore circle around again and snatch the girl from the stroller. The pink unicorn balloon floated skyward as the mother screamed.

"And watch Merlin," Arthur ordered as he scrambled to his feet, already sprinting after the beast. He dodged through the crowd, scanning the sky. He glimpsed the manticore weaving past the Ferris wheel and roller coaster, working hard to stay aloft with the child in its claws.

Arthur jumped the turnstile to the rides, chain mail rattling as he landed. He was hot and sweating, but fear for the girl made him put on more speed. The creature was flying lower now, wings angling in a way that predicted a landing. Arthur sprinted toward the Merry Minstrel restaurant, fearing the worst.

The manticore landed in the middle of the restaurant's patio. Terrified patrons streaked past, barely noticing a man holding a huge sword. More were scrambling to crawl over the glass pony wall that separated the eatery from the crowds.

Chairs and tables tipped over. Food was strewn everywhere. In the middle crouched the manticore, the little girl trapped between its front paws. The child was sobbing, long wails punctuated by red-faced hiccups. She had sunshine hair like Gwen's, Arthur thought, hating Talvaric all the more.

Arthur delivered a single swift kick to the pony wall. The Plexiglas panel flew off its brackets with a clatter, bouncing once before it came to rest. When it saw Arthur, the manticore rose to its feet, looming over the child. Arthur couldn't help but glance at the stump of its tail.

"If you choose to return to your home in peace, I will see to it you get there in safety." Arthur made the words clear and loud, hoping manticores spoke English. He repeated himself in French, Greek and Latin, just in case.

There was no flicker of recognition in the creature's eyes. If anything, they looked insane, filled with formless rage. This wouldn't be as easy as helping the talking fox, who had been content with a can of tuna and an old shirt to sleep on. Worse, Arthur could hear the child's mother sobbing somewhere behind him.

This was up to Arthur. Merlin was down, the other knights were chasing their own monsters and Medievaland's security guards were—perhaps fortunately—nowhere in sight. He began advancing with slow, deliberate steps. This would either spook the creature or provoke it, but either way he had to get close enough to grab the girl. Why had the beast taken her? As a hostage? Parental instinct? Dinner? By the drool dripping from the creature's fangs, Arthur assumed the last.

"Let her go," he said softly, not sure he could be heard over the wailing child and the thousand clicks of smartphones taking pictures. He just kept talking, his voice as smooth and quiet as Excalibur was sharp.

The manticore snarled, the nightmarish teeth on full display. While the fangs were appalling, Arthur paid more attention to its stance, watching for any sudden shifts in weight that meant it was about to pounce. Of all its mismatched parts, the lion was at its core. It would be those instincts he had to watch out for. "Just back away," he said. "Then we can all go home."

Miraculously, it did take a step back. But then the manticore rushed him, bowling the girl over as it raced forward. Arthur barely got his sword up in time. Alarm surged through him as the manticore reared up, displaying paws like dinner plates. The thing cuffed him hard, claws scraping on his mail shirt. The links tore, slashing claws flaying the flesh beneath. Arthur staggered, his shoulder suddenly numb. Excalibur dropped to the ground, but before he could dive for it, the manticore lunged, knocking him flat. It landed with rib-cracking weight on his chest, but Arthur slid away, using speed to outmaneuver it. Confused, the manticore looked around for its prey but Arthur grabbed its rounded ears.

Arthur felt an instant of regret, but he twisted its head sharply. Bone crunched and the creature collapsed, neck broken. Arthur sagged, his mind and soul a blank for one heartbeat before the world rushed in.

Then he backed away from the monster and went to the small girl, who was still crying. Ignoring his wounded shoulder, Arthur gathered her up from where she was stranded amid the broken china and carried her out of the mess. Her warm, soft weight was comforting, but he didn't get to hold her long. The child's mother was there, sobbing words that Arthur couldn't unravel through his exhaustion. She put her arms out for her daughter, relief and gratitude in every line of her body. Arthur surrendered the child.

"I suppose you want me to clean up the mess?" Merlin asked drily.

Arthur spun. "How are you up and walking?"

The enchanter's face was the shade of curdled milk. "I don't recommend manticore venom. It's like the hangover you get after a drinking party with trolls."

Merlin said something under his breath, and the manticore's body imploded into a pile of dust. Half a dozen curious onlookers leaped backward in alarm.

"The glamor fell when you were unconscious," Arthur said.

"My apologies. It's back under control," Merlin replied, his lips white with strain. "All but the most observant will think this was no more than a clever bit of showmanship."

Arthur put a hand on his shoulder to steady him. "Come with me. You need to sit down."

"We don't have time for that."

"I need a better plan," said Arthur.

"You think I can give you one?"

"I need you to open a portal. Gwen needs rescuing and Talvaric needs killing."

Merlin shrugged. "I think your plan is just fine."

Chapter 26

"The good news is that I know where Talvaric took Gwen," Merlin announced. They were in Arthur's SUV, speeding back to the hotel. "I had a look at the portal. He didn't bother to hide the new destination."

"Careless or overconfident." Arthur wasn't sure which was worse. Both said Talvaric wasn't concerned about retaliation. "What's the bad news?"

"Everything else."

That killed conversation for a few minutes. Eventually, Merlin cleared his throat. "Are you sure you want to do this?"

"I thought you said my plan was fine."

"In principle. I'm not liking the logistics. The moment you walk through the portal, you're on Talvaric's turf." Merlin's eyes drifted shut. With a wrench of guilt, Arthur saw the enchanter was still weak.

"There are many reasons I would rather not walk through the portal," Arthur said quietly.

"You prefer to fight on your own ground."

"I do." There was no point in lying. "And I know asking you to open it is a drain of power when you can least afford it."

Merlin chuckled. "It takes more than a manticore to put me out of action."

"You're my oldest friend." Arthur slowed for a red light, loathing modern traffic rules. "I don't take your well-being lightly."

"Appreciated, but I know you," Merlin agreed. "There's a reason you left your men behind to mop up the monsters, including the ones with microphones. You're sneaking off. Owen might be in his own particular zoological heaven with all the beasts at large, but the others would rather be at your side. Logically, they should be."

The light changed and Arthur stepped on the gas. "So?"

"The reason you're going solo is that Gwen is a problem only you can solve. This is really about you and her. Talvaric just happened to step in the middle of it."

"Talvaric is a maniac who wants to slaughter me on television," Arthur grumbled.

"He wants to kill a king," said Merlin. "He made it personal when he took your wife."

Arthur cast a glance at Merlin, whose amber eyes were open now. A familiar irritation crept over Arthur. Talking to Merlin was a mixed experience—half enlightenment, half confusion. "I don't see the difference."

"You're the King of Camelot, but you're also Arthur. And there is the real problem you face, beyond fae and lunatics and monsters. You've always been too much a king, and Gwen too little the queen. She's tried to wear the crown, to find her own way of fulfilling her role, but you haven't truly let her."

Arthur clenched the steering wheel in frustration. Gwen had said pretty much the same thing. "I've tried to protect her."

"Perhaps you should show her how to protect herself." Merlin's eyes drifted shut again. "Don't take away her self-respect."

Arthur's chest tightened. Gwen had been about to walk away and start her own life without him. All at once, the enormity of that unthinkable future hit him. Without her, there would be no adventures to conquer trolls, no clever solutions, no romance under the stars, none of her creative, curious spirit. She was beautiful, yes, but she was brave, stubborn, ingenious and always seeking new and better ways to look at everything, even if it was just a way to keep foxes out of the chicken coop. If she were gone, he'd be bereft.

She was his partner. Arthur's thoughts skipped a beat as he realized the truth. He'd never seen it before. *And I love her. This is what loving someone actually means.* What if she didn't want him now? What if—

Arthur pulled the SUV into the hotel parking lot and killed the motor. Merlin was right—his true challenge was making things right with Gwen. She would either forgive him, or he would have nothing.

Merlin shifted in his seat, easing his wounded side. "You need someone to remind you to be a man as well as a king. You need someone to share your burdens. Without that, it's easy to lose your way. And a lost monarch becomes little more than a tyrant."

Arthur was silent. *This is why Camelot requires a queen.* He sucked in a breath. "We had an arranged marriage. She never actually agreed to wed me."

"Fix it. You need her," Merlin added. "And that's why I'll risk sending you to Talvaric's home."

The knot in Arthur's gut eased. "Thank you, old friend." He'd faced Talvaric as a king, with defiance and principles. The next time they met, Arthur would face him as a man, battling to save the woman he loved.

"Then let's go." Merlin reached for the door handle when his phone rang. When he looked at the caller ID, his expression filled with an irritated disgust. "It's Clary."

The enchanter put the phone on speaker. "Aren't you supposed to be dragon-sitting?"

"I thought you said the magic on Rukon's cave would hold even if you fell asleep." Clary's voice was sharp.

"Of course it will," Merlin retorted, and then a horrified look stole over his features. "Although the fact that I was poisoned and passed out probably changed things."

"Whatever. Rukon isn't in his cage any longer," Clary said in the strained tone of one dealing with a very large lizard, "and he says he wants to go home now."

Arthur instantly saw the possibilities. He hadn't planned on taking backup, but... "Tell him I think we can arrange that."

The jeweled comb in Gwen's hand had long teeth that slid easily into the lock of her cell door. Unfortunately, they were carved from bone and didn't hold up to her attempts to force the pins. Gwen heard the snap of another tooth breaking. With a curse, she pulled the comb back through the bars and examined the damage. The comb was of fae design, rimmed in sapphires and very pretty. Unfortunately, it was now missing three teeth. Despondently, Gwen pushed it into her hair to hide the damage.

Gwen had washed and changed into the clothes Talvaric had provided, and the sapphire comb had come with the gown. She had put off changing for as long as possible, but eventually grime and stale sweat had made her reconsider. Besides that, defying Talvaric without a good reason was foolish.

As if merely thinking about the fae drew him forth, Talvaric's steps rang on the stone floor. Gwen straightened, shaking out her skirts. When he came into view, a pair of dryads followed at a respectful distance, their heads bowed.

"Aren't you a picture?" he said with a sly smile.

The tunic he wore was the same blue as her gown, with the same silver cord around the neck and wrists. The symbolism was plain, even if Clary would have condemned the coordinated outfits as too matchy-matchy. His green gaze swept from her hem to the combs in her hair. Gwen had seen that look before—possession, and it wasn't even for her own sake. Talvaric simply wanted to outrage Arthur.

Her skin crawled with disgust. *This is just another adventure,* she told herself. It was like being in the troll's lair, only worse because she was alone. She wanted Arthur's presence so badly it hurt. She'd been afraid in the mines, but there was a vast difference between then and now. Here, no one had her back.

Talvaric studied her expression with a faint smile. Cruelty lurked beneath the curve of his lips, a blade disguised but by no means sheathed. "Come. I have something to show you."

He took a key from his belt and unlocked the door. There only seemed to be one key, she noticed, but was careful to appear uninterested when he put it away and handed her out of her cage. They set off toward a different part of the house, the silent dryads shadowing their steps.

"I paid your world a visit today," he said conversationally.

"Did your journey have a purpose, my lord?" Gwen asked in her most polite tone.

"Certainly," he said, and added nothing more.

He was baiting her with the vague answer, but she refused to bite.

They passed through a gallery, where pictures might have hung. Instead, there were a lot of swords and she guessed he used it as a practice room for fencing. At the other end, a short flight of steps led to an octagonal chamber surrounded with windows. While most surfaces in the manor were painted white, the floor was a colorful pattern of blue and orange. The design was a starburst in a circle of hammered bronze and in the center was a plinth holding a crystal globe. Gwen knew at once it was a room for working magic. She had no powers of her own, but the energy in the air prickled her arms.

Talvaric stepped up to the globe and made a swiping gesture with one hand. The crystal fogged for an instant, and then the mist parted to reveal an outdoor scene of utter mayhem. A crowd of ordinary people milled about, ducking and screaming and trying to snap pictures with their phones. Above them, gargoyles flicked to and fro, diving with the speed and agility of swallows. Gwen's shoulders tensed. The creatures were harmless, until they weren't. In a pack, they could be savage.

"My world doesn't have live gargoyles," she said, doing her best to smother her horror. "What did you do?"

"I gave Camelot something to chew on. It wasn't my first intention, but Arthur refused to take me seriously."

Gwen looked up with a frown. "I find that hard to believe." Arthur despised the fae, but he would never discount them.

"Perhaps I'm saying this the wrong way. Let me try again." Talvaric tapped his chin with one finger, mimicking someone deep in thought. "He refused to give himself up to save your life, so I sent my beasts to show how serious I truly am. Does that make more sense?"

The fae's smirk deepened. *He refused to give himself up to save your life.* That was what Talvaric wanted her to hear. She wasn't loved. No one would come to rescue her.

Sick despair froze her veins. Arthur was king. Of course, he couldn't drop everything to mount a rescue. Wife or not, she was just one woman. One woman who would never give him the heir he needed. A woman who couldn't find it in her heart to trust him. The question wasn't whether Arthur would come, but why he would bother.

"You could have asked," she said lightly, even though her knees shook. "I could have told you he can't be manipulated for my sake."

Talvaric's eyes narrowed, a flush of anger creeping up his cheeks. "Then what good are you?"

None. "You should have sent spies to check your

facts. If you want to be King of Faery, you should know that every good king has spies."

"I have this." Talvaric pointed to the crystal ball. "What I saw between you looked like love to me."

And love was a weapon he could use.

Gwen swallowed, thinking of the past days with Arthur, and trying not to think of Talvaric watching them through his crystal ball. What she'd shared with Arthur might have been love and maybe even a brief partnership, but she would never admit it to this monster. "You have no soul. What would you know of true affection?"

Talvaric's eyes met hers, and there was murder in them. Gwen's blood turned to ice, but she set her jaw. Pride refused to let her look away.

Then the windows behind them shattered. Shards of glass fountained in a thousand tiny, stinging pieces, catching in clothes and hair and biting exposed skin. Gwen ducked, shielding her face as her ears rang with a deafening roar. A sudden rush of wind brought the scent of forest and smoke. Dragon smoke.

A furtive glance told her Talvaric had forgotten her. His pale face was slack, eyes transfixed on whatever was behind her. Gwen spun around to see Rukon's giant green form outside the window. The dragon was flapping in place, toothy jaws bared in a snarl.

Gwen bolted. After enjoying the freedom of light modern clothes, the gown felt unbearably heavy, tangling her feet as she moved. All the same, she flew through the gallery with the swords, bursting past a clutch of dryads. They watched her with curiosity, but didn't move to stop her.

"Run!" Gwen called out. "The dragon has come for Talvaric."

She had a small window of time to get out of the manor house and find the portal Rukon had used. Hopefully, it would take her home.

She turned, and turned again, frustrated because every room and corridor was the same featureless white. Before long Gwen suspected she was going in circles.

One more burst of speed took her into a long, long hallway that sloped downward. It was wide and high ceilinged, more of a tunnel than any household corridor. Her first instinct was to retreat. This wasn't the way outside, and she'd had bad luck with underground lairs. Still, she stopped, poised on tiptoe and holding her breath. There was a sound coming from the darkness that reminded her of…peeping chicks?

Given what she'd seen in Talvaric's manor, there was no telling what was down there. Gwen wished she'd grabbed a sword when she'd raced through the weapons room, but all she'd been thinking about was freedom. Which was what she should have been thinking about now, except it wasn't just her own safety that mattered. She had to consider all the creatures in Talvaric's zoo. Some of them were dangerous, but none of them deserved to be his captive—and whatever was down here sounded as if it was very, very young.

She ran forward on light feet, glad the passageway was smooth and straight. There was a soft, rosy light coming from the other end, throwing just enough illumination to find her way. A slight crook at the end of the tunnel angled into a large natural cave. Gwen stopped, grabbing the stone wall for support. Her lips parted in surprise.

Elosta, the blue dragon, lay curled around a clutch of eggs, and they were hatching.

Chapter 27

The fight was on, and Arthur was betting that a willing dragon was far deadlier than a dragon forced to obey.

Whatever magical leash the fae used on Rukon had been weakened by exposure to Merlin's spells. As for the rest of the fae's hold—it was a two-edged sword. Talvaric had Rukon's mate. That was a powerful control, but it was also a reason to fight.

Merlin had opened a new portal—one big enough for a dragon—that sent them just outside Talvaric's manor, on the lush green of the lawn. Rukon had gone through first, but only by seconds, and was aiming for the north end of the house. As Arthur followed, the portal snapped shut, magic tingling like the air before a storm. Arthur took off at a run, aiming for the other end of the sprawling structure. If Talvaric had any wits, he'd run in the opposite direction from the dragon's attack—and straight onto Arthur's blade.

Arthur circled the perimeter of the place, looking for a way in with no success. Frustration mounted quickly. The house didn't simply lack a formal entry—there wasn't even a tradesman's door. With a stable and gardens and large property to maintain, there should have been many ways for the servants to come and go. Unfortunately, they were invisible.

Arthur drew Excalibur and stood with his back to the manor. In the sword's bright blade, the reflection of the house was clear and, as always, the charmed sword cut through magic. Arthur saw the entry and its guard—a creature that resembled something between an insect and a uniformed footman. As he turned and stormed toward the entry, the glamor broken, the creature scuttled away.

The door wasn't locked, and Arthur was inside just in time to hear Rukon's outraged roar. A surge of panic sharpened his focus. If he was going to find Gwen, he would have to work quickly.

Gwen stood openmouthed. The eggs were so large she could have barely held one in both her arms, and the shells were iridescent shades of blues, purples and greens. The colors reminded her of the riches of the goblins' treasure hoard, but this was even more wonderful. The rosy light was coming from the eggs themselves. The gentle heat of the cavern was boosted every so often when Elosta breathed licks of flame into the air.

The tiny dragonets nearly made her laugh out loud. They were as big as full-grown cats, if cats had bat wings and necks as long as their tails—but they were clearly newborns. Four or five were tumbling around the clutch, clumsy but determined, with their translucent wings spread wide for balance. If all the eggs were viable, there would be a dozen young, each matching the color of its shell.

Arthur's story of Elosta plummeting from the sky jarred Gwen's memory. She had nearly perished, and these eggs would have gone cold and dead. A glance at the dragon showed her wings were charred, the fine membranes that webbed them in tatters.

"Human?" Elosta said, the single word filled with warning. Gwen had never heard a female dragon speak. The voice was feminine, but as resonant as Rukon's.

"Pardon me," said Gwen, giving a curtsy because she was the intruder in this mother's very private domain. "I am Guinevere, Queen of Camelot."

"Why are you here?" the dragon asked, clearly suspicious.

There was no time to waste, so Gwen explained as quickly as she could. "I'm glad to see you well," she finished.

"I was spared from death so that my eggs might live. The fae is careful of his investment." Her tone was dark with anger.

"Perhaps he did this one thing right. Your children are beautiful."

The dragon made a soft crooning noise that didn't fit with her size or the sharpness of her teeth. Or maybe it did, Gwen thought as Elosta righted a floundering youngster with her long snout.

"Thank you, human, your words are courteous," said the dragon. "Someday your children will be beautiful, as well."

The statement made Gwen flinch. "I'm afraid not."

"No? I see the shadows of younglings around you. Dragons are rarely mistaken in these things."

"I was cursed by a witch." Gwen drew breath with effort. "Even Talvaric said I will mother no heirs."

The fae's name drew a plume of angry smoke from the dragon's snout. "He has no gift of prophecy, but he thrives on the ability to see another's fears. Do not take his word on this."

A tiny blue dragon peeped agreement—or perhaps it just peeped. Gwen wasn't sure when they began to understand spoken language.

"How did you find my den, Queen of Camelot?"

"I am seeking the way out of this place. Rukon is attacking the house and I got away."

"Rukon is here?" Elosta rose to her feet in excitement, though she was still careful where she placed her talons.

It was then Gwen saw the slender gold chain that bound the dragon's hind foot to the cavern wall. It had to be magic, because nothing that flimsy would have worked otherwise. The dragon saw her looking. "Yes, he has me bound, and one day he will bind my heart by stealing my children."

"No," said Gwen. "Not if Rukon has any say in the matter. He's coming for you."

"And where is the King of Camelot?" asked Elosta. "Surely he is coming for his queen?"

Gwen straightened her shoulders. "A king is wherever his people need him the most." But she wasn't certain of her husband.

Arthur was looking for Gwen, but he found Talvaric first. He'd just entered a long room hung with weapons when the fae slid to a stop at the other end of the space, panting. Arthur drew up short, surprised. The fae's singed appearance spoke of a narrow escape. Tiny shards of glass glittered on his hair and clothes as he moved.

A roar shook the manor, shaking plaster loose from the walls. Talvaric's panicked gaze swept from Arthur to the windows. A dark shadow flicked over the lawn, marking the circling dragon's passage.

"You've annoyed a lot of people," Arthur observed. "Especially the wrong ones."

Talvaric's response was to dart to the wall and snatch a blade from a rack of swords. He moved with a limp—had that cut come from the dragon, or perhaps the glass?—but Arthur knew better than to count that too heavily in a fight. Fae could fight past pain like no others.

"What have you done with my wife?" Arthur asked, swishing Excalibur to loosen his injured shoulder.

"So you came for her, after all. How endearing." Talvaric grinned, his panic suspended long enough to enjoy the gibe.

"Gwen was always coming home."

"Not when you refuse to obey my rules."

Arthur made a disgusted noise. "Grow up. Answer the question. Where is she?"

Talvaric's lip curled. "Beat it out of me."

With pleasure. Arthur grinned as Talvaric launched toward him. Their skirmish at Medievaland had been intense, but this fight was the one that mattered.

They were staggeringly different swordsmen, with distinct styles and weapons. Arthur was quick for a man in armor, but Talvaric's attack was like water—swift, changeable, seeking the tiniest gaps in Arthur's guard. Arthur's blows hammered in return. A two-handed great sword like Excalibur was made for strength, not speed.

Arthur brought Excalibur down in a mighty, two-handed slash. Talvaric dodged and rolled, laughing as he did it. The fae was a natural acrobat, and knew it. The fae lunged, turning the motion into a cutting blow with a twist of his wrist. It caught the underside of Arthur's arm, finding a slight gap between mail and plate. Arthur roared in pain, but used the sound as a distraction. With a backslash, he left a wide slice along Talvaric's ribs. The fae screamed.

Talvaric's blue tunic was instantly soaked in red, but he moved as fast as ever, shrinking back from Arthur with a string of Faery invective. Arthur swung again, but Excalibur whistled through empty air. Talvaric bolted for safety. With an angry roar, Arthur charged after him.

He was not as fast, and in armor he was nowhere as quiet. He kept the fae in sight for several turnings through the anonymous white house, catching a glimpse of the blue tunic or the swing of Talvaric's long white braid. Eventually, though, Arthur was left panting and lost. Humans could never match a fae in a footrace. However, they weren't helpless.

Arthur's gaze fell on the trail of scarlet drops on the stark white floor. Talvaric had drunk a mortal soul, and was experiencing emotions after a long time without. Apparently, he'd forgotten how panic could make one careless. Arthur began to run again, but this time he knew exactly where to go. He hoped, desperately, that the fae would lead him to Gwen.

The blood drops led past cages filled with creatures that left him sad and disturbed. A barguest, black furred and red eyed, peered from the back of its cage, shuddering in fright. He passed dryads standing helpless, as if their wills had been ripped away. They should have been dancing in the woods, far beyond the sight of anyone but the moon. But then he heard Rukon's frustrated roar, and the crash of the dragon smashing its way into the manor. There would be justice.

When the path descended down a long, broad tunnel leading under the earth, Arthur heard the roar of another dragon. The sound rang off the walls, the echoes magnifying it until it became a physical force. After that he slowed, sword raised to strike. He could smell smoke and blood and the leathery scent of a dragon's lair. The last time he'd ventured into one, he'd been reminded that humans were a nice-sized snack.

He swung around the corner, ready for anything. A glance took in the female dragon, her young and Talvaric holding a sword to Gwen's throat. Gwen's eyes were wide, the blue almost shocking in her pale face.

Arthur did not stop to think. He moved with a speed Talvaric did not, could not expect. The sword went flying from the fae's hand, taken by the heavy great sword with the delicacy of a rapier. It shouldn't have been possible, but Arthur was first among the mortal swordsmen for a reason. He understood the value of surprise.

He could have killed the fae then, but he reached for Gwen instead. Talvaric thrust her into Arthur's arms and ran, crossing just out of the reach of Elosta's snapping jaws. Arthur caught Gwen's weight against him for a delicious moment, savored the scent of her skin and hair. It was only for a single heartbeat, but it was long enough for the fae to snatch up his blade.

Arthur spun with a snarl, pushing Gwen to safety behind him. Talvaric's eyes flew wide at the sound, delivered with the savagery of a man at his limit. When the fae had taken Gwen, he'd pushed Arthur beyond any expectation of mercy. One more time, the fae fled.

But Rukon was at the other end of the tunnel, and he was coming to protect his mate. Talvaric stopped, arms flying wide in an effort to stop his forward motion. Eyes red with fury glared from the darkness. The fae raised his blade and turned to face Arthur, ready to make one final defense.

A series of images flashed through Arthur's mind: Rukon, Elosta, the barguest, the dryads, Senec wounded and trembling. Gwen, with the blade to her throat. Feeling its even, perfect balance, Arthur swung Excalibur, showing what a great sword was made for. Talvaric's head flew wide.

Silence rang as loud as any roar. Fountaining blood, the fae's body fell. Arthur took a step back, and then another as Rukon's flames turned the remains to ash, scouring the world clean of Talvaric's presence. But Arthur was not quite done. He spun on his heel, once more hefting the long blade that was so much a part of him. With a shout of victory, he slashed it downward, severing the chain that bound the blue dragon. Light flared as Excalibur's power severed the spell, burning the links apart. Elosta roared in triumph, bounding free to twine her long, sinuous neck with Rukon's.

Slowly, Arthur let the weight of Excalibur drag down his arm until the point dug into the stone floor. Gradually, his pounding heart slowed, the furious thunder abating until he could breathe at a normal pace. He leaned into his sword hilt, exhaustion finally making its claws felt.

Gentle hands touched his arm and he lifted his head. Gwen was there, her eyes shining with tears. "You came for me." Her voice was soft, almost wondering. "You saved my life."

"Of course I did." He tried to make it sound matter-of-fact, but his voice shook.

She cupped her hands around his face, leaning close so their foreheads touched and breath mingled. "Thank you," she whispered.

Arthur said nothing. He could not, with Gwen's tears burning against his skin. Common words would have been sacrilege.

Chapter 28

The dragon's fire had destroyed the key to the cages, and it took time to find the spare. It was dark when the creatures were finally freed. Not one made any move to harm their fellows, and each bowed before the King and Queen of Camelot, for he bore the name and duty of the Pendragon, protector of magical beasts. After they paid homage, they ran one by one into the darkness, vanishing back to wherever they belonged. Only the barguest stayed an extra moment to lick Gwen's hand before he fled.

"He knows I like dogs," Gwen said, but Arthur looked dubious.

The only part of the manor that remained occupied was Elosta's underground cavern. She could not fly until her wings healed, and she had to remain until the eggs were fully hatched. But that was safe beneath the ground, and it was time for the dryads to have their say. Gwen watched from a safe distance as they placed their long fingers against the walls and seemed to grow into the stonework, long tendrils crumbling the structure just as roots crack pavement. But rather than taking years, the process took minutes. In no time, Talvaric's manor—and prison—was reduced to rubble. The dryads cleared the tunnel mouth for the dragons to come and go, and then they, too, vanished into the woods.

After that, Arthur and Gwen used the portal to return home. Clary, who had been waiting, drove them to Arthur's apartment. The destination was Gwen's choice. "I can't go back to the hotel," she said. "I know Talvaric's gone, but I'd still be jumping at shadows."

Still, the apartment held memories, too. Their reunion. The first awkward night when she'd shut Arthur out of his bedroom. Walking out to face the knights who'd left her behind while they'd traveled to the future.

Gwen stood in the living room, still in the blue gown Talvaric had made her wear. It was dark outside, the city lights beautiful but as alien to Gwen as the place she'd just left. Someday this world would look like home, she supposed. Just not yet.

Arthur came out of his office. "I phoned Merlin to let him know we're safely home. He'll tell the others."

"Good," she replied.

"The knights rounded up most of the creatures," Arthur added. "Merlin and Clary have been sending them back through the portal. Some probably got away, but no one's sure."

"No innocents were hurt?"

"Not seriously, or not that we know of. We were lucky." He looked tired, his hair rumpled and his feet bare. His armor was piled in the corner, waiting to be cleaned.

They stared at one another for a long moment, neither wanting to say more. The crisis was past, the villain vanquished and even the barguest was safe. She should have been content.

And yet nothing had changed. Not really. The last time they'd been together, they'd parted in anger. "I'm sorry," she said, her voice cracking on the words. "I don't know if I can change who I am."

If the shift in topic startled him, he didn't show it. "Would you be surprised if I said I don't want you to?" His smile was wistful. "You keep me humble."

She wasn't certain how to take that, and stiffened. "I'm not your possession. I can't be put on display or locked up whenever you like."

His gaze lowered, a flush spreading over his cheekbones. "No."

She could see he was sorry, but her hurt went too deep for a single word to cure it. He'd left her too many times. "I can't be the queen you want."

"And who is she?"

"Someone else."

He choked a laugh. "I don't want someone else. I want the difficult woman who fought beside me in Zorath's mine."

Her breath caught, not sure she could trust the intensity in his eyes. "You never wanted her before."

"I never let myself know her until now." He reached forward, running his fingers down the length of her arm. The featherlight touch made her shiver. "I want that woman, every day and every night."

"Are you sure?"

"Only the best of my knights have your wits and nerve. You and I make good partners."

In other words, she'd proven something in the Crystal Mountains. She suspected they'd both changed perspectives over the last few days. "Do I deserve such praise after keeping secrets from you?"

His expression grew grave. "What you're really asking is whether you can finally trust me."

"And whether you'll ever trust me back," she said in a small voice. It was true. Everything he said was true. "In some ways, I've been selfish. I'm one person, and I never understood how many lives you touch. I wanted too much from you."

"No." He shook his head. "If anyone deserved my best, it was you. I'm the one at fault, and I would give much to atone for that."

"I don't want to be right at your expense. That was never what I wanted."

He didn't answer. Instead, he went to the corner, where his armor lay in a jumble, and picked up Excalibur. When he turned back to her, he held the blade balanced across his palms.

"There are moments of faith. Moments when the only choice is to leap into the future. Should I pull the sword from the stone and rule Camelot, or walk away and live a peaceful life? Those decisions make us what we are, and nothing should ever take them away."

Gwen stood very still, barely breathing, and wondered where he was going with this.

"You were never given a choice about your future. When it came time to wed, others selected a husband for you. That wasn't just."

He fell to one knee, offering Excalibur in outstretched

hands. Reflexively, she took the sword, balancing the weight with care.

"My lady, this blade is everything I am—my weapon, my power, the symbol of my rank and right to rule. I surrender it to you as a king to his queen, and as a man to his woman. Return Excalibur to me when I prove myself the husband you deserve."

He reached up, cupping her hands where she held the sword, helping her bear the weight of it. "Will you marry me, Gwen?"

He was giving her a choice, the freedom to go or stay. She'd never had this decision, never known what she might have chosen if her father hadn't sent her to Camelot to be the queen. And here, in this modern age, the options were beyond counting. If she struck out on her own, she could be anything.

Yet this wasn't a flight from the familiar into the unknown. It was from one unknown to another. Camelot was utterly changed, even if the dangers facing it were just as deadly as before. The knights lived in secret, using their wits as much as their blades. The trappings of monarchy meant nothing here. If she stayed, she would have to work hard to help this new Camelot thrive.

Gwen was numb, her body tingling with shock. Arthur was giving her the power to direct her future. This was her moment to pull her own sword from the stone, and leap.

She met his blue eyes. There was uncertainty in them, but there was also hope—and love. He was the same man that he had always been, but in this strange time and place they had finally seen the truth in each other.

It was like coming home, but to the home and the husband she'd always wanted.

"Yes," Gwen said, and pressed Excalibur into his hands.

His eyes grew darker as he lowered the sword to the floor. It rattled slightly as he released it, the sound loud in the sudden, profound silence. It was as if the air had suddenly grown thick.

Arthur rose and stepped over the sword to take her in his arms. "Gwen," he whispered. "My wife and queen."

His hands slid from her waist up her ribs, caressing her. She felt suddenly fragile, as if made of eggshell or the finest glass. And yet, here she was, spanning centuries to be in his arms again. Queen Guinevere wasn't so easy to leave behind as all that. The thought made her laugh even as her throat ached with tears. It wasn't unhappiness, just the relief of a long journey successfully completed.

"What are you thinking?" he asked. "You have the oddest expression."

"I belong with you." When it really mattered, he'd crossed worlds to come for her, to be her hero.

"Yes." His smile was confident. "I never doubted it."

"My character is flawed," she said. "I'm independent and willful."

"I know. I've always made the error of trying to control you. I think I'll count on you instead."

He stopped her mouth with his before she could say more. When she closed her eyes, she saw him opening cage after cage of beasts, great and small, horrifying and beautiful. He had saved them all, and he had held her hand as they watched them run free. Finally, in that moment, she'd understood why he was king, but also who he was as a man.

The kiss lasted a very long time, and her hands found the hem of his T-shirt, warming themselves against the heat of his bare skin. The sensation brought tension to her belly, as if the fire in him had passed through her palms and into her core. Impatience prompted her to finger the buckle at his waist. His stomach tightened at her touch, hard and vulnerable at once. She stroked the ridged muscle with her fingertips, pleased by his intake of breath.

His lips ran down her throat, tasting her. She let her head fall back, nuzzling the softness of his hair as it fell against her cheek. And then his mouth was on her collarbone and his thumbs stroking over the swell of her breasts. She leaned into it, the sweet ache inside her turning liquid. When his caress roved over her nipples, she shivered. Moaning softly, she arched her back for more.

"Are you going to shut the door on me tonight?" he teased.

"Perhaps not." She nipped the lobe of his ear. "Prove to me you're worthy of entrance to my bower."

"Shall I come as a supplicant to Your Majesty?"

"Supplicants are as common as sheep in the field. I think something with more resolve."

In a swift motion, he caught her up in his arms. Gwen's stomach swooped as her feet left the floor and she instinctively clung to his shoulders as he carried her into his bedroom. The bedside lamp was on. She hadn't seen the room since she'd slept in it, and a bit of the confusion from that first night returned—but only for an instant. As soon as her toes touched the carpet, she was in his arms once more—and when Arthur kissed, it was impossible to think about anything but him.

He pulled off his shirt, revealing the angry, scored flesh where the manticore had clawed him. She traced the skin around the hurt, then over the swell of his chest, where older scars seamed his skin. He had a warrior's physique, muscled from the long use of weapons. Her mouth went dry, as it always did when he offered his body for her pleasure. Even after years together, each time seemed new.

"He gave you this dress?" Arthur asked, his voice so low she barely heard the words.

"Yes."

He gripped the wide neck of the gown and tore it in a single, angry wrench. When he released the fabric, the garment fell away, leaving Gwen in her chemise. She instantly felt cleaner. Nothing of Talvaric's had a place here. "Thank you," she said.

The rest of their clothes vanished soon after. Gwen fell on the bed, reaching up for Arthur to join her. He stretched out beside her, the length of him a hot line against her side. For a moment, she was lost in the sensation of touch—smooth and rough, firm and yielding, the crispness of hair and softness of lips. He arched over her, settling her back into the pillow. The musk of his skin was a familiar mix of leather, steel and man. She buried her face in his shoulder, wanting more.

His palms found her breasts, kneading and caressing until her core burned with new heat. Gwen bowed her back, stretching her arms above her head and inviting him to do more. She felt flushed and heavy, her nipples aching from his attention. He nuzzled her, licking and sucking and loving her until she grew restless, needing to feel him in other places.

His hand stroked her belly, working its way down and down until he found the wetness between her legs. She startled under his touch, sparks of sensation firing through her. But he didn't hurry to slake that need, nibbling his way over her skin instead, every touch of tongue and teeth building the tension inside her. She kissed and squirmed and rubbed him back, the taste of him like a drug. She was lost in him, hypnotized and addicted.

When he at last turned his full attention to her aching core, Gwen was slick with sweat. His mouth teased her, parting flesh that tingled with every gust of his breath. As his fingers slid inside, her body tried to grip them, but they weren't nearly enough to satisfy. She was slick and swollen and greedy. His thumb stroked her into spasms of pleasure as tears of release escaped her lids, trickling down her temples and into her hair.

"Please," she begged, just once because she was a queen, and because his mouth covered hers before more words were possible.

He slid inside, the fullness of it coaxing a groan from her throat. She gripped him, digging her fingers into the hard planes of his back. He loomed over her, but she wrapped herself around him, binding herself with desire. She was already drunk on it, loose and eager with the heat of their bodies. When he began to move, they surged as one.

Gwen's mind slipped then, blank of everything but the need to move with him, to release the gnawing wildness spiraling up inside her. Her breasts brushed against the roughness of his chest, the sensation a pleasure and a goad at once. She bit his shoulder. There was no explanation for it beyond savage glee.

Cursing at the pain, Arthur held her hips, angling her body. He had given, and now he took possession. With driving thrusts, his rhythm quickened and broke as he plundered her. The mad thing inside Gwen sprang free. She cried out, speared on the sharp pleasure of her surrender. He plunged once, twice more before he stiffened and shuddered.

Afterward, they curled together like a single being, their limbs tangled. Gwen's face buried in the crook of Arthur's shoulder, the world beyond the bed a strange and distant thing. She listened to Arthur's slow, deep breathing as sleep claimed him. The darkness wrapped them like a soft, black cloak.

For once, Gwen's thoughts were still. She had drawn her sword and leaped, and she had landed in the arms of the man who was meant to catch her. With a smile tugging at her lips, the Queen of Camelot drifted into peaceful slumber.

Chapter 29

Arthur woke to a kiss. It was an excellent kiss, bringing him to full wakefulness in seconds. Some dim and distant part of him was aware of aches and bruises from yesterday's battles, but all of him that mattered was focused elsewhere. Guinevere was naked and wrapping her clever fingers around his shaft.

The morning light bathed her, making her skin glow as if white fire burned inside. Pale blue veins showed in the most tender places—her temples, her throat, her breasts. He kissed them all, keenly aware of the life flowing so close to his lips. Gwen was a never-ending wealth of sensory experience. Soft skin tempted him and the rich scent of her tantalized him. Fair hair sheeted like a gold river around her, teasing as it swung to obscure the most interesting views.

He was hard in her hands, every part of him straining

to claim her again. But this time, she was in command, her hot tongue refining his desires. "What are you planning, woman?" he asked, his voice dropping into the region of a growl.

She drew herself up, straddling his waist. "You know I have an interest in how things work," she said lightly, lowering herself so that she slid neatly over him.

He swore, the tight heat of her so perfect that his pulse stuttered with pleasure. But then she rolled her hips. He reached up and she caught his hands, placing them over her breasts. Telling him what she wanted. As a knight sworn to serve his lady, Arthur had to obey. He caressed her as she caressed him, exploring and testing every angle and motion. Arthur held himself in careful control, letting her discover her pleasure, but he had to clench his teeth.

When she began pushing and rocking, he thought he might die. She sat high and proud like the Amazons of legend. Every undulating motion rippled her belly and swayed her breasts, the nipples winking from the curtain of her hair. Years in the saddle had made Gwen fit and strong, and the glove of her body around him squeezed with every move.

She came with a soft, gasping cry and then sank, draping herself across his chest in a pool of silken hair. He loved her languor and the elasticity of her pleasured body, but mostly he loved the fact she'd taken what she wanted. He rolled her over so that she spread out beneath him, boneless and sated.

"Did you solve your engineering problem?" he murmured in her ear.

She gasped a laugh, surging to life beneath him. "What do you think?"

"A theory has to be tested more than once."

She wriggled away, playing now. Her eyes sparked with laughter. The sight of it shook him deep and hard, for it had been so long since he'd seen that look. When she slid off the bed, he followed, drawn by an invisible thread that refused to allow distance between them.

He caught her, trapping her between his body and the cool white of the bedroom wall. She kissed him standing on her toes and holding his face in her hands. It was frank, her lust unfettered. He was tinder in its path.

Arthur hitched her up, hooking her legs around his hips and bracing her back against the wall. Her nails dug into his shoulders as he pushed into her. Her head flung back, throat bare to him. He pushed and pushed, stirring her as he might a banked fire. A flush of heat crept up her pale skin, staining it pink. Only then did he let go, releasing himself and filling her as she melted against him, hot, sensual and shivering with pleasure.

"Gwen," he whispered.

"I don't think I can stand." She let loose a throaty giggle as she drooped against him. Her eyes were closed, the sweep of her lashes like wing tips against her cheeks.

Arthur's chest ached with the miracle of her. He had stepped between worlds for her, but it seemed such a paltry thing compared to her courage. He had lost everything—his kingdom, his castles and his armies. No one in this time recognized him as their king. All he had left was his war against the fae.

But Gwen had stayed. When it had counted most, she had chosen him.

He kissed her softly, reverently, loving her with all his being. "What can I do to please you?"

She twined her arms around his neck. "I'm still new to this world. Show me what you like."

"I'd love a hot shower."

Their eyes met, and he could see her working out the possibilities. Watching her think was arousing all on its own.

"Together?" she asked.

"Of course."

Her grin was wicked.

"I think," said Merlin, fussing with the sleeves of his brand-new enchanter's robes, "the happiest person in all the realms is Medievaland's accountant."

"The park is certainly busy," Gwen agreed, eyeing Merlin's costume. The park had hired him as part of the troupe of entertainers, and wearing the outfit was part of the job. The robes were covered with moons and stars and had come with a tall staff and a pointed hat that he refused to wear.

It was nearly two months since Talvaric's defeat. The knights and ladies of Camelot were waiting inside the service building next to the tourney grounds. Outside, a noisy throng of guests filled the large white pavilion where that day's event would be held. Banquets at Medievaland had always been sellout events, but now there was a waiting list for tickets. The recent media attention, for good or ill, had brought the theme park to national attention.

"What about the lawsuits?" she asked nervously.

Merlin shrugged. "No one was actually hurt beyond a good scare, and there's no physical evidence that any of Talvaric's beasts were anything but fancy puppets. The park settled with the family of the child the manticore abducted, and they're paying a fine for some sort of violation of the peace, but they'll make the money up a hundred times over with increased sales."

Merlin turned to Clary, who was wearing a medieval costume but still typing on her smartphone. "What do the mysterious gods of the interwebs say?"

"We're still trending on the top five things to know about King Arthur. There are always a few trolls, but—"

"Trolls?" Gawain spun around from where he was chatting with his brother.

Beaumains put a hand on his sword. "Where?"

Clary rolled her eyes. "Not that kind."

The conversation was interrupted by Arthur's arrival. He was wearing a tunic and cloak of deep claret trimmed with gold. Excalibur hung at his side. When he saw Gwen, his step quickened and a smile dawned in his eyes. She held out her hands and he took them, kissing her lightly.

"You look breathtaking," he said, his gaze drinking her in as if they had been apart for weeks, not hours.

"Thank you." She'd had a dress made for the banquet, though she'd added some of her own touches. The fabric was a shimmering confection of palest yellow—definitely not a product of her own time, but authenticity was hardly required. If she could have the best of both worlds, she would.

He looped her hand over his arm, still smiling. They'd both done a lot of that in the past few weeks. "Any last words of advice for a debut performer?" she asked. This was the first time she'd appear in a Medievaland show.

"Just remember they all want to fall in love with you, and who can blame them?"

With that, he gave a signal, and trumpets sounded

the arrival of the king and queen. They stepped into the night and walked beneath garlands of glittering lights. Arm in arm, they were the head of a procession, followed by Merlin and Clary and then the other knights falling in behind. Fans cheered and cameras flashed. For a moment, Gwen was startled, but then she realized she already knew what to do. She'd been a queen before, and this was just the same. She smiled and waved, and caught the glances of as many people as she could, giving them a moment of personal connection.

They sat at the high table, while the guests were seated around trestle tables that formed an open square inside the tent. Senec the fox sat in Sir Owen's lap, pointed snout sniffing the air as platters were brought by liveried servants. The pair had been inseparable since the knight had bound the animal's wounds. With some coaxing, Senec had been convinced not to speak in public, but he'd refused to be left out of the fun—or the food. Gwen watched the fox snag a chicken wing and disappear under the table. The sight gave her a feeling of contentment—Camelot might no longer be a sprawling kingdom, but those who needed its protection still found welcome.

A servant offered her a basket of rolls and she took one. Even after many meals in the modern age, she marveled at the light texture of the bread. "So," she said to Arthur, "what is it that Merlin will do here?"

"Special effects," Arthur said with a twinkle. "At first he said pandering to the entertainment industry was beneath him, but even an enchanter has to eat. Compared to his other clients, we're schoolchildren."

Gwen frowned. "Who are these other clients?"

"Those members of the hidden world with no other place to go."

In other words, outcasts and criminals. She shivered slightly, and Arthur picked up her hand, kissing it. "We've had our difficulties with Merlin. Do you mind that he is once again in our circle?"

"No." She was a little surprised to find she meant it. "He's proud and difficult, but he cares for you. I am grateful for that devotion."

Arthur's smile was lopsided. "He's also made a deal with Rukon to do the occasional flyby. Medievaland's reputation for dragons is secured."

Their conversation ended as the entertainment began. Singers, jugglers, storytellers and magicians each took their turn. Palomedes and Beaumains picked a mock fight over one of the pretty young guests and staged a bit of swordplay. The public cheered and wept and swooned exactly as they should, their problems forgotten for the night. It reminded Gwen of the times when traveling minstrels visited her father's castle, and everyone gathered in the great hall to hear love songs and tales of mighty heroes. People hadn't changed much.

Her opinion was confirmed later, when she made the rounds of the guests. All members of Arthur's court, including the king and queen, spent a few minutes at each table to make the diners welcome. Gwen enjoyed the experience, answering endless questions about what it was like to live in a castle. Young girls asked a great many questions about the knights. It was delightful.

When she returned to her seat, Arthur was doing an interview outside the tent, but Clary was there. "How do you like celebrity?" Clary asked. "I see you and Arthur made the front page of the entertainment magazine."

"It's interesting," Gwen said. "But I can't wait to get into school. I'm not giving up on that plan."

"You shouldn't," said the witch. "Every time the fae strike, there's a new twist. We need a lot of different skills to combat them. You have a great deal to offer."

"Having something to work toward makes me feel rooted." That was important, coming from such a different world. But even more vital was that for the first time in her life, Gwen was shaping her own future with the support of the man she loved.

Clary watched her with a curious expression. "Did you say once that you were cursed?"

Gwen went still, her pleasant mood wavering. That wasn't something she cared to discuss in a public place. "Yes."

"May I ask what kind of curse?"

"It was of a very personal nature." Though she was almost certain Clary had guessed what it was.

"Uh-huh." Clary shrugged. "For what it's worth, witches can see most curses. I don't see one."

What was it Elosta had said? *I see the shadows of younglings around you. Dragons are rarely mistaken in these things.* "That is good news," Gwen said carefully, reaching for a glass of wine.

Clary put a hand over hers. "I wouldn't touch that."

"Why not?"

"Even if you were cursed back in the day, most such spells don't last more than a hundred years. It would have dissipated centuries ago."

She rose, kissed Gwen's cheek and wandered off to beg Merlin one more time to teach her the proper way to open a portal. Gwen sat very still, the untasted glass of wine just outside her reach. She withdrew her hand, folding her fingers in her lap. The sound of the banquet seemed to meld into a solid roar as she considered what Clary had said, and what she hadn't.

A piece of knowledge, one of the million random facts Merlin's spell had put in her head, said alcohol and babies didn't mix. Gwen shot another look at the witch, wondering exactly what that intense gaze of hers had meant. Clary looked up and winked.

It was impossible to block the parade of thoughts that rushed through her mind. How many weeks had she been here? How many times had she been in Arthur's bed and on Arthur's couch and in the shower and… They had been well and truly reunited. Still, it was very early.

But witches were witches, and they saw what was hidden. She'd missed her monthly courses, but after being turned to stone for centuries, wouldn't her body take time to adjust? And wouldn't it be normal if unfamiliar food sometimes made her queasy?

Feeling more than a little shaky, Gwen rose and left the banquet, glad of the fresh autumn air outside the tent. She saw Arthur at once, bidding the reporter farewell. For an instant she saw her husband as a silhouette, the lights strung in the trees rendering him in black and white. But then he turned and saw her, and in an instant his arm was around her waist.

"How did it go?" she asked.

"Well enough." He smiled, but it was rueful. "I think the young lad wanted to know how to sign on as one of the knights."

"Perhaps training new knights is not the worst idea," she mused, but her mind was elsewhere. "I need to speak to you alone."

His brow creased, but he led her away to a stand of trees that gave them shelter and privacy. He held her close, his fingers linked behind her back. She wanted nothing more than to lean into his warmth, but held herself back so that she could look into his face.

"What is it?" he asked.

"We've talked a bit about the future," she said, "and all the things that must be done. Protecting this world from the fae, finding more of the knights and waking them from the stone sleep and running these shows at Medievaland so that we can pay for food and shelter."

"And you have your schooling," he reminded her. "Don't forget that."

"I won't," Gwen said. "I want all of it. I'm happier than I've ever been."

"As am I." He kissed her forehead. "Leading you into the banquet tonight, as my wife and queen and partner, was one of my most joyous moments. Everything was right."

"I have one more responsibility to add to that future list," she said softly.

She took his hand and pressed it to her stomach. "It is very soon. I am going on the word of a witch."

She wasn't sure what his reaction would be. All kings required an heir, but Arthur was a man. Since their last real fight, she'd learned to expect honesty from him. That was healthy, but sometimes uncomfortable.

A child was a new vulnerability and, as she said, another responsibility. Arthur didn't need more.

But she needn't have worried for one instant. Arthur picked her up, spinning her around with a joyous whoop that made the park workers stop and stare.

"Hush!" Gwen put a hand over Arthur's mouth.

His eyes went wide, as if he would explode with the news. She laughed, contradicting the tears that suddenly blurred her vision. She wanted to laugh and cry and dissolve all at once. The happiness seemed too much, but she would fight like a tigress to keep it all.

This was her kingdom, and she would make her home and raise her babies in it. She would study and build marvels and take part in the fight to keep it safe. And she would do it in the arms of this man, this king and her husband.

Some days, it was good to be queen.

* * * * *